Mercy

FORBIDDEN DESIRES OF PCH
BOOK ONE

CHELLE ROSE

CHELLE ROSE BOOKS

This book is dedicated to all the Smut Sluts out there. You are my people.

"We are all born sexual creatures, thank God, but it's a pity so many people despise and crush this natural gift." — Marilyn Monroe

Triggers

This book is a work of fiction. Names, characters, places, and incidents are the product of the author's imagination or are used fictitiously. Any resemblance to actual events, locations, or persons, living or dead, is coincidental. This book is intended for a mature audience 18+. There may be some violence, drug use, or other triggers. Please be aware if you have any of those triggers.

This book has content that is not suitable for all readers. Please read through the triggers before deciding to keep reading.

Triggers:

~ Ridiculous amount of sex (Seriously)
    ~ MFC calls MMC Daddy.
    ~ Kidnapping
    ~ Violence
    ~ Cancer (Adults and children. No children die from cancer in this book)
    ~ Death

One

MERCY

MOST MEN THINK I'm just a pretty girl. After all, a woman can't be both pretty and intelligent. I roll my eyes, thinking about all the men that have underestimated me through the years. Maybe I am pretty, but there's more to me, a lot more. I finished high school at sixteen and graduated with my master's degree in Social Work at twenty-three. There are things I want, and I'm not afraid to go after them. One of them is Dr. Liam Lexington. I've spent seven long years wanting this man and I will get him.

I'm working my last shift at the On-Call Room, a bar owned by Dr. Xander Kane, a Pocono Children's Hospital doctor. Most of the patrons are doctors or women that are fascinated by the idea of snagging one. It's comical to watch them throw themselves at these men. Normally, they get shot down. However, occasionally, one of them gets lucky. Although it's never like what I read in romance novels. There's never a happily ever after, just an orgasm or two, and then it's over by morning light.

It's funny how people celebrate when someone leaves a job, but to commemorate my new position, the staff brought me cupcakes—delicious chocolate filled with whipped cream. I have spent the summer working here after graduating college. I bonded with several members of the staff nearly instantaneously. It's bittersweet knowing that it's almost over.

Standing behind the bar, stacking glasses on the shelf, *he* comes in-my heart races, and my breath hitches, as I attempt to control my shaky hands. This is what he does to me, Dr. Liam Lexington makes me weak in the knees. He's my best friend's father, and I know I shouldn't watch him the way I am for that reason alone. It's been seven years since I saw him last prior to this summer. He hasn't aged a day, his dark just fucked hair hangs to his collar, his emerald-green eyes with gold flecks have barely a wrinkle. He has his sleeves rolled up exposing his muscular fore-arms. And those hands. Holy fuck. How can hands be so sexy? I've seen him here a handful of times over the past few months, yet this is the first time our eyes have made contact. His heated gaze moves up and down my body as he shifts uncomfortably in his seat. *Do you want to play, Dr. Lexington?* Picking up my cupcake I take a bite. I stick my finger into the middle of the cupcake, I scoop up the whipped cream as I lock my eyes on his, licking my finger to the tip. When I stick my finger in my mouth and suck off the remaining cream, he looks like he might explode. Liam and Xander sit in Maribel's section. Damn lucky, Maribel. He glances at Xander and then back up at me, his gaze following my mouth. His tongue darts up and slowly slides across his bottom lip. Fuck. I'm going to come just watching him. My eyes travel down his body, and I'm delighted to notice his chest rising and falling faster than before.

Finally, customers sit in my section ending our eye-fucking. I walk over to the table, pasting a fake smile on my face.

"Good evening, I'm Mercy. I'll be your server tonight. Can I get you something to drink?"

"Two beers, whatever's on tap is fine," the blond man says, both of them smile at me as if I'll be, tonight's meal. I get hit on all the time, they'll get nowhere with me, because I'm saving myself for the man at table eight. Only Liam. I can't hide my smile as I walk away, glancing at the table I wanted. His eyes follow me as I walk back to the bar. We play this cat-and-mouse game the entire time he's here. He's tracking me with his stunning blue orbs as if he's waiting for the perfect moment to pounce. He probably doesn't remember me, but I remember him. The last time I saw him was at his son Nash's sixteenth birthday party before

I went to college. I was captivated by him then, but I knew he would not get involved with a sixteen-year-old. It would have been an emphatic hell no. Besides, I'm sure my braces, thick glasses and under-developed body were not exactly a turn-on. So, I've bided my time, waiting, and the way he's staring at me tonight, the time is about right. Just a little longer until I set my plan in motion. I need to be patient. *He will be mine.*

After several drinks, the object of my affection and Dr. Kane rise from their seats to leave. As Liam walks to the door, he glances back, his eyes gazing up and down my body before settling on my face one last time. Shaking his head as if trying to snap himself out of a trance, his lips form a tight line, and he turns, walking out the door. My breathing returns to normal after several minutes. Could he tell, what he did to me? I internally pat myself on the back for keeping my shit together while he was here or at least appearing to.

Mirabel walks up to me as I clean my last table. "What was that about?" she asks.

"What?" I glance up at her feigning confusion even though I know exactly what she's referring to.

"Dr. Lexington, the way he stared at you, holy shit, I thought the place was going to catch on fire. Do you know him?" She fans herself dramatically.

I smile, "Not really."

The topic of Liam and I are on a need-to-know basis and gossipy as fuck Mirabel does not need to know. I like her just fine, but I know anything I tell her is likely to be repeated to everyone in the bar which then will move across the street to the hospital which is not what I need right now.

"Oh girl, he wants more than to know you."

I giggle, "Have a good night, Mirabel. I'm out."

"You too, sweetie. I'm going to miss you."

She pulls me into a hug, "I hope you're going to visit."

A smile creeps across my face, "A pack of wild horses couldn't keep me away."

After gathering my things and counting down my register, I'm done working here. Tomorrow, I start my first day as a social worker, officially. Earlier today, I had orientation and a tour of the hospital. I've wanted to be a social worker since I was eleven, when a social worker came into my school on career day. When cancer snatched my little sister from me, I knew this is where I'd end up.

With trembling hands, I wipe a tear from my cheek, my heart is heavy as I try to keep it together. As a social worker, I know there's no time limit on grief, but it's been nine years. I would have expected not to feel like this by now. Still, memories flash before me, us shopping together, goofing around, swimming in the pool, and then her in a hospital bed, dying. Pulling into my parking spot, I park the car, allowing the sorrow to consume me as it frequently does.

I crawl into the bed beside her frail body, pulling her into my arms. I'm as gentle as possible. She whispers, "I don't want to leave you." "Laney, I know, but you just worry about yourself. I'll be okay. You'll always be with me. Baby sister, you'll never be gone, because you're cemented in my heart."

My mom looks on with tears streaming down her face.

"When you're ready to go, you just go. I love you so much. You've been the best sister I could've ever dreamed of. Thank you."

A tear falls from her hazel eyes that match mine to a T. Our eyes are why everyone always thinks we're twins.

"I love you too. Always together. Even death can't tear us apart," she said.

That's something we've said to each other since I was seven. But now, the words have never been truer. I pull her tighter as the tears fall relentlessly.

Those were her last words as she died in my arms. At fifteen, I lost my fourteen-year-old sister. And the pain has never subsided. It lives within me, a raging inferno in my heart, never to be extinguished.

Finally, I make it to my apartment and collapse on my bed. The tears I've cried have exhausted me, so I fall into a slumber.

* * *

LIAM

. . .

I lie in bed thinking about the woman at the bar. I asked Xander about her, but he told me she starts working at the hospital tomorrow, so to leave her alone. I think his words were, 'Keep your dick out of the workplace.' I know he's not wrong. It's never a great idea to tie up and spank your co-workers into submission. He knows what I'm like. We've known each other since ninth grade when he moved to the Pocono Mountains. I don't do relationships other than sexual ones. Love is not a word I've ever uttered, other than to my son since his mother died twenty-three years ago. The darker side of sex appeals to me. I'm not gentle. It's not something I'm even capable of. She's too young for me, and I know that. Yet, when I saw what she did to that fucking cupcake, I nearly lost my damn mind. I need to see my cum on her lips in the worst fucking way.

When I was in medical school, I went to a therapist, she said I needed to change my treatment of women, no more spanking or controlling behavior. Fuck that. I'm fine just the way I am. For the record, I don't beat women. Spank, maybe, but I'd never really hurt them, well, at least not without consent. I do, however, fuck them. Normally, only once because the women frequently make that choice, 'you're too rough.' I've never found a woman that can match my sexual appetite. I know at the age of forty I probably never will. If it were going to happen it would've happened by now.

Xander said to leave her alone. But fuck, I can't get those eyes out of my mind. Dark, seductive, hazel-they drew me in and wouldn't let go. I couldn't avert my gaze as hard as I tried. And that body, fuck me, it was ravishing. She appeared to be about five-eight, wearing a naughty nurse costume, it's what all the waitresses wear but fuck she made it look so hot, her long creamy legs pulled my attention from my friend, her tits spilling out the top, begging for my tongue. It's her face that did me in, those stunning eyes that I could get lost in for days, those pouty lips, and even her fucking cheekbones are sexy. I'm not sure that I've ever been more attracted to a woman in my life. She looked young. I know I need to leave her alone. But that doesn't stop my hand from reaching into my boxer shorts and pulling my cock out.

She walks up to me in the empty bar; I'm standing beside a table when she asks me what I'd like to drink. "What do you want to drink?" I ask her. She takes her lip between her perfect teeth before responding, "You, Daddy." My shock is apparent. "Excuse me?" I ask her. "Every single drop," she smiles seductively. Kneeling in front of me, she undoes my pants and takes my cock out, gazing up at me from under her thick lashes. She licks the pre-cum from the head of my dick while moaning appreciatively before taking me inch by inch into her throat. I slide my hands into her dark waist-length hair, winding it in my fists, pulling hard as she slides my length down her throat, and whimpers. Tears stream down her cheeks as she gags, but I don't let up; I keep fucking her perfect mouth.

I stroke myself faster. I'm so close as I think about shooting my seed down her beautiful throat. A few more pumps and cum shoots onto my stomach, as I convulse with the best orgasm I've had in years, by my own fucking hand, thinking about this mystery woman. She is driving me fucking crazy and I don't even know her name. Maybe I like the mystery. I could have very easily asked Xander her name, but I didn't.

Two

LIAM

WAKING UP THE NEXT MORNING, I do what I do every day. I head down to my gym in the basement to work out my frustrations of life.

As music blasts in my earbuds, I adjust my stance for my next round of shoulder presses. I move to the beat of the music, oblivious to the world around me. Anyone who knows me knows not to disturb me when I work out. Everyone except my son Nash. He knows better, but he just doesn't care. It's always about what dad can do for him, everything is always about Nash. An earbud gets yanked from my ear. I set the weight down and spin around with a glare.

"Nash."

"Dad," he nods at me.

"What is it? What do you want now?" I say, pausing my music.

I know I sound cold towards my only child, but he infuriates me, to say the least. If he's here, it's not to see his father. There's only one reason Nash shows his face these days, he wants something.

He laughs, "I wanted to talk to you."

"What do you need money for this time?"

Reaching to my right, I grab a towel from my towel rack and wipe the sweat from my brow.

"I don't need money. I want to have a party."

"So have a party, you have your own apartment, you don't need my permission."

He pinches the bridge of his nose, "No, I want to have it here."

"Why?"

"Well, it's summer, and you can't have a pool party in an apartment without a pool."

I sigh as I run my hand through my hair, "A bunch of kids at my house, I don't know."

"Dad, I'm twenty-three. We aren't kids anymore. We're adults."

I roll my eyes; he certainly doesn't act like an adult. He lives off daddy's money and has never worked a day in his life. These visits normally involve him asking for more money. I pay for his apartment, car, food, utilities, everything, but somehow, it's never enough.

"How many people?"

"Thirty for the party, but I thought that a few of us could stay from Thursday until Tuesday after it's done."

"How many are a few?"

"Three."

"Alright, fine," I say. This is exactly what I need, a bunch of drunk kids at my house.

"Thanks, Dad!"

I yell, "Get a job, will you?" as he walks back upstairs to leave.

He shakes his head but doesn't respond, he rarely does.

"Damn kids," I say to myself. Sometimes I think he is this way because I give him too much. I know I should be tougher with him. I've always been gentler because he doesn't have a mom. I wonder if she were still here if he'd have his shit together. Most days, it seems I'm lacking as a father. I love a little too hard when it comes to Nash.

Walking up to my home office, I sit at my large cherry wood desk. I've got a patient, a little girl, that has acute myeloid (AML), cancer of the bone and blood. I've been treating her since she was one. She's had a rough life, going through chemotherapy at such a young age. I remember her ringing the bell when she went into remission. She is the cutest five-year-old I have ever seen. When you spend years treating the same patient, you can't help but form an attachment. It's inevitable. Last night, her sweet little face haunted my dreams. Her cancer is back, and the profound sadness in her eyes cut through me like a knife. The chemotherapy was so hard on her little body the first time, there were a few days when I thought we might lose her. Now, here we are again.

After finishing the treatment plan, I shower and prepare for the day. Today, I am not wearing my normal work clothes.

I pull on my princess scrubs, just for five-year-old Ivy. I am sure I look ridiculous, but it'll make her smile. That's the most important thing right now.

Walking through the door to the garage, I slide into my black Escalade. Opening the garage door, I back out, wind down my driveway, and head out the gate. It's about a thirty-minute drive to the children's hospital. After fumbling with the radio, I finally find a station that I like and crank it up. I drive into the doctor's parking lot and pull into my reserved spot.

As I walk into the hospital, many of the nurses smile and wave. They are much better behaved now that I've been here for a while. When I first started here, they called me Doc Delicious behind my back. They slid panties under the on-call room door. I put an end to that shit quickly. They still glance my way with fuck-me eyes that all go ignored. I'm a doctor, not a fuck boy. Besides, I am sure they couldn't handle the experience. I knock on Ivy's door before opening it slowly.

"Dr. L," she yells!

I can't help the chuckle that bubbles out of my chest.

Pulling up a stool beside her bed, I take a seat. I nod to her mom, who stands on the other side of her bed, appearing to be ready to make a mad dash out of this hospital room.

Ivy pulls on the hem of my shirt. "You're wearing princesses!" She squeals excitedly.

My lips turn up into a grin that spreads from ear to ear. "Do you like them?"

A very serious expression crosses her face. "Dr. L, I love princesses. They are my favorite. Especially Elsa," she says, pointing at the princess on my shirt.

I smile, "How are you, sweetheart?"

"I'm sad that I have cancer again," she hangs her head low as she twists her knotted fingers.

"Me too, Ivy. But guess what?" I say, trying to sound upbeat.

Her eyes snap to mine with a questioning look.

"You're going to kick cancer's butt twice! Right?" I arch an eyebrow at her expectantly.

"Yes! Super Ivy!"

I chuckle as she giggles. "That's right, sweetheart."

"Can I talk to your mom for a minute?"

"Will you come back?" Her eyes are practically begging me to say yes.

"They are going to come in and put your port in while I see other patients. I'll tell you what, let's have lunch together. What do you want?"

"I'll have a cheeseburger and fries before I get sick again," she says with unshed tears in her eyes. It breaks my heart that she knows the sickness that's sure to be coming. I won't give her false hope though, she is going to get sick, really sick.

"You've got it, kiddo." I smile and nod to her mom, who follows me to the hall.

"We're going to do chemo again as well as targeted drug therapy."

"What's that?" she asks.

"Simply put, it targets the cancer cells, and the goal is that it stops them from growing and ultimately kills them."

"Okay," she says with an annoyed expression on her face. "That sounds very expensive."

I sigh, "It will be. However, there are payment plans available if you talk to billing. Also, like last time I will not be charging my fees." When Ivy went through chemo last time, I knew finances were an issue. My fees were all waived. It's something I do whenever I have patients in this type of situation. I don't need the money. I could retire today and never want for anything. Money is not why I'm a pediatric oncologist. If there was a hospital that provided free treatment I'd work, there. I hate the pharmaceutical companies that get rich off poor, dying people. It makes me sick.

She folds her arms across her chest in obvious annoyance.

I nod to the social worker, and she comes over.

"This is Ivy's mom, Linda. Maybe you could show her to the billing office?"

She smiles, "Of course, doctor."

I put my hand on Linda's shoulder. "It's going to be okay."

I'm rewarded with a scowl, "That's easy for you to say. You're not the one that has to pay for this."

I paste a fake smile on my face, "I'll be back for lunch."

I go to the doctor's on-call room to take a breath before my consultation. Days like this are hard for me. You never want to see a cancer patient relapse. It's almost worse than when they first get diagnosed because they know what the road will look like. I sit on the bed as I shake my head.

I try to distract myself for a moment, I read through my emails. There is one that catches my eye in an instant, 'Welcome to Our New Employees'. Opening it I scan it looking for one person. My dick twitches when I see her picture. Fuck, she's so beautiful. Mercy Madison. I can't. She's working here now, and damn, she's young. She would get hurt, this much I know. I'm an asshole, but even I have lines that I won't cross. What is it with this woman? Why can't I get her out of my head? I pull up Instagram and search for her now that I know her name. Fuck me, this picture of her in a gold bikini is going to do me in. God, she's stunning. She's beautiful in such a natural way. Mercy doesn't wear a ton of makeup to cover her flaws. I'm not sure she has any. And those curves... I love a woman with meat on her bones and damn does she have the perfect amount.

The last woman I was with wanted vanilla, candles, flowers, a gentle lover, all the shit I simply don't do. I know it works for most people, but it does nothing for me. The other problem is I don't do relationships, sex only for me. I'm simply not cut out for relationships; I can't be *that* guy. I've never been in one other than Nash's mom, and back then, I was too young to know what I wanted. I wouldn't know how to start. Besides, if cancer has taught me anything, it's that getting attached to people is dangerous. Everyone around me seems to die.

I grab my phone off the bed and put it in my pocket, and I can't get that face out of my damn head. I'm sure a woman like that has a boyfriend, anyway. I drag my hand down my face and rise off the bed and head to my next patient.

The morning races by in a flash, and it's lunchtime. I ordered hamburgers, French fries, and dessert from a nearby steakhouse. My phone goes off, letting me know the Uber driver has dropped it off, so I grab it from the nurse's station before heading to Ivy's room.

I knock on Ivy's door and walk in, "Lunch time!"

She beams at me as she puts down the iPad in her hands. She squeals, "It smells so good! I'm starving to death."

Her mother has a disinterested expression. Something is off there, but I can't put my finger on it.

I pull up a seat beside Ivy and take the food out, handing hers to her first.

"A steakhouse?" Linda asks, her pitch slightly raised, "You didn't have to do that. The cafeteria would have been fine."

"I wanted steakhouse hamburgers. Have you had the food in the cafeteria?" I shudder dramatically.

Ivy giggles as she takes a bite of her hamburger.

As we sit there eating, my phone chimes, and I fetch it from my pocket to see who it is.

Nash: We'll be there tonight, just so you know.

I groan. Great, thanks for the notice, kid. He had said they'd be at my house tomorrow. I guess he can't wait to torture his old man.

Linda looks at me questioningly.

I chuckle, "Spoiler alert. They don't get any easier when they're grown up."

She smiles but it doesn't reach her eyes.

I'm tempted to stay at a hotel while his friends are there, but I also want to make sure he doesn't destroy my damn house. I'm sure now that they're old enough, there will be alcohol and sex.

Taking the last bite of my hamburger, I toss my trash in the bag. Ivy ate almost all her food; she must have been quite hungry.

"That was so good, Dr. L. Thank you!"

"You're so welcome, Princess."

Her ear-to-ear grin soothes my black heart.

I fell in love with Nash's mom in high school, she was my entire fucking world, then she got cancer. They diagnosed her with ovarian cancer after she got pregnant with Nash. We were advised she'd need to have an abortion so she could start chemo, but she refused. There was no talking her out of having him. She loved him so much from the moment we found out she was pregnant; she sacrificed her life for him. Nash was born three weeks early by induction. Her body couldn't wait any longer. They thought she might die before he was born, which would risk his life. Within minutes of her giving birth, she died in that hospital room. She held him, looked into his eyes, and said, "I love you, baby boy. I'll be watching you," then she was gone, it happened so fast. It was as if she held on just to deliver him and look at him, once. I took Nash into my arms as they attempted to revive her. Somehow, my world ended and began on the same day. It was a lot for a seventeen-year-old kid to take in. In one day, I lost my girlfriend and gained a son, becoming a single parent. I was lucky that my parents were there for me. I don't know what would have happened to us if they weren't. They made it possible for me to attend medical school and provide Nash with the life he knows today. I'm lucky to have them. They adopted me when I was three days old and never treated me as if I wasn't theirs.

I guess that's why I get so pissed off when I see him squandering his life. She lost hers as he was gifted his. I love my son with everything I have. I just wish he'd do more with this gift. Another thing cancer taught me is that life is precious and can vanish in a breath.

I squeeze Ivy's hand and glance at her, "Okay, sweetheart. We will start chemo tomorrow. I talked to your mom about the medication we are adding. We're going to kill those cancer cells, right?"

She nods, a tear escaping from her eye.

"Every day, when you wake up, I want you to say, today, I'm going to kill cancer cells! Can you do that for me?"

Her lips turn up into a slight smile.

"Yes, Dr. L, I promise."

I wink at her, "I'll be working from home until Tuesday, so we'll do our chats on video. Is that okay?"

She nods.

"Okay, I'll talk to you tomorrow."

"Okay," she says in a quiet, shaky voice.

"Linda, can you walk me to the elevator?"

Rising from her seat, she glances at Ivy, "I'll be right back."

As we walk, I wait to talk until we are out of earshot.

"It's important for Ivy to keep a positive attitude. I probably had this conversation with you before, but it bears repeating. The mind is closely linked to the body. I believe if she stays positive, she'll have a far better outcome."

"I'm not sure I can do this again."

What the fuck is wrong with this woman? I completely understand that cancer is hard on the loved ones. But it's not about her, it's about her daughter. She needs to stay strong for that little girl. She isn't sure if she can do this again? How does she thinks Ivy feels?

"You don't have a choice. We are here to support you. You will get through this. Call me if you need anything. Otherwise, I'll talk to you both tomorrow."

"Thank you."

"You're welcome. I'll see you tomorrow."

She walks away as I press the button for the elevator. I'm heading home because I want to set some ground rules for my son.

Three

LIAM

WALKING INTO MY HOUSE, I head to my bathroom to take a shower and change into something other than my princess scrubs. I don't want his friends to see me like this. It's difficult to take a man wearing princess clothes seriously. I throw my phone on the bed and step to my bathroom. It's the master bathroom in my bedroom, so I'm not expecting anyone to be there.

Mercy is standing in front of me with a towel in her hand, but not covering her body. I can't control myself, I should walk away, but I won't. I can't.

My gaze takes her stunning body in, traveling up, down, and back up again. My God, she's beautiful from fucking head to toe. Her long, wet, wavy, brown hair hangs to her waist, her hazel eyes penetrate mine, her breasts, those fucking breasts. My pants are suddenly uncomfortable, my dick so rigid it's painful.

"Dr. Lexington," she says as she exhales a sharp breath. Her chest rises and falls rapidly.

I am fighting with everything I have not to grab and kiss her, taking her right here in my fucking bathroom.

Moving closer to her, I run my fingers down her arm. She shivers beneath my touch, making me only crave her more.

"Tell me, baby girl, why are you naked in my bathroom?" She swallows hard, and the way her throat bobs when she does, is making me crazy. How can this even be possible? I don't know her, yet I ache for her as if I've waited a lifetime for her to be close enough to touch. Midlife crisis maybe?

"Nash is my best friend. He invited me," she squeaks.

Fuck me, she's young, works at the hospital, and is my son's best friend. How much more fucking off-limits can she get? And why isn't that stopping me?

I run my finger from her jaw down to her neck, and her eyes close as she moans.

Fuck me.

Forbidden. Off-limits. Stop fucking touching her!

I touch her bottom lip, and she whimpers. Every sound she makes is driving me to the brink of insanity. Then she takes her bottom lip between her teeth just as I fantasized, she would. I'm about two seconds from doing something I know I shouldn't, when my brain finally overcomes my starving body. It's been a long time for me, and I don't think I've ever been this fucking horny. I've fantasized about her non-stop since I saw her in the bar. Now she's materialized, naked in my bathroom like the most delicious temptation that she is. Fuck me.

"Baby girl, you better go before I lose my damn mind and do something we'll both regret."

"Yes, sir. I'm sorry, Dr. Lexington."

Yes, sir, she's trying to kill me.

"Liam is fine, Mercy."

"Liam," she whispers, as if she's testing out my name on her tongue.

It's at this exact moment, I know this woman is going to have me begging for mercy.

"Liam, can I get dressed first?"

"Of course," as if I'm going to have her walk through the house naked on full display for the other boys here. I'm not sure why but the thought of other men looking at her enrages me, which, of course, makes no sense whatsoever.

Her eyes are begging me to fuck her. There's nothing I'd love more than to do exactly that, but I know it's not an option. Before, it was just a bad idea but now that I know she's friends with my son? It's not just a bad idea. It's fucking impossible.

Why did he have to bring *her*?

I grab my bottle from my nightstand and make myself a drink. I make quick work of downing the amber liquid. After our encounter, my nerves are shot. My dick is so hard I am not sure it'll ever go down. Her naked body is anchored into my brain, and it's not going anywhere, anytime soon.

She comes out of the bathroom, and while she isn't naked, she's still so sensual in a metallic purple bikini, drawing me in, like the apple called to Eve. I pour myself another drink as she walks up to me. She takes the glass from my hand and takes a drink. I watch her mouth as she takes a long sip and then moans, licking her lips. The way she sounds, fuck, I could listen to her moaning all day and never tire of it.

"That's so good. Thank you, Liam." she says, her voice sounding sweet, but her lips curve into a sinister grin.

She runs her fingers down my chest as she smirks at me.

"Princesses. I never pictured you as a princess kind of guy. Have you ever read any of the smutty fairy tales, Liam? I have, and they always make me wet."

As I run a hand through my hair, she flashes me a sexy smile as she reaches out and strokes my jaw, her fingers rubbing my stubble.

"I'll see you later," she says in a low, sultry tone.

She turns and walks out of my bedroom, leaving me with the bluest balls any man has ever had. Oh, she's a bad girl. She knows exactly what she's doing to me. All I can think about is punishing her, taking a belt to her ass until she safe words.

I wander into the kitchen and grab the leftover pot roast my chef prepared earlier. As I stand at the island eating my dinner, Mercy stands behind me, pressing her body into mine.

She moans, "It's good, isn't it?"

I reach around my back, grab her by her wrists, and pull her to me. "Baby girl, I don't know what game you're playing, but you're my son's best friend, so it's not happening."

She gazes at me with those bedroom eyes, "Forbidden fruit is always the sweetest, don't you think?" I release her hands, and she giggles as she walks away.

I know that the next week is going to be pure torture. What is this girl after? Is she like so many, fixated on hooking up with a doctor? I'll never understand the fascination. Too many medical dramas, probably. *Fucking Grey's Anatomy.*

I finish my dinner and rinse my plate, putting it in the dishwasher. Walking into the living room, I spot Nash and his friends watching TV. They are all on the couch except Mercy is lying on the floor, on her stomach. Her ass, my God, her ass, is delectable. I want nothing more than to get on the floor with her and fuck her until she screams. When she laughs at the reality show they are watching, something twists in my stomach. Her laugh is perfect, high pitched, a giggle, really. And suddenly, I don't know if I want to fuck her or make her laugh again. *What the fuck, Liam?*

I take my sex-crazed ass back to my bedroom. I have not been this horny since I was a teenager. I can't walk past my bathroom without thinking of her tiny, naked body standing there, moans escaping from her soft lips. Lips that I am dying to taste but tell myself I never will. I can't.

A few drinks later, I settle into bed with a book about treating cancer in children. I want to make sure there's nothing I'm missing. I hold young lives in my hands. So, I stay up to date on all the new treatments, never wanting to fall behind on fresh new developments.

I read for a few hours before my eyes get heavy, and I place the book on the end table beside my bed before falling asleep.

Four

LIAM

RISING out of bed at six o'clock in the morning, I head to the kitchen to make coffee. Nash and all his friends are at the table. What the hell are they doing up so early? Aren't young twenty-somethings supposed to sleep all day? I nod to them as I make my coffee.

I pour myself a cup and sip it as I stand there in my own little world. Nash's voice snaps me out of my daydream about a certain woman I found in my bathroom yesterday.

"Dad?"

I turn around, facing Nash, arching an eyebrow at him.

"This is Jessica. You know Matt, and do you remember Mercy?"

Pasting a fake smile on my face, "I do."

I didn't, but obviously, I'm acquainted with her now. Did I know her before? Nash seems to think so, but I sure as hell do not remember meeting her before seeing her in the bar. Somehow, I can't imagine I would have ever met her and not remembered her. She's unforgettable.

She blushes crimson. Fuck me. I'm staring at her; I can't help it. She's wearing that gold bikini from the Instagram picture. It shows off her body perfectly, all of her curves are on display, her creamy white complexion, my eyes roam her body, taking it all in. When I get to her tits nearly spilling out of the top, I salivate. This is slow, sweet torture. I

19

imagine, slowly peeling that gold bikini off her pale skin. I bet her ass will look incredible with red marks on it. *Her soft moans echo in my ears while I trail my tongue down her body, inhaling her scent, making her come on my tongue—her hands in my hair as she trembles in ecstasy.*

"Umm Dad?"

My eyes snap to Nash, "Sorry, I was lost in thought for a minute."

Uncontrollably, my sight goes back to Mercy as she bites her lip like she can read my mind, and I glance back to Nash. After clearing my throat and my sexual thoughts I say, "I'll see you kids later. I have work to do."

"Dr. Lexington?"

I sigh, damn it, I was so close to escaping.

"I was wondering if I could pick your brain about being an oncologist?"

Nash beams with pride, "Mercy graduated with a degree in social work. She just started at the children's hospital."

"Wouldn't it be better to pick the brain of a social worker, then?"

She smiles sweetly, "I'd love to know more about what it's like from a doctor's perspective. The medical aspect."

I run a hand through my hair, "Of course. Anytime, Mercy. My office is upstairs. I'm working from home for the next few days."

I'm sure if my son knew how badly I want to fuck his friend he wouldn't be pushing us together. I'm trying to stay away from her, but now I'm going to be cornered into being alone with her in my office. I bet she'd look beautiful bent over my desk. My dick jumps in excitement. *You settle down, it's not fucking happening.*

Picking up my coffee cup, I walk up to my office. I'm in my pajama pants, no shirt—the pleasure of working from home. Of course, when I have video chats with patients, I have to be in proper attire, but this is fine for now. Well, until the knock at my door.

Glancing up, Mercy walks through my office door, this girl does not waste time. Her lips turn up into a sweet smile. "Dr. Lexington." I'm not sure why but when she calls me doctor, my dick instantly swells.

"Mercy, just call me Liam."

Her cheeks get pink, and I have to adjust myself slightly behind my desk. Damn, she's so alluring. Her dark hair hangs to her waist, her bikini shows off her curves, curves that I want to run my fingers down. She stares at me with intense hazel eyes as she bites her lip. Fuck me.

"Liam, thank you for taking time out of your day for me."

Rising from my chair, I stalk towards her like a madman. My fingers grip the top of her bikini, and she stares at me in surprise. I rip her top from her body, and she gasps. Cupping her beautiful breasts, I go right to them, feasting on them. Never taking my mouth off her perfect pink bud, I bite down, running my hands up her legs, I untie her bottoms. She moans, "Yes, please fuck me." I yank my pants down, freeing my cock, thrusting into her. With my hand on her throat and holding her against the wall, I continue fucking her hard while she whimpers my name.

"Liam?"

Snatched from my daydream, I clear my throat, "Sorry, my mind was somewhere else. Have a seat, Mercy."

She sits on my couch and crosses her legs, making me drool. The way her thigh is stretched over her other leg, I am dying to spread her legs and touch her bottoms. Are they wet? Fuck, I'd like to find out.

"Is it difficult to work with sick children day in and day out?"

"Of course, it is," that was a stupid question. And I know this girl is smarter than this.

She nods as she fidgets with her knotted hands.

I rise out of my chair and walk around my desk, leaning against it, I stand in front of her. As I watch her, I force my mind to stay pure while gripping my desk on either side of me to stay grounded.

"How do you deal with it?"

"I just do. I'm there to take care of them compassionately."

Darting her tongue out, she licks and then bites her bottom lip.

Her hands move to the strings on her bikini. She rubs a finger along the stitching, driving me insane.

"Mercy. What's this about? Why are you in my office?"

She swallows hard and rises off the couch and moves over to me, placing a hand over the skin covering my heart.

"I think we both know why I'm here." Her fingertips trail down my bare chest. She draws circles around my nipple, my racing pulse and ragged breathing give me away. I know she's aware of how she affects me. Fuck.

"You're the poison infecting every cell in my body. But you're also the antidote. My body aches for yours, Dr. Lexington." She whispers.

Stepping closer, her body is pressed against mine, she places her hands around my neck, stands on her tiptoes, and pulls me down, putting her lips against my throat. Dashing her tongue out, she slides it downward. And I swear to God, I'm about to fucking lose all control. Her tongue is warm, wet, and everything I want on every inch of my body. I never want it to end, I want more, so much more. My dick aches for her mouth with an indescribable need. Then I remember why I can't do this. Nash. Fuck. I can't let this continue.

"Mercy, stop."

She gazes at me with dark eyes, "Liam, I know you want me as much as I want you."

"No. It's not happening, not now, not ever," she presses against my hungry cock.

"Why?"

"You are twenty-three years old; I am forty and you are my son's best friend."

"He doesn't need to know. And I'm old enough to make you feel good," she said. "Let me make you feel good," she whispers. *Fuck, baby girl, I want that so much, but I can't. Please stop torturing me.*

Her fingers wrap tightly around my cock as she strokes me through my pants. My control is hanging on by a fine thread. I'm dangerously close to snapping the proverbial thread.

I grab her wrists, "No, Mercy. No."

Backing away, she looks defeated.

"I can't," I say regretfully.

I'm about two seconds away from doing something I really shouldn't do. So, I walk back behind my desk and sit down. "You should go. I have work to do. Close the door on your way out," this is what I have to do. I must shut this down. This can't happen between us. There's too much as stake. Fuck. I bet her pussy would feel so good on my cock.

"Yes, sir," she says with irritation.

Fuck. She doesn't know it, but if she had called me sir about two minutes ago, with her hand on my cock, I wouldn't have been able to turn her down. I would've fucked her senseless, but then I would've regretted it the second I had to look my son in the face. A good father does not fuck his son's friends.

I drag my hand down my face, I can't get her mouth out of my head. The things I wish I could do to her but can't. *Back to work, Liam.*

I pour over my patient charts; six kids are starting chemo today. They've all had ports put in and are ready to go. Chemo with kids is a little different. Adults know about cancer and chemo even if they haven't experienced it personally; these kids mostly learn about it as they go. When they are told they will get sick, they don't understand how sick they will get because they've never known sickness like chemo. Kids figure it out quickly, of course. It's hard on them, it's hard on their families, and it's even difficult for the medical staff. As a doctor specializing in kids with cancer, I see the devastation cancer leaves in its wake daily. When these little souls struggle and sometimes die, it destroys everything in its path. You never fully recover from a loss like that. So, I do my best to prevent that from happening. My goal is to provide compassionate care to these children and their families. But, if I'm honest, sometimes it becomes a little much; that's where my much-needed release comes in. *Fuck, Liam, get her out of your head.*

People think I'm crazy sometimes for losing so many to cancer and becoming an oncologist. Sometimes I agree with them, but after my twin brother died from leukemia, I knew I would do this with my life. I know the grief firsthand, so I think I contribute something different than some of my colleagues.

Placing a call to one of my favorite nurses, I check on my patients. So far so good, but it's early. The sickness will normally start four to six hours after treatment.

Next up is my buddy, Javiar. He's a genius computer programmer, and has been helping me develop a game for the kids at the hospital. It'll be called "Kill Cancer", it's a game that has them kill the cancer cells with different colored drugs. Think *Dr. Mario* but for smaller kids. I hope that the positive messages at the end of each level will keep them going on days when it's easy to lose hope. It's not something we will ever sell, it's just for *my kids*. Some of these children spend months in the hospital. They get bored, and many love games, especially when they are too sick to get out of bed.

"Javiar. Where are we?"

He laughs. I've been asking him that same question for two years now. "You're gonna be happy, doc. It's ready."

"Wonderful," I said.

"If you bring the tablets to me, I'll install it on all of them."

"I'll see you soon," I say with a ridiculous grin. I've waited impatiently for this day, hounding him on a near daily basis.

Five

LIAM

RISING FROM MY DESK, Nash walks in.

"Hey, son. I'm getting ready to leave to have the chemo game installed on the tablets for the kids. Did you need something?"

"No, but maybe you could take Mercy. It will mean a lot to me if you'd help her settle in at the hospital."

I slide my hands into my pockets trying to hide my irritation.

"Nash, I don't think that's a great idea."

"Why?"

Of course, I can't tell him why, so I just say, "Fine."

"Great, thanks Dad. I'll go tell her, "He beams at me. Fucking beams at me because of Mercy. Is there something going on between them? And why does that single thought have my blood boiling? *She's not yours, she never will be. Whatever and whoever she does is not of your damn business.*

I drag my hand down my face as he leaves, I'm not happy about this. I'm trying to stay away from this woman, not be forced closer to her.

I head downstairs to my bathroom and jump in the shower to prepare for the day. All I can fucking think about is finding Mercy naked here. Standing under the hot spray, I put my hands on the wall and try to clear my brain. The water falls down my back, and damn it, it's not relaxing me at all. Stepping back from the spray, I take my cock in my hand and stroke it while thinking about Mercy's naked body. In my mind, she's in the shower with me, kneeling, begging for my dick. I stroke faster. This new fantasy is my favorite. Leaning my back against the shower wall for support, I'm about to come undone when I catch movement through my shower door to my left. Mercy is staring at me with my cock in my hand.

What the hell is wrong with this woman?

"Have you no boundaries, whatsoever, Mercy?"

She smiles, staring down at my dick in my hand with her lips parted.

"Wait in the bedroom, please."

Licking her lips, she says, "Yes, sir."

Turning off the water, I step out of the shower and dry off. I pull my boxers on and step into the bedroom.

"What the fuck is wrong with you?" I bite.

She smirks at me, "I hope you at least got to finish."

Pushing her up against the wall, I grab her throat, holding her in place. "Listen here baby girl, keep pushing and you'll learn more about me than you ever wanted to know. You're playing with fucking fire. Fuck around and find out, little girl," she moans. I've got her by her fucking throat, and she moans like she's going to come. "Stop fucking with me." I let her go and walk to my closet to get dressed.

Her voice travels through the room. "Do you think that scared me, Liam?"

I sigh a deep breath; this woman is exasperating.

"All it did was make me wet and want you more."

I get my suit pants, socks, and shoes and get them on as I shake my head. "Mercy, you're impossible."

Glancing over at her, she giggles, "I know what I want, and I'm not afraid to go after it."

"Even if it costs you your job?" I arch an eyebrow at her.

She giggles. I could easily make one quick phone call that would end her employment. She certainly doesn't appear concerned.

I pull on a white dress shirt and put it on as she watches me with an intense gaze. After putting on my suit, I glance at her while slipping my shoes on, "Let's go."

She smiles, "Yes, sir."

"Would you stop calling me that?"

She throws me a seductive look, and says, "I think you like it."

Ignoring her comment, I walk out to the garage with her following me. We get in, and I drive away.

Trying to make small talk, I ask her, "What made you get into social work? And why kids' with cancer?"

There's pain in her expression when I glance at her.

"I lost my sister to cancer eight years ago. After that happened, I felt like I could have extra compassion for people going through the same thing. I always knew I wanted to be a therapist, help people, but it was then that I knew it needed to be kids with cancer."

"I'm sorry, Mercy."

Glancing over at her again, I see the ache and it's heartbreaking.

"She fought a long, hard battle. At least she's not in pain now. But I really miss her. She was my best friend. We did everything together. Someday, I want to open a cancer center that will provide free treatment and counseling for families affected by cancer that can't afford it."

I'm speechless. There's more to this overbearing sexual creature than I realized.

"That's wonderful and very much needed," I said.

She nods, "What about you? What made you get into pediatric oncology?"

"I always knew I wanted to be a doctor. When I lost my brother to leukemia, then I lost Nash's mom to cancer, and then my grandmother, an aunt, the list goes on. I knew I needed to be an oncologist, but when I was in medical school, I met a little boy that altered my world. He was going through chemo; he didn't make it. It was at his funeral that it came to me. Maybe I could've saved him. I was a cocky young man, but I believed I could've made a difference. There were other treatments that could've been done, not just chemo alone. I've always believed he needed more, and that might have made the difference between life and death. That little boy changed my life."

"What was his name?"

I smile, remembering him fondly, "Charlie."

We arrive at the hospital, and I find my usual parking spot. Getting out, we walk up to the door, and I hold it open for her.

"You're the Chief of Pediatric Oncology?" She says loudly.

"So, my parking spot says," I reply flatly.

"Wow, that's really impressive for such a young doctor," she says.

"Come on, I want to introduce you to someone before we pick up the tablets."

As we stand outside of Ivy's room Mercy starts to shake and backs away slowly. I watch her as tears run down her face. She fidgets with her shirt in clear agitation. Her eyes dart back and forth as her breathing gets heavy.

"I can't go in...there." She turns and sprints back toward the door.

What just happened?

I follow her out to the parking lot to find her sitting on a bench outside with her face in her hands, sobbing.

Quietly I sit beside her.

I watch the most beautiful woman I've ever seen break down before me. I don't know what to do, how to help. But something in me breaks seeing her like this. I want to take whatever this pain is away.

I know better than to touch her, but I have no choice. I pull her closer to me and rub her back.

"Shhh... I've got you."

She lays her head on my arm and fuck it feels good to have her so close.

"I'm sorry, Liam."

I kiss the top of her head, "What happened in there?"

"Room one twelve. My sister died in that room."

"Mercy, I didn't know. I'm sorry. I didn't even know your sister had been a patient here."

She looks up at me and smiles weakly.

"You were here, Liam."

Jesus Christ. This is not happening.

"What was her name?"

"Laney Madison."

It all comes rushing back. Laney had a sister barely older than her. We had to pry her away from Laney when she died. It took four grown men to separate them. I held Mercy while she cried. I had known her and the mother. She was Nash's best friend. Mercy was a cute kid, braces, glasses. I never would've imagined she'd turn into the stunning woman she is today. She looks so different.

"I'm sorry, I didn't save her. I was early in my career. At that point I did what I was told by my supervising oncologist. But that's no excuse, I'm sorry."

She smiles, "I've never blamed you. Honestly, you did everything you could. No one could have saved her. It wasn't detected until she was stage three. There is nothing you could have done, Liam."

Blowing out a breath she says, "You really didn't remember me?"

I chuckle, "You don't look anything like you did then. Even your hair color is different. You were a cute kid but I never imagined you'd grow into a woman this...beautiful."

She wipes her tears and kisses me on the cheek. "Thank you. Let's try this again."

"Mercy, you don't have to."

She sighs, "Actually, I do. If I'm going to be working here, I will have to go into that room. But I'm glad that I don't have to do it alone."

I open the door and we walk back into the hospital, I stay behind her letting her dictate the pace.

When we get to Ivy's room she stops, touches the door frame and exhales a loud sigh, "I'm ready," she says.

We walk into Ivy's room, and she lights up like a damn Christmas tree. "Dr. L!"

I smile at her, "Hi, sweetheart."

"I thought you weren't coming in for a few days."

"Well, I had to pick up the tablets so we can install the game I was telling you about. And I couldn't come here and not see my best girl."

She giggles, "It's finally ready?"

"It's finally ready. I want you to meet someone. This is Mercy. She's going to be working here. Mercy, this is Ivy."

A smile crosses her sweet little face, "It's nice to meet you. Are you a doctor too?"

"It's nice to meet you too, Ivy. I'm not a doctor. I'm a social worker."

"A social worker?" Ivy asks.

"Like Abby, she'll talk about the different feelings you might have while going through this."

"Yeah, Abby talks about 'big' feelings," she giggles. "Are you Dr. L's... *girlfriend*?" she asks in a sing-song voice.

"No," I said quickly. "How are you feeling today, Ivy?"

"I'm okay. I'll probably start getting sick soon, though."

I grab her chart and look it over; everything seems fine now. "Where's your mom today?"

Ivy sighs as she looks away, "Work. She can't afford to be off work this time. Mommy said we went broke last time."

I rub the stubble on my jaw as I wonder if she ever talked to billing.

"Dr. Lexington, can I talk to you outside for a minute?"

I wink at Ivy, "I'll be right back, okay?"

She giggles, "Go talk to your *girlfriend*."

Shaking my head at her, I walk out to the hall. "What is it, Mercy?"

"Can you go by yourself to get the games installed? I was thinking I could stay here with Ivy; I hate to see her alone. Maybe you could swing back by to pick me up?"

"Mercy, you don't have to work for free."

She smiles a radiant smile that makes me weak. "I really want to. It's not work, I'm just hanging out."

"Are you going to be okay in that room?"

"I'm okay now, I promise. It was just a shock."

"That's fine. I have to bring the tablets back, anyway. I can pick you up then."

I add, "You should know, she really likes princesses, almost to the point of obsession."

She laughs and fuck me, the way her eyes light up, "Completely normal."

"Really? Because I remember someone making fun of my princess clothes."

I grin as she smirks at me.

"Well, doctor, I have a couple things to say in response to that. First, I happen to love your princess scrubs. They are quite sexy on you. And second, were you just being friendly with me? I didn't know Mr. Grumpy could be so pleasant."

Arching an eyebrow as I feign shock, "Did you just call me grumpy?"

Walking back in, Mercy goes up to Ivy's bed and asks, "Would it be okay if I hung out for a little while?"

"Can we play until I get sick?"

"Anything you want," Mercy says.

I smile at them both. I suddenly see that there's more to Mercy than I originally thought. Still, it isn't happening, but seeing her like this makes my heart race.

"I'll see you ladies in a little while."

Mercy waves, and Ivy yells, "Bye, Dr. L!"

I laugh as I walk out the door to go pick up my pet project.

Six

MERCY

"WHAT DO you want to do first, Ivy?"

She touches her finger to her lips, clearly thinking hard.

"Can we go to the playroom? There are barbies there, but you have to be with a grown up. And the nurses are always too busy."

"Let me check with Dr. L."

I text Nash to get his father's number, and luckily, he replies immediately. So, I call Liam, delicious Liam. I've been in love with him since I was sixteen years old, okay maybe it was lust. I've never stopped thinking about him through the years, even when I didn't see him or Nash because of school. I was too young then, but I'm not now. Every fantasy I've ever had revolves around Liam Lexington. I want his hands on my body in the most excruciating way. The way he looks at me, I know he wants it too. Shaking my head to snap out of my thoughts, I dial his number.

"Dr. Lexington," he answers.

Even over the phone, he sounds sexy and makes my clit throb.

"It's Mercy. Can Ivy go to the playroom?"

"Mercy, you know very well the nurses could have answered that question."

A smirk crosses my face. I secretly love it when he's grumpy with me,

"Maybe, but you're on the phone so maybe you could just answer this lowly peasant's question really quick," I bite.

He sighs, "Yes, if she isn't sick. Bring a wheelchair, there should be one in her bathroom. If she refuses the wheelchair which she will, she can't go. When she gets sick it'll be sudden and hit her like a ton of bricks."

I grin, "Thank you, doctor."

He disconnects the call; I save his number on my phone; I'll definitely use it again.

Walking into the bathroom, I grab the wheelchair and bring it over to her bed.

"Not the wheelchair," she whines, "I can walk."

"Doctors orders, honey."

"Fine!" she yells with a scowl on her cute little face. She is an adorable little girl, with big brown eyes and long brown, curly hair. Little Ivy looks like a *Disney* character with those large, expressive eyes.

She gets into the wheelchair, and we go to the playroom. I help her out of the chair, and we sit on the floor with our legs crossed. First, we play barbies, but she gets bored rather easily.

"Can we paint?"

I nod, "We can do anything you want to."

"Not anything," she frowns, "All I want to do is go home and play with my friends." Her little hands are balled into fists.

"I know it must be hard being here."

"I love it when Dr. L comes to see me. But I hate it here. And my mom isn't here. I want my mommy." A tear rolls down her cheek.

My heart is shattering into a million different pieces.

"I have an idea that might help a little bit."

She gazes up at me with an inquisitive expression.

"What if you drew or painted a picture every day to show how you're feeling."

"Some days they might be ugly pictures," she said with a frown.

She fiddles with the barbie she still has in her hands. I think it's a reaction to anxiety as I observe her moving their limbs back and forth absentmindedly.

"That's okay. Sometimes we have ugly feelings."

With wide eyes, she gazes at me, "You have ugly feelings?"

"Everybody has ugly feelings, Ivy. Honey, everybody has hard days. What you feel is completely normal. Feelings are neither right or wrong, they are just feelings."

"Mommy says to paint pretty pictures," she said.

"Well, I think if you're painting a picture for someone it should be pretty. But when I paint it helps me get my feelings out. And sometimes, the ugly has to come out too. Do you want to try it?" I ask.

She nods, "Okay."

"Let me get the paint."

I get all the supplies we'll need off the top shelf of the cabinet and take them over to the art table.

"Okay here we go. Can I paint too?"

She beams at me, "Yes!" I help her get up off the floor and we sit at the table together.

I paint a little but mostly watch her to see how I can help. First, she paints a woman walking out a door, a small person; I assume it's her, crying. She's quite the artist, and she even paints an IV pole. This little girl is hurting, and not just from cancer, it goes deeper than that.

She paints mostly black and a little dark purple. She puts the paintbrush down, stares at the picture, and starts sobbing. Picking the paintbrush back up, she angrily swipes black paint over the people in her picture. She puts the brush back down again, balls up her fists, and sobs uncontrollably. I pull her into my arms and hold her to my chest. She cries between sobs, "I'm getting paint all over you."

"It doesn't matter," I say as I stroke her hair.

She cries for the longest time, and each sob tears another piece of my heart. But I don't let go. I will sit with her for as long as it takes.

Glancing up at the door, I see Liam standing in the doorway, watching us with concern etched on his face. I motion for him to come in, and he does. He squats down so he's eye level with Ivy.

"What's going on with my best girl?" he said.

"I'm sad," she says, staring up at him.

"I can see that, sweetheart. But why are you sad?"

"I miss mommy. I don't even know when she's coming back," she said.

"It's hard when your mommy has to work when you need her here, isn't it?" he asks. This man has such a gentle side when it comes to this little girl. I assume he's like this with all his patients, although I've only seen him with her. But it's beautiful. I wish all doctors had this bedside manner.

She nods.

"Did painting help at all?"

"Yes, it made me cry. But I feel better." She wipes her tears with her sleeve.

"How about if I come in every day and paint with you, as long as you feel up to it?"

She smiles but it doesn't reach her eyes, "Okay."

"I don't feel good. Can I go back to my room?"

"Of course."

Liam lifts her into the wheelchair, and we walk her back to her room, where Liam lifts her into bed.

"Get some sleep, sweet girl," he said.

"I'll see you tomorrow," I said.

Her face is ashen as she waves weakly. On our way out, he instructs the nurses to check in on her through the remainder of the day. We walk outside, and he turns to me as we step to his car.

"Why are you committing to coming to see her every day?"

"Because she needs someone, Liam."

"You don't have to. It's not your responsibility."

I smile, "I know. But I want to."

He pulls me into his arms tight against his chest, "Thank you."

I wrap my arms around him, "I didn't do it for you, but you're welcome."

He kisses me on the forehead, and a shiver runs down my spine.

Lifting my head, I gaze up at him. The air crackles between us and it's as if there's a force stronger than either of us, pulling us together. His gaze lowers to my lips, as he darts his tongue out and swipes his bottom lip.

He pushes me back against his car, taking my face in his hands, and leans down, sweeping his tongue across my lips. I part my lips as I moan, and he darts his tongue in my mouth, his dancing with mine with the perfect amount of suction. He moves his hands from my face to my hair. He pulls with force, and kisses me harder, as I melt into him. His lips move from my mouth down my neck, licking and biting as he growls. Pulling back suddenly, he looks dazed. Dragging his hand down his face, he says, "I'm so sorry, Mercy. I don't know why I did that. Fuck, I'm sorry. It won't happen again, let's go."

The best kiss of my entire life, and he's sorry. This man is infuriating. I get into the vehicle and stare out the window; I close my eyes and take a deep breath as I grip the armrest. There's this clear attraction between us that he wants to constantly deny. Then he finally kisses me, and he's fucking sorry.

"You're mad at me," he said as he drove away.

"You think?"

"I'm sorry, Mercy. I shouldn't have done that."

"I'm not mad that you kissed me, Liam. I never wanted it to end. I'm mad because you're sorry, and you want to pretend there's nothing between us. This attraction is not one-sided, and we both know it."

I know his son is my best friend, but we aren't married; this man is so frustrating. Why won't he let this go? He kissed me. I thought I was so close to getting what I've wanted for so long but now back to nothing.

He sighs as he turns onto the highway. "I wish it didn't exist, but it does. Mercy, I still can't act on it. That's why I apologized."

"Do you have a girlfriend or something?"

He laughs, "No, I don't have a girlfriend." Running his hand through his hair, "You know why. Nash. It would hurt him, so I can't. Besides, you're young. Mercy, I'm forty years old, and not the person you think I am. I'm not the kind of man you need. I'd only hurt you."

I raise my eyebrows as I stare at him, "How?"

He grips the steering wheel tight.

"I have a tendency of pushing women away with sex. I like things rough, Mercy. I'm not normal. Sex with me hurts. Trust me, baby girl, you don't want to go there with me."

"I'll take my chances, Liam. I'm not afraid of you. Bring it. I can handle anything you throw my way."

He pulls to the side of the road, his eyes blazing, "I won't be gentle with you, Mercy."

"Don't be," I said.

"Take your seatbelt off, now."

I do as I keep staring at him.

He pulls me over his lap, "Ass up. Now."

Liam pulls my skirt up, exposing my ass.

"Such a bad girl. You need to be punished."

"For what?" I stammer.

He growls as he slams his open hand against my ass.

"For tempting me so much," again he hits me in the same spot.

"Fucking dirty girl," he growls as his hand comes down again, stinging my flesh.

"Get up here," he commands.

I climb over the console and straddle him. Pulling my hair with force, he yanks my head back, exposing my neck. Running his tongue up my neck, I moan, then he bites, hard.

"Liam, yes."

"It's Daddy to you, my fucking slut."

Daddy? Well then. That's a new one. But if he fucks me, I'll call him whatever the hell he wants.

"Do you understand?" he asks.

"Yes, Daddy," I whisper, and it sounds bizarre coming out of my mouth.

"Good girl."

What in the world? My clit pulsates from two words that I would never expect to cause that kind of reaction from my body.

Placing his hands on my thighs, he spreads them with force.

He lifts my skirt and pulls my panties to the side and thrusts two fingers into me. I gasp audibly from the delicious intrusion.

"I'm rough, but if you want me to stop just tell me to stop."

I shake my head as he slams his fingers in me again, "Please don't ever stop."

"Such a fucking willing slut."

He leans forward, licking between my breasts, as he keeps thrusting his fingers into me so hard that I fear I might lose my virginity this way. I roll my hips as I moan loudly.

"I'm so close. Please, Daddy, can I come?"

He cocks his head at me in surprise, he swallows hard, "Yes, baby girl, come for me."

I reach my hand between my legs and circle my clit with my finger as he continues finger fucking me so hard, that I can barely see. He bites my bottom lip, and that's all it takes. I'm coming so hard, my back arches as I throw my head back, screaming for him. Taking his fingers out, he sucks them clean while staring into my eyes. Fuck, everything he does, everything he says sets my body on fire.

"Fuck. Why does my son's friend have to be so sexy?" he says.

"This has nothing to do with Nash. Leave him out of it."

"Are you a submissive?"

I shake my head, "No."

"Then how did you know to ask permission to come?"

I giggle, "I read."

"He can't know about this, Mercy."

"I know," I said.

"Good girl."

I bite my lip, "Thank you, Daddy."

He drags his hand down his face, "Fuck, what did I just do? This is wrong in every way."

Reaching down underneath me, I stroke his cock through his pants.

"I think part of you disagrees."

"Get back to your seat before I spank your ass again."

"Promises, promises." I say as I shuffle back into my seat.

Reaching over, he strokes my thigh as he starts driving, "You're so fucking beautiful."

I blush, "Thank you, sir."

"And perfect," he said.

I smile at him; he's so sexy, everything about him, arouses me.

"But we won't do that again, I can't."

My smile falls. I've never wanted to strangle someone more than I do right now.

We get to the house, and I see my friends and tell them all about my day. I tell them about Ivy but, of course, I leave out the parts about Liam.

Sitting in the living room, drinking, and talking, Nash pulls me into his arms, "I'm so proud of you, Mercy."

I smile, "Thank you."

He's been hugging me a lot, and it's kind of weird. He never did before, Jessica gives me a look each time he does. I mean, he's my best friend, so it's not a big deal; it's just weird. We spend the evening planning out the party. They're all disappointed when I tell them I'll be going to the hospital every day. But Ivy has no one right now, and that's more important. No child should spend their days in a hospital bed going through chemo, alone.

We all finish watching TV and head to bed. I wish I were closer to Liam's room. He may be Nash's dad but damn, he's sexy. His hair is dark with silver specks, I want to run my hands through it as he buries himself inside me. When he called me a good girl, I melted. I know he wants me too. I saw his eyes move up and down my body with desire. When he had his fingers inside me, his expression told me a story his words won't dare express. He wants me. I want him. I will have him. If Nash finds out, he'll get over it. We've been friends for a long time. Besides, it's not like I'm going to marry him and become Nash's step-mom. I just want to fuck him, mostly.

I come up with a plan, hopefully, Liam reacts the way I want him to. As I rise out of bed, I can't stifle the grin on my face. I put on a bathrobe in case I get caught. I find my way to Liam's room, quiet as a mouse. I open the door to his room and close it quietly, and let out a breath I didn't realize I'd been holding in. He's sound asleep, the blankets hanging below his hips. Taking a moment, I stare at his chest, my mouth watering. He's gorgeous with a strong muscular chest, my eyes travel down to that perfect 'V', then to his hard cock. The sheet over him does nothing to hide it, he's huge. Dropping the robe to the floor, I slide into the bed; I climb on top of him. He's really out, he moans but doesn't wake up. I press my lips to his and slip my tongue into his mouth as I run my hands through his hair. In one swift movement, he's on top of me, straddling me, holding my wrists above my head. His dark green eyes are filled with a darkness I can't decipher. Anger? Lust? I'm not sure.

Seven

MERCY

"WHAT DO you think you're doing, baby girl?"

I turn my head to the side, filled with shame. Okay, maybe this was not my brightest idea.

"You will look at me when I speak to you, unless you're told otherwise."

Where's my nerve now? It's completely gone. When I glance up into his eyes, my heart pounds against his chest as I tremble uncontrollably.

"Are you scared?"

I nod as I bite my lip.

He moves his hands off my wrists and slides them down my sides.

"Good. You should be," he said.

There's no way to abandon my plan at this point so I grab him by his hair and pull his mouth to mine. I bite his lip, and a growl rumbles through his chest. Sliding my tongue into his mouth, I expect him to pull away, but he becomes ravenous. His tongue fights with mine as if they are at war with each other. I know he's at war with himself. I need him more than I've ever needed anything. I won't stop this if he doesn't. Pulling back from our kiss, his gaze meets mine.

"You're sure you want this? I will be rough; I won't go easy on you. I won't be gentle. I don't know how. It will hurt."

"I want this. Be as rough as you want to be," but I'm terrified. I've never done this before. I know it's going to hurt, I just don't know how much. I've fooled around with boys before, but I've never had intercourse. I've been saving it for this man, boys have tried but I wasn't willing to give them all of me.

Moving his mouth to my neck, he bites, licks, and bites me again, causing a whimper to escape from my lips.

"Liam."

He growls, "It's Daddy to you. Do you understand?"

"Yes, Daddy."

He groans as he moves lower down my body, stopping at my breasts.

"These tits are fucking perfect. When I saw you in that damn bikini, I couldn't stop thinking about fucking you right here." He slides his finger between my breasts.

A satisfied smile crosses my lips.

I moan as he takes a pink bud into his mouth and pinches the other between his thumb and middle finger, hard. He continues moving downward, kissing, licking, and biting along the way. As he moves to the apex of my thighs, I shiver with anticipation. His eyes snap to mine, and for a moment, he just stares.

"Earlier in the car it struck me that you must be a dirty fucking girl, aren't you? No hair, this cunt is just waiting to be eaten. Do you want me to lick your pussy, baby girl?"

"Yes, please, Daddy."

"Tonight, you're my little slut. I'm going to fuck you so hard any way I want to. Maybe we can get each other out of our systems."

I moan, "Daddy, please."

Another growl escapes from his throat.

My heart sinks at his words, 'out of our systems,' I don't want to be out of his system, and I know he'll never be out of mine. Yet, I still won't walk away from this even though I know he'd stop if I asked him to. I will take what I can get from Liam, the man I've fantasized about for years, even if it's just this one night, hoping there will be more.

He attacks my pussy like a starving man, watching my face the entire time. I put my hands in his hair as he slides his tongue up my slit. This isn't the first time I've done this, but this is the first time I've felt anything this intense. Messing around with boys my age didn't prepare me for this. He's no boy, all man, Liam knows exactly what he's doing. Licking my clit in circles, he thrusts three fingers inside me. Moving his fingers in and out, he never stops licking me, staring at me. When he does a scissor motion with his fingers I nearly scream at the top of my lungs. No one has ever done that before. He removes his fingers from my pussy and gently strokes my back hole.

"Jesus Christ, you taste so fucking good."

He continues to eat me out like this is everything he has ever wanted. It's a heady feeling being desired like this. This isn't for me; this is for him. Dr. Lexington enjoys the taste of a woman. Has he been thinking about doing this to me? His lips move to my clit, and he sucks softly at first as he watches my reaction. Then he sucks hard as I grip my hands in his hair, trembling underneath him, as I fly into my orgasm that threatens to rip me to shreds.

He removes his fingers from my pussy and gently strokes my back hole.

"Has anybody ever fucked your ass?"

My eyes go wide, "No."

"Tonight, I will."

I swallow hard. I've never even had sex let alone anal sex. The thought of it terrifies me but it's Liam. There is nothing I would say no to.

"Are you going to let me?"

"Yes, Daddy."

"Such a good girl."

Getting up, he goes into his drawer, gets a condom out, and sets it on the foot of the bed along with a bottle of lube.

"Good girls get rewarded, bad girls get punished. I think we both know which you've been."

Standing at the foot of the bed, he grabs my legs and pulls me down, so my ass is at the edge of the mattress.

"What's your safe word?"

"I don't have a safe word."

"Your safe word is mercy. Saying stop will not make me stop. Only your safe word will work. I trust you can remember your own name."

I nod as I bite my lip. He takes his boxer shorts off and stands in front of me naked in all his glory and he is glorious. His cock is huge, my god. It's swollen and angry looking and no way will that fit inside me. I watch him as he opens the condom and rolls it onto his massive length. I'm not sure if it's the length I'm more worried about or the girth. Both are bigger than I've ever seen.

"Last chance to back out."

"I want this. I want you." I breathe.

"I'm going to fucking hell," he says as he slides into me.

"Fuck, you're so tight. Relax, let me in."

Placing his hands on my hips, he slams into me with such force that it knocks the wind out of me, sending a bolt of burning pain through me. Holy fuck this hurts.

"How are you so tight?"

I don't say a word not wanting to freak him out.

"Tell me you're not a virgin."

"I'm not a virgin," I squeak out because I'm not now. I lost my virginity the second he slammed into me with the force of a freight train. I have a feeling if I tell him I was a virgin we are done. I want this so I don't say more.

The pain is excruciating for the first few minutes, but I hide it from him. The way he looks at me with that hooded gaze makes it all worthwhile. He watches my body as he fucks me, making me feel sexy. I've never had a man look at me like this.

"You're so beautiful, every inch of you. Your pussy was made for my cock."

"Please, don't stop. You feel so good."

"Come for me, baby girl. Come on Daddy's cock."

He moves one hand and rubs my clit, while moving his hips side to side and the sensation makes me go crazy, thrusting my hips, digging my fingers into the sheets and screaming for him repeatedly. My back arches, and my body tenses as my orgasm seizes me, stronger than I've ever felt. He pulls out, and I feel such emptiness.

"Turn over. On all fours."

"Yes, sir."

I turn over and do as ordered.

He slams into me, grabbing a fistful of my hair, and pulls hard.

"What kind of a girl comes into a man's bedroom naked in the middle of the night?" he growls. He pulls my hair tighter, "Fucking answer me."

"A bad one."

"I think you deserve to be punished. Don't you?"

He has a tight hold on my head and my breathing gets heavy.

"Yes, Daddy," I whimper.

"You will count after each hit you get. There will be three. Next time it'll be with a belt. Do you understand?"

"Yes," I gasp. A belt? What the fuck.

He slams his open hand down on my right ass cheek.

"Ow," I cry.

"Count. Or I will start over."

"One," I say.

He hits me again, harder.

"Two," I cry out.

Another slap to my ass, and it doesn't really hurt, it just stings.

"Three."

He starts thrusting again.

"Such a good girl, taking my punishment without complaint."

He runs his hand down my back and squeezes my ass. He stops, and I hear what sounds like a plastic bottle opening. Then there's wetness at my back hole as he sinks a finger into me. I freeze.

"Don't clench, baby girl. Relax. It'll feel good in a few minutes."

I try to relax, but it hurts.

As he thrusts his fingers in and out, breaking through the ring of muscle, I start to moan and push back on him. God, it feels good, he was right. He inserts another finger, waits a few minutes before inserting a third. I pant and moan his name repeatedly as I rock my hips, slamming back onto his fingers and his cock.

"Do you like that, baby girl?"

"Yes, Daddy, yes."

He pulls his dick out of my pussy and slowly replaces his fingers with it in my back hole. The sensation is far different from his fingers. I try to relax as he slowly inserts himself.

"Good girl. Take my cock, baby."

I've read about this, it's a praise kink. I always kind of thought the characters in the books I read were weird being into it. But, when he calls me a good girl, it makes my heart race and my pussy clench. It's a content, happy feeling that I don't quite understand. I know in this instant that I would do anything to please him, to hear those words of praise again and again.

He grabs my hips and starts fucking me, every thrust a little faster than the one before. It quickly turns from pain to unadulterated pleasure. Before I know it, I'm pushing back onto him, hard.

"Do you like that?"

"Yes, harder Daddy, please."

He pulls my hair hard as he slams into me repeatedly. "Play with your clit."

I move one hand to my pussy and rub my clit, he pushes my face into the mattress and holds my head down.

Turning my head to the side, I gasp as he squeezes my neck.

"Tonight, you're my perfect little slut. I told you I wouldn't go easy on you."

"Yes," I whimper.

My body is experiencing things it never has before. I am not prepared for my next orgasm. My body shakes uncontrollably, as I crumble toward ecstasy. I can't hold back my screams. I hope no one hears us but at this moment I don't care.

"Daddy, yes, oh my God."

He grabs my hips, digging his fingers into my skin, "Fuck yes, baby girl," he groans as his dick jerks inside me.

His voice is breathy, and I know it's what my fantasies will be fueled by going forward.

Pulling out of me, he gets up and disposes of the condom and washes his hands.

I collapse on the bed, he comes back and lies down beside me, pulling me into his arms, he rubs my ass.

"Thank you, Daddy."

"You're welcome but, Mercy, you know this won't happen again, right?"

"Why?" I ask.

"You know why, don't make me say it again. I was weak. This should not have happened. Obviously I should be locking my door."

"Did you not enjoy it?" I brace for the painful answer.

"It was perfect, you're perfect. But it can't be more than one night. I can't do this to Nash."

"I see. I'm going to go," I said.

"Mercy. It's not you. If I had met you any other way, I'd pursue the hell out of you."

"I understand. I won't come in here again. I'm sorry. This was a huge mistake."

Rising off the bed, I stop and grab my bathrobe, put it on, and leave his room. I walk back to my room feeling like such a fool. What was I thinking? That might have been the stupidest shit I've done in a long time. Of course, a man like him wouldn't want me for more than one night. For him, it was just sex, but I've been pining away for this man for seven long years. It was so much more to me.

Throwing myself on the bed, I reach over to the end table and grab my phone. I snap a photo, tears streaming down my face. I caption it, 'Stupid girls do stupid things...' and post it on Instagram but not Facebook. I don't want Nash to see it and luckily for me he doesn't use Instagram. I lay there, staring at the impossibly naïve girl on the screen when I get a message on Instagram. It's from Liam. My heart races out of control.

Liam: Baby girl, please don't cry, not because of me especially.
Me: I'm fine.
Liam: I wish things were different. If it weren't for Nash, I'd want to take you out, show you off, and get to know all of you.
Me: I'm going to bed.
Liam: Please don't leave things like this.
Me: It's no big deal. Just forget about it. I got exactly what I asked for. I'm not mad at you, I'm mad at myself.

I can't get the images of being with him out of my head. It was so much more than I ever expected, and I want it to happen again and again. I want to be *his*. The way he kissed me, I know no man will ever measure up. One night with Liam Lexington has ruined me. I'll never experience that feeling again, pure bliss. He owns me even though he doesn't want me. Still, I don't have any regrets. I'd do it all again.

Eight

LIAM

FUCK! *Liam, you asshole. You made her cry.*

The last thing I wanted to do was hurt or make her feel bad. I want to go in there right now and take her into my arms while I kiss every single tear away. I can't, as much as I want to, I need to reign myself in. What I need most is to forget about Mercy. I'm no good for her, and I can't do that to Nash. It has to stop. The way her pussy gripped my cock will haunt me forever, she tasted like honey, and dripped with sensuality. Kissing has always been a means to an end. It's never been something that I've craved but when her lips were pressed to mine, her tongue in my mouth it did something to me. I could've kissed her for hours.

As hard as I try, I can't sleep. Thoughts of her flood my brain, she won't leave me alone. So, I get up at three o'clock in the morning and go to the kitchen to get a drink of water. Mercy is standing at the counter, her head hanging down.

"Mercy."

She turns to face me, her heated glare cuts through me, "I couldn't sleep," she huffs.

"Can we talk?" I ask.

"No, *Daddy*," she says with a spiteful tongue.

Running a hand through my hair, I expel a loud sigh. Even with red-rimmed eyes, she's so beautiful.

"I'm sorry," I say. That's all I've got. I don't know how to make this right. What's done is done, I guess I can't.

"Fuck you, Liam," she says.

I snap, no one talks to me like that. Walking up to her, I grab her hair and pull, forcing her to look at my face.

"Listen here, baby girl. You're the one that climbed into my fucking bed without an invitation. You can be mad at me, but this is as much your fault as it is mine. I gave you ample opportunity to walk out. You said you wanted it. I never told you there would be more, I did not lie to you or mislead you."

She softens under my glare, "I'm sorry," she whispers with tears in her eyes.

"I want to take you back to my bed right now and fuck you until you do forget your own name. I so badly want to see you on your knees, looking up at me, sucking my cock. I want you. Nothing has changed but we can't."

Reaching up, she strokes my chest, and her small hands send sparks up my spine. I need to get the hell out of here before I can't resist her. I'm dangerously close to carrying her to my room and repeating the events of a few hours ago. Releasing her, I step back and take her in one last time. This is it, I swear—just one kiss. I step back toward her and crash my lips to hers. She moans as she parts her lips, I plunge my tongue into her mouth, sliding my hands into her hair, I wind her hair around my hand and pull hard, as I deepen our kiss. She runs her hands down my chest, digging her nails into my skin, kissing me back with the same desperation I feel for her. I pull back after I'm out of air, both of us breathing heavily.

She gazes at me with wanting eyes, "Liam, I need you."

I shake my head, "I can't."

She grabs my erection and strokes me through my boxers. "You can, you're *choosing* not to."

"Mercy, we have to stop this."

"I'll never tell him," she said.

"I don't want to hide things from him," I respond matter-of-factly.

She pulls down my boxers in a swift movement as she kneels.

Fuck. Mercy on her knees is an alluring sight. I'm going to make her stop, I have to.

"Let me make you feel good one last time. I want to do this for you." We are in my kitchen, where anybody could walk in and catch us, Nash could walk in and see this. Why does that make me want this even more? That should make me force her to stop, but it doesn't. *What the hell is wrong with me?*

She licks the underside of my cock from base to tip, then strokes me as she circles the head with her tongue. I gaze down at her through hooded eyes, "Yes, baby girl."

Lowering her mouth over my cock she moves her head up and down, and fuck, her mouth feels amazing. I grab onto the counter to hold myself up, she's going to make me come fast.

Grabbing her head, I move her faster, she starts to gag, but I don't stop, I stare down at her, relishing the tears in her eyes.

"Yes, I love it when you gag on my dick, baby girl."

I hold her head in my hands as I thrust myself into her mouth over and over hitting the back of her throat every time. She grabs my balls, massaging them gently and I'm about to come undone.

She moans, and it vibrates against my cock, sending me over the edge. I grip her head even tighter, forcefully as I shoot cum down her pretty throat, my body shaking with spasms.

I release her head and she slides her mouth off me.

Looking up at me with sweet eyes, she licks her lips, "Thank you, Liam." She stands and gazes at me seriously, "I'm done chasing you. If you want me, you'll have to make the next move."

"Mercy, I won't. I can't."

"Then this is goodbye, Liam."

One last time, I pull her into my arms, inhaling her addictive scent. I kiss her on the neck, "Goodbye, Mercy."

Releasing her, she stares at me momentarily, and then tears her gaze away and walks back to her room.

Walking back to my room, I throw myself on the bed as if I'm a moody teenager. I slide between the sheets and can't fall asleep. This shit with Mercy has to stop, I can't do this. Nash may never forgive me, and

I can't lose my son. Besides, she's too young to deal with my baggage. I will never be able to give her what she wants out of life. Why does the right thing have to feel so fucking wrong? *Do the right thing, Liam.* But how? Every time she's near me, I can't control myself. *Show some restraint, asshole.*

Finally, I fall asleep, although it's a restless sleep. Dreaming of dying patients, then Nash's mom, and finally, Mercy begging me to fuck her. Why does she have to be so fixated on me? Although, if I'm honest with myself, and I don't want to be, I am just as fixated on her.

I have a couple of patients to check in with today, but I'm not working unless I get called in. I climb out of bed, grab my gym shorts, and get changed for a long workout.

Jessica and Mercy sit at the table as I walk into the kitchen to get coffee before exercising.

"Wow, Dr. Lexington, you have an incredible body for an older guy," Jessica said.

I roll my eyes.

Mercy snaps, "Jessica stop! Don't talk like that."

"Why because he's yours?" She giggles.

Through gritted teeth, Mercy says, "Jessica."

They talk as if I'm not even here and it doesn't take long for it to get old.

"Ladies, you do realize I can hear you, right?"

Glancing at Mercy, her cheeks are red, fuck I love that so much.

Before my cock starts talking for me, telling all my secrets, I head down to the gym.

I spend two hours working out, and I'm quite grateful that nobody disturbs me. I half expected Mercy to come down, but she did say she was done chasing me. Maybe, she really is done. And why does that bother me so much? What the hell is wrong with me? The thought of never having her in my arms again isn't something I like. The idea of her in another man's arms is even worse.

After my workout, I head upstairs, shower, and then do the most ridiculous thing. I stand looking out my window and watch Mercy in the pool like the pervert I have become. When Xander, my colleague and best friend since high school calls, I'm thrilled for the distraction.

After changing into jeans and a blue Henley, I head downstairs to leave. Nash stops me on my way to the garage.

"Done in the pool?" I ask.

"For now, where are you going? I thought you might want to play a game with us."

"A game?" I snicker. "I'm past the age of spin the bottle, son."

"Seriously dad."

"Sorry, I have plans."

"A date?" Nash asks, with a shocked expression.

"Son."

Glancing at Mercy, a pained expression crosses her face as she averts my gaze. Do I clarify that it's a male friend? Do I let her think I have a date, so she'll move on to someone more appropriate for her? Jessica glares at me, puts her arm around Mercy, and they walk to the bedroom. Shit. Jessica knows. This is exactly what I was afraid of. Nash finding out and Mercy getting hurt. The two things I worried most about are going to happen.

Running a hand through my hair, I glance at Nash, "I'll see you later."

"Okay, I'm going to go find out what's wrong with Mercy. Bye dad."

Fuck. Fuck. Fuck.

Arriving at On-Call, I sit in the booth across from Xander, and he arches an eyebrow at me.

Within a few minutes, the waitress brings us a couple of beers. Sitting with the owner does have its perks.

"What?" I ask.

"You look like hell, Liam. What's going on?"

Exhaling a deep sigh, I shake my head, "I fucked up so bad, Xander."

I take a long gulp of my beer and am pleasantly surprised. Sometimes, he orders some off-the-wall garbage. I'm not a fan of craft beer. I prefer the normal shit.

"What did you do?"

Running a hand through my hair, "I shouldn't even talk about it," I said.

"Well, you certainly look like you need to talk to someone."

He's not wrong, in the least.

I tell him about Mercy, Nash, and her work at the hospital. And this asshole has the gall to appear amused. He rubs his chin with his thumb and finger as his lips turn into a smirk.

"I never thought I'd live to see it. Liam Lexington is in love."

"Xander, I am not. It's just sex."

He shakes his head, an expression of disbelief on his face as he arches an eyebrow. "No, I have seen you with just sex. What I haven't ever seen is you so torn up about a woman. I've never seen you so worried about them getting hurt."

"Are you going to help me or not?"

He laughs, "I get the Nash thing. But is she, his girlfriend?"

"No, well, according to her they've only ever been friends."

"Wow, Nash hasn't tapped that?"

Glaring at him I bite, "Don't fucking talk about her like that."

"Settle down, Liam. Can you at least admit that you have feelings for her?"

"It's just sex, Xander, I barely know her," I said.

He raises an eyebrow, "Well then, it's an easy solution. Let her go. Problem solved."

I groan, "I've tried. Every time I say, 'that's it' and every time I'm a liar."

Picking up my glass, I take a gulp of my beer.

He shakes his head, "Because you have feelings for her."

I finish my beer and get the waitress's attention to bring me another. When she brings me the next one, I ask her for Whiskey because beer is just not strong enough.

"Is she good in bed?"

Rolling my eyes at him, I say, "None of your business but very."

He chuckles as he puts his finger on his chin, looking deep in thought. "Imagine if you trained her how good she'd be. I assume you're still into that weird kinky shit."

I can't stifle my grin, "Yeah, I am."

"How did she feel about all of that?"

I expel a sigh, "Xander, she was totally into it. I thought that would be the end of it because it normally is. I intentionally did things to her that most women say no to, thinking it would turn her off. But nope." I pop the p to emphasize my annoyance.

"And you're going to let that go?"

Rubbing the stubble on my cheek, I say, "I don't have a choice."

"You do have a choice. Nash is not a kid anymore. Tell me this," he said with a thoughtful expression.

"If she weren't Nash's friend, would you still only want sex with her?"

"Oh, I'd have so much sex with her. But no not only sex. I'm dying to take her out, I want to take care of her."

"Liam, Liam, Liam. You are so fucking in love and don't even know it."

"I just met her. Well, after not seeing her for years apparently."

He shrugs his shoulders, "Sometimes it happens fast. It doesn't change how you feel. Look, you need to make sure there's nothing between her and Nash. And if not, in my opinion you should go for it."

Rubbing my temples, "You aren't making this easier. You were supposed to say something to snap me the hell out of this shit."

He laughs, "I want you to be as happy as I am with Isabella."

"Both of us can't win the lottery. The odds are astronomical."

Xander and Isabella are like a dirty fucking Hallmark movie. I've never seen two people so in love and utterly obsessed with each other. It's nauseating.

The waitress brings over two more shots, "I down them one after the other."

"You know, drinking is not going to help, right?"

I nod. Of course, I know that, I'm not an idiot. But I need something to numb everything that I can't afford to be feeling.

"Okay let's go. I'm driving you home, you've had too much to drink. You can get an Uber tomorrow and pick up your car."

"I'm fine," I said.

"Friends don't let friends drive drunk. And you, my friend, are drunk."

A serious look crosses his face and I know it's not open for discussion.

"Let's get you home Doc Delicious."

I shoot him a glare, "Don't start your shit."

He chuckles, "All these years later and that's still hilarious."

"What a gentleman you are, Dr. Kane," I said as he helped me into his car.

He smirks at me, "Are you going to need help getting into the house too, drunk ass?"

"No, I'll be alright," I stammer.

He pulls up to the house, and somehow, I manage to get out of the vehicle just fine and approach my door. Entering, I walk in and go through my living room, but as I begin to turn left to make my way to my bedroom, I see what I'll never be able to unsee. Mercy is in Nash's arms, his lips pressed to hers, her hands on his chest. I stand there like an idiot, just staring.

And then I hear the words that gut me.

"Merce, I've been in love with you since we were five. I'm tired of trying to pretend I'm not."

Once my breathing starts again, I go to move, but my legs go out, I hit the wall, and a picture of Nash goes flying, and glass shatters. Mercy jumps away from Nash and stares at me with regretful eyes.

My words slur, "I'm just going to my bedroom. Continue. Don't let me interrupt your fucking love fest."

After I slam my door, I strip down to my boxers and lay on the bed as the room spins. Fuck. Nash is in love with her. I fucked the girl my son loves. And the horrible man that I am, I'm dying to do it again. Pussy is never worth losing your kid for no matter how good it is. I vow to myself right now, never again. I'm done with Mercy.

I grab my phone when I hear it chime with a text alert.

Mercy: I don't love him, his declarations change nothing for me.

Me: It changes everything for me.

Nine

MERCY

IT'S BEEN three months since I left Liam's house. He was done with me, and I couldn't stomach being around Nash either so I left before the party even happened. He ruined everything. Maybe I shouldn't be angry about him simply telling me his feelings, but I am. Liam doesn't respond to any of my messages, he pretends I don't even exist at the hospital. It's painful, to say the least, he obviously didn't feel anything for me. It was completely one-sided. I was nothing more than a good lay, one and done. Still, my feelings haven't changed, I love him. But I've given up on the hope that one day we'll be together. I deserve better than this. For the first few weeks I fantasized that I'd see him in the hospital, and he'd look at me and suddenly know he couldn't live without me. Stupid, I know. But it's been three months, ninety days and he still can't even be bothered to respond to a simple text message, so I'm over it, done. People will treat you how you allow them to treat you. I am aware that climbing into his bed in the middle of the night, acting like a slut didn't exactly help matters. I told him that I got what I wanted and that was not true. I wanted more, so much more.

I'm standing in the break room, it's a simple room with a few tables and a couple of coffee machines. I'm brewing fresh coffee because I can't stand shit that's been sitting around for hours.

The whisper of a breath reaches my neck and I freeze. My stupid brain is convinced that it's Liam's breath but somewhere deep down I know better.

"Have mercy, you look beautiful today."

I roll my eyes as I spin around to come face to face with Dr. Jacobs.

"That's so original. I've never heard that before," I quip sarcastically.

He grins as he invades my personal space, taking my hand in his, "Go out with me tonight."

Dr. Jacobs is a handsome man, but he's no Liam. He's got dark hair that falls to the top of his collar, perfectly styled, parted to the right. Brown eyes that are simply generic, nothing special. And when he looks at me, I know he wants to fuck me. But I want more. I want a man that looks at me like he can't take another breath without me. Unrealistic, I know. I mean I just met him a week ago.

Turning away from him I pour my cup of coffee, add a little splash of hazelnut cream and stir it before taking a long sip, burning my tongue. Ow!

"Just a drink," he says.

Facing him again with my coffee in my hands, I sigh, "I'm sorry, I have plans."

He shakes his head, "A date?"

I laugh, it's really none of his damn business what my plans are. "No, nothing like that. I'm going to the On-Call room with my best friend."

"Raincheck then?" he smiles.

I nod, "Sure."

"I have to go, Dr. Jacobs. I have a patient to see."

"I'll walk you."

We walk to Ivy's room, and as we approach, Liam comes out of her room and stops in his tracks glaring at me, his jaw clenched, nostrils flared. I swallow hard and attempt to pretend he's not there.

"Thank you, Dr. Jacobs," I say with a forced smile.

"Maybe, I'll see you tonight, Mercy."

I nod, clearly, I shouldn't have told him where I was going. I can't deal with Liam Lexington's many moods right now. He's frozen, like a wall of stone, and I walk around him and go into Ivy's room. I don't know what his issue is but right now I need to focus on her.

"MERCY!"

I can't help but laugh, as I walk to the head of her bed, this little girl is so special. There's nothing quite like someone always being happy to see you.

"Hi, sweetheart. How are you feeling?"

"I'm weak, I'm not allowed to leave my room. So, we can't paint," she says with a frown.

"Well, what if we color instead of paint? We can do that here."

She taps her finger on her lip. "If you take me, I won't tell Dr. L."

I shake my head, "Oh no missy. Doctors orders are doctors orders. Besides, it would break my heart if you got hurt. Should I get the supplies?"

"I guess," she sighs.

This tiny little girl has such a fierce personality. It's going to take her far in life.

"I'll be back."

Walking to the playroom to get the art supplies, I can't stifle the grin on my face. I adore this tiny human with everything I have. I can't wait until she's cancer free. When she rings that bell, I plan on being here.

Reaching up on the top shelf, I grab the crayons and paper.

"What do you think you're doing, baby girl?"

I gasp, "Liam." Spinning around, he's close enough I can feel his breath on my face. I focus my gaze to the floor. If I look at him, I'm done for.

"I... I'm getting art supplies for Ivy," I stammer.

"You will look at me when I'm speaking to you."

Casting my eyes up to his, instantly, I'm weak in the knees. I'm supposed to be angry, damn it. One look into his eyes and my body threatens to melt into a puddle at his feet.

"What do you want, Liam?" I try to sound stronger than I am.

He arches an eyebrow, "What are you doing with Jacobs?"

God, he smells so good. I miss the taste of his tongue on my lips. Who am I kidding? I miss everything about this man. *No Mercy. Stop. Don't think about him like that.* "Nothing," I respond flatly.

"I don't like seeing you with him."

Something in me snaps, I see red, placing my hand on his chest I push him back. "You haven't spoken to me in three fucking months. I'm not even worthy enough to get a simple reply to a text message. So, you know what Liam, I don't honestly care what you like and what you don't. I will see and fuck whoever I want, it does not affect you in the least."

"I miss you," he whispers.

"No. You don't get to do this to me. It was just sex, you made that abundantly clear. It was easy for you to walk away. I gave you all of me, I let you do things to me that I'd never let any other man do and you didn't want me. You don't get to come back three months later claiming that you miss me. No. It's done, Liam. Whatever we were, it's over. Now if you'll excuse me, you're interrupting my time with a patient."

"It wasn't just sex."

I stop momentarily in the doorway without turning back to him. Why does he say everything I've wanted to hear now? It's too late. Shaking my head I respond, "It doesn't matter what it was, Liam. It's over."

As I walk to Ivy's room I swipe angrily at the tears on my face. I hate him, how dare he. It's all about what he wants. He's never considered what I want, how his actions affect me. I paste a big, fake smile on my face as I walk back into her room.

"Here you can use this to draw on," I roll the bedside table over her bed.

I hand her the crayons and paper, "Okay my budding artist, show me what you've got."

She giggles, first she takes a black crayon and draws an outline of a man. I watch her quietly, not wanting to disturb her.

Once she draws princesses on his clothes and a stethoscope, I know this is Liam. But he's holding what seems to be a paper bag.

"What's in the bag that he's holding?"

"The cure for cancer."

I swallow hard, if only he had the cure for cancer. She thinks he hung the moon and the stars, she has so much faith in him. It's beautiful to witness the purest love this little girl has for such a complicated man. Of course, she doesn't know the negative side of him like I do. She only knows the doctor that works tirelessly to save as many innocent children as he possibly can.

"Are you going to give this to him? It's a beautiful picture."

She nods, "Yes. I hope he likes it."

Stuffing down my emotions I simply state, "He's going to love it, I have no doubt."

"I know he doesn't really have the cure for cancer," she says with unshed tears in her eyes.

"I heard your mom was here yesterday."

"Yeah, it was weird," she says as she shakes her head like she's trying to shake something off.

"Weird, how?"

"She's doing this funeral thing where she can... payments she called it." The tears fall down her chubby cheeks, "Mercy, what's the box called that you go in when you die?"

"Box?"

"Yeah, they bury you in it."

"A casket?"

"Yeah, casket, she made me pick one."

"Jesus."

She arches an eyebrow at me, "You are not supposed to say that."

"I'm so sorry, you're right, I apologize. It won't happen again."

I should never have shown any emotion. It was a simple reaction before I could even think. What kind of person makes a little kid going through chemo pick out their fucking casket? It doesn't take a degree in social work to know how wrong that is. The more I learn about this woman the more I hate her. The more I worry about Ivy eventually going home with her.

"How did that make you feel?"

She turns away from me, staring at the wall, "Like I'm going to die."

"That's how it would make me feel too, I think. But you are not terminal Ivy. We aren't hiding anything from you. I'm sure, Dr. L will be happy to talk to you about it. Remember what he says about staying positive."

"Can I ask you something, but you can't lie?"

"I will never lie to you, sweet girl. Ask me anything."

"Do you think I am going to die?"

I expel a big breath, "I'm going to treat you like a grown up for a minute and give you the total truth. And then we can talk about how you feel about it, okay?"

She nods but stays quiet.

"You have cancer, things can go wrong. There is no guarantee that anyone will survive this. We simply can't promise anything. But there is a far higher chance that you live through this than there is that you die. Sixty-eight percent, Ivy. There's a sixty-eight percent chance that you'll live through this. Sixty-eight kids out of one hundred will survive. That's really high odds. While I can't guarantee anything, I think your mom is wasting money on something she'll never need."

"Thank you," she smiles.

"You're welcome. Get some rest. I'll see you tomorrow."

As I rise, she stares at me with relief painted on her sweet little face. I smile and walk out of her room. I have one more patient to see before I'm ready to go out with Jessica.

Ten

LIAM

I'M in the gym at my house. I need to get rid of some of this tension. I turn on my iPod and Def Leppard's "Too Late for Love" starts playing. The irony is not lost on me. I'm not in love with her. Xander was wrong about that. But on some level, I need her. It's like a slow never-ending ache that I haven't even begun to understand. I begin to lift free weights but I'm not in the zone, not today. My mind is on Mercy and only her. Fuck, I miss her. I was sure after I let her go that she and Nash would make a go of it. But they didn't, according to him they've barely spoken.

Standing so close to her today made me crave her in such a desperate way. When I saw her with Jacobs the rage burned through me leaving me reeling. I had to fight everything in me not to attack him, reminding myself that I was in a children's hospital. She's mine, he can't have her. The only problem is she's not mine anymore. Was she ever? Not really. Well, she definitely isn't now, I made sure of that. If I believe what she said she never will be, it's too late. The only woman in two fucking decades that gave me everything I wanted, and I ruined it. She matches my sexual appetite, something I was sure I'd never find. I broke her heart and now she's moving on without me. The thought of her with another man makes me irrational. I want to kidnap her and never let her leave. I know I'm a little unhinged, but I need her, like a fish needs fucking water.

I place my free weights on the rack and give up on releasing tension, it's here to stay. I go upstairs to take a shower and get ready. I'm meeting Xander at the On-Call Room in an hour.

Finally, I'm dressed and ready to go when I get a text message.

Xander: Man, maybe you should stay home. I can come over there if you want.

Me: Why? I'm ready, I'm leaving, Relax.

Xander: No, it's not that. It's not a good idea.

Me: What the fuck, man. Why is it not a good idea?

Xander: Mercy is here. She's not alone, I don't want a scene at my bar.

Me: Jacobs?

Xander: Yeah. Trust me you don't want to see it.

Me: On my way.

Xander: Fantastic.

I run out to my car, get in, and nearly race out of my driveway. If his hands are on her, I'm breaking his fingers. I'm not generally a violent man, but nobody touches what's mine. Mercy may not fucking realize it, but she is mine, she was a month ago, and she always will be. Hopefully, my driving doesn't get me pulled over, as I weave in and out of traffic, I know it's a possibility. A Beamer lays on his horn but I don't care. I'm terrified that she's going to leave with him before I get there to try to stop her. If she leaves with him, I know exactly what they'll be doing. Bile fills my stomach at the mere thought.

I park in the back and rush around to the front, I yank the door open hitting the brick with the metal handle, my blood boils as I prepare for what I know I'm going to see. Xander is waiting for me, but I push past him, in a huff.

"Liam!"

Jessica is at the door leaving with Dr. Griffin, the resident whore of the hospital. That man would fuck a snake if it would hold still long enough. Xander calls my name again. Ignoring him, I walk to the tables and find Mercy with Jacobs and instantly see red. He has his hand on her thigh as he kisses her neck. Her eyes are closed, she's actually enjoying this. The bile from my stomach rises in my throat, I swallow hard forcing it back down.

"Take your fucking hands off her."

Jacobs pops his head up and arches an eyebrow staring at me with a stoic expression. "And if I don't?" He challenges.

"You don't want to know the answer to that question."

"Come, Mercy."

He blurts out, "She's not your obedient lap dog. She's a grown woman and can make her own decisions."

He grips her thigh as she sits there staring at me, regret reflecting in her gaze.

"Mercy, now. Let's go."

She pulls his hand from her leg, "I have to go, Shane. I'm sorry."

His mouth opens as he stares at her. This is not what he was expecting, I'm sure. But relief floods me.

I take her by the hand and walk briskly through the bar, out to my car. Without a word, I open the door for her, and she gets in. As I sit in the driver's seat I put the car into drive, and my hands grip the steering wheel with white knuckle force. I speed out into the traffic heading home. The anger threatens to consume me, she let him put his mouth and hands all over her body. Maybe it's my own fault after how I treated her, but I'm still filled with so much rage that I don't know how to contain it. And it hits me like a fucking brick wall.

"Was this the first time?"

"What?" she responds but I know damn well she knows what I'm asking.

"Have you fucked him?" I bite.

Sighing she says, "No, Liam. I have not."

She stares out the window with her body turned to the door giving me the silent treatment the rest of the way to my house.

I pull into my driveway after a stressful drive. You could cut the tension with a knife.

"Now what?" she asks, throwing her hands in the air.

"We're going inside, let's go."

We walk in the front door together and she stands just inside the doorway with her arms folded across her chest. I close the door behind her.

"Why am I here, Liam?"

"Because I want you to be," I said. And to be fucking punished for your behavior, I think to myself. I have never wanted to take a belt to a woman like I want to at this moment. The only reason I won't is because the fear of losing her is far greater than my need to punish her.

She moves her hands to her sides in a rigid stance, balling her hands into fists. "What about what I want?" she asks, with unshed tears in her eyes.

My heart drops like an elevator that goes from the fiftieth floor straight to the first. She doesn't want to be here with me. I was so consumed by what I wanted, I never gave it any thought. I never considered what she wanted, that I may no longer be it for her. Fuck. I may have really lost her. This might be it. She told me at the hospital that it was over, but I couldn't accept it. I drove to that bar to claim what was mine, never even considering that she wanted nothing to do with me.

I move closer to her, leaving only inches between us, as I slide my hand into her hair and run my nose along her neck, she shivers. Fuck. Her scent does things to me that no other woman has. I place my lips on the shell of her ear as I whisper, "Baby girl, I want you more than you can imagine. But if you don't want me, say the word, I'll drive you back to your car."

Her voice is shaky, "Liam, you know I want you. But nothing has changed. Nash is still your son and my best friend."

I run my lips across her jaw to her mouth. "I don't want to lose my son. But I don't want to lose you either. I'm risking everything for you, knowing it's a gamble worth taking. You're worth the chance. You're the first woman that left me unraveled without you. I need you."

"Liam," she says in a whisper.

I press my lips to hers softly. When she moans into my mouth, I lose my mind. I grab her face as I deepen our kiss. It's a demanding, desperate, needy kiss. Never removing my lips from hers, I undo my pants and push them to my knees. Reaching up under her skirt, I grab hold of her panties, and rip them off her.

Pushing her against the door, I lift her, putting her legs over my forearms, holding her up as I plunge into her. A groan escapes from somewhere deep inside me. Feeling her again after over three months is everything I want. It has felt like a fucking eternity.

She wraps her legs around my waist and digs her nails into my shoulders through my shirt. "I need this shirt off of you, Liam."

I groan with displeasure but take her off me and set her down. "Bedroom, now."

She giggles as she practically runs to the bedroom.

I take my pants off at the door and remove my shirt before going into the bedroom.

When I walk into the room, I can't believe my eyes. The most beautiful sight lies before me. She's naked, on my bed with her legs spread, rubbing her clit with one hand and pinching a nipple with the other.

I stop in the doorway, admiring her. I could watch her do this all day long.

"You're fucking stunning. Is this what you've done for the last three months?"

"Yes," she gasps with a harsh breath.

"Hands off, baby girl. That's mine, every fucking inch of you is mine. And I'll be the one to make you come."

I settle between her legs on my stomach and thrust my tongue inside her. She tastes fucking divine.

"Fuck, Liam!"

I pull my tongue out and pinch her clit, hard and she yelps.

"What's my name?"

"Daddy, I'm sorry, Daddy."

"That's better, now be a good girl and come on my tongue," I say with an arched brow.

I slide my tongue back into her beautiful cunt. Pressing my thumb to her clit, she arches her back as she screams and bucks her hips, clawing into the bedsheets, she comes on my tongue. Fuck, she's like a wild animal tonight, and it makes me crazy with desire.

As I climb up between her legs, my eyes travel the length of her body, drinking her in.

"Just fucking gorgeous. But I need to be inside you."

"Yes, Daddy, fuck me."

I slam into her without warning, causing her to cry out. I close her legs together and hold her thighs shut as I push into her hard and fast.

"Yes, Daddy, I'm going to come."

"Good girl. Come all over Daddy's cock."

She grips the sheets again, and writhes underneath me, screaming so loud, coming completely undone. I could nearly come just from watching her unravel for me. I spread her legs, so I could get closer to her face.

"I lo-"

"Don't!" she interrupts me.

"Don't Liam. Don't."

I pull out of her and lay on my back beside her.

I want to pull her into my arms, but I don't make a move, and neither does she. We both lay, worlds apart, in complete silence. Sometime in the middle of the night, I finally fall asleep.

Eleven

MERCY

I LAY there watching Liam sleep, and damn, he's a beautiful man. I can't get out of my head the way he wouldn't even speak to me, as if I were gum on the bottom of his shoe, nothing more than an annoyance. For years I believed that Liam was everything I wanted in a man. But I was young, foolish, and so wrong. I grab his prescription pad and leave him a note.

Dear Liam,

I went to get my car, so I could go home. The words you came so close to speaking rattled me. You were going to say them even though we both know they weren't true. Love is not ignoring someone for three months and then laying claim to them when you see them with someone new. That's not love.

Maybe we can see each other occasionally just to scratch an itch. But I can't give you more than that. I have been in love with you since I was sixteen. Loving you means hurting myself. I deserve better.

I'm sorry.

~ Mercy

. . .

I run out to the waiting cab, so I can pick up my car, and go home. Leaving Liam like this feels wrong but it's something I must do. It hurt when he wouldn't even speak to me after Nash expressed his feelings for me, I had never felt so unimportant in my life. As far as he was concerned, we couldn't be together because of Nash, I understood that. But to not even be willing to speak to me? Even at work, he wouldn't say a word to me. Everything had to be communicated through nurses or other social work staff. I can handle being spanked, hell I can even handle the belt that he has threatened, but to punish me by shutting me out completely, isn't something I can deal with. Why was I even being punished at all? It's not my fault that Nash decided to reveal his feelings for me. I'm like a kid's toy at a yard sale. He doesn't want me, but when he notices someone else's eye on me, I'm his and no one else can have me.

The truth is, I'm not interested in Dr. Jacobs. He's handsome, but I don't *feel* things for him like I do with Liam. I let him touch and kiss me because I needed to feel alive for a moment. I wanted to picture Liam as his lips grazed my neck. But his mouth didn't feel like Liam's, his sounds were not the same, and it didn't work. When Liam appeared and told me to come with him, it was like some force beyond my control. My body obeyed even though my mind knew better. He has some sort of gravitational pull when it comes to my body. It doesn't matter what my brain tells me, my body, it obeys.

I hand the driver money for my fare and cross the empty parking lot. Sliding into my vehicle, I try to turn my emotions off as I drive home, but it's a failed attempt. I can't stop thinking about the way he touched me last night and the words he came so close to saying. The words would have never meant a thing because they aren't the truth. He loves fucking me perhaps, but he doesn't love *me*. I wish the last three months never happened and he did love me, wishing doesn't make it so.

After the short drive to my apartment, I park and walk up to the third floor. I dig my keys out and walk to my door and stop abruptly. Liam stands in front of my door with his arms folded across his chest.

My heart pounds as I swallow hard. I don't have to guess why he's here; I already know.

"I thought you might call, but showing up at my door? How do you even know where I live?"

He arches his eyebrow through a narrowed glare. "Then you don't know me very well. I have a friend in IT," he says through a clenched jaw.

"Can you move so I can get into my apartment? In fact, go home Liam."

He moves to the side so I can unlock my door, but it's clear as day he's not going anywhere.

I move inside, and he follows me, closing the door behind him.

"Liam, why are you here?"

"You said goodbye," he says and then swallows hard, his body tense, his gaze darts around the room as if he can't look at me.

"Liam, I meant what I said, we can't be together."

He paces back and forth as he rubs the stubble on his jawline.

"Can you sit down? You're making me nervous."

For a moment, he stops and stares at me as if he can read every thought and emotion I'm going through. It's unnerving when he looks at me this way.

He sits on the couch, his muscular legs spread, elbows on his knees. "If I have to sit, so do you," he whispers.

I nod, sitting beside him, but leaving space between us.

"Liam," he pops his face to the side and gazes at me, "we can't be-"

"No! Mercy, no," he shakes his head, as if he can shake my words away. I mean these words, and it doesn't matter if he accepts it.

He pushes me down on the couch as he straddles me, his face less than an inch from mine.

"Baby girl, I'm sorry I hurt you. I fucked up. I didn't have experience falling in love with my son's best friend, someone that he also loves. There's no guidebook for that. I've never really been in love; I know that now. I didn't know what to do. I thought I could forget you, but I can't. Please don't ask me to."

He presses his lips to mine with a tenderness I didn't know he was capable of. He gently slides his tongue against mine before his kiss turns wild and desperate. Sliding one hand in my hair, he groans into my mouth as I wrap my arms around his neck and stroke the back of his hair.

What the hell am I doing? I'm sending him mixed signals. I meant what I said. I turn my face to the side, "Liam, get off me."

He does, with a wide-eyed expression on his face. "I'm not letting you go again. I can't. I won't. I love you, baby girl. I can't let you go, not for anything."

"As always with you, what I want doesn't matter," I say as I sit up.

He laughs, but it's not sincere, it's born out of frustration.

"You do want me," he says with a serious expression. "I bet you're soaking wet."

"No. My body wants you, but my mind says otherwise."

"What about your heart?"

"My heart doesn't get a vote in this, Liam. My mind is making the decision because it's the only part of me that can be trusted when it comes to you."

"No, I need you."

"I'm sorry. You had your chance. Be honest with yourself, Liam. You didn't even want me until you saw me with someone else."

"Is that what you believe?" He says, blinking rapidly, as if he's trying to make sense of my words.

"Yes," a tear rolls down my cheek.

"Baby, I'm sorry."

"I know you are, what's done is done, we can't go back. It's too late."

He stands up and starts pacing again. I try to read his emotions, fear, panic, sadness? I'm unable to figure him out, but it's strong, whichever it is.

Dragging his hand down his face, he stares at me hard before speaking again. "I will not fucking let you go. I made a mistake, it's called forgiveness."

I shake my head as I hold my hands in my lap. "I forgive you but that doesn't mean I can trust you. I can't go through that again, Liam. I won't."

"Goddamn it, Mercy!" He glares at me with dark eyes.

"Liam, it's time for you to go."

"Fine, just tell me one thing?" He says with a raised eyebrow.

"What?"

I stand, go to the door, and open it for him to leave.

"Why won't you give me another chance? I didn't cheat on you; I wasn't with anyone else when we weren't speaking. Mercy, I need you more than I need air."

"I just can't, Liam. Please go." Unshed tears fill his eyes as he turns toward the door.

"I'm sorry, baby girl. I'm so fucking sorry."

He walks away, and I close the door, finally able to fall apart. I press my back against the door, sliding to the floor, and sob. Five minutes into a crying fest, he bangs on my door. "Mercy, open the door. Now!"

I stand up and stare at the door, willing him with a glare, to go away. As if he can see me through the damn door. How long has he been outside my door? Could he hear me crying like a wounded animal?

"It's Ivy, open the fucking door!" he yells.

Twelve

LIAM

SHE OPENS THE DOOR, and it's obvious she's been crying. Her cheeks are red, and tear stained. It breaks my heart, but I can't deal with our shit right now.

"I got a call on my way to my car. Ivy is sick, really sick. She has a staph infection. I'm going to the hospital. Do you want to-"

"Yes, I'm coming. Let's go," she says, as she picks up her keys and purse from the counter.

We walk together out to my car, I open the door, and she slides in.

I drive fast, even though I know getting there quickly won't change a damn thing.

After several minutes in silence, she asks, "How bad is it, Liam?"

"It's bad. She's in emergency surgery to remove the infected tissue. Xander believes there will be several more surgeries required."

"Is she going to-?"

She doesn't finish her sentence, but I know what she was going to ask. Ivy has become important to her. They have a special bond; I've seen it many times.

"I don't know, baby. It could go either way to be honest with you. Xander is very good at what he does but the infection is spreading like fucking wildfire."

"Where is the surgery?"

"Her left arm. The concern is that it'll spread to her heart."

"How are you so calm?"

"I am not calm. Ivy is a special patient to me. Of course, I always want all of my patients to survive. But she has burrowed a little space in my heart."

She sighs loudly.

"I'll repeat what you've heard me tell patients' families over and over again. It's important that we stay positive for her. She can't see us filled with panic. Her spirit needs to stay high. If you have a weak moment, you'll need to leave her room."

She nods, but I can see how much she's struggling with this. I take her hand in mine, and to my surprise, she doesn't recoil.

"Her birthday is in three weeks, I hope she's better, I was planning on throwing her a party," she says with her shoulders hunched and her gaze fixed on her lap.

I can't help but smile as I pull into the parking lot, "I think that's a wonderful idea."

She gets out of the car before I can open the door for her. Again, I go to take her hand, but this time, she pulls away.

"I'm here for Ivy, Liam. This changes nothing between us, please don't think it does."

"Of course," I say with a nod, but obviously, this isn't what I wanted her to say. I don't say anything further because this isn't about me. This is about Ivy, she's completely right. How did I fuck things up so badly? And why did I just assume she'd be waiting for me when I got my shit together?

After scanning my badge at the doctor's entrance, I hold the door open for her.

She says, "Thank you," but her expression is one I can't read at all. Her lips form a tight line as if she's holding herself together best as she's capable of. Is it me that's causing it? Ivy? It's probably Ivy, I tell myself. After all, she's done with me.

We walk in complete silence to Ivy's room, but she isn't back yet.

"Take a seat. I'll call and get an update on the surgery."

74

She nods and sits in the chair that normally is placed beside Ivy's bed.

"I'll be back, I'm going to call from the nurse's station."

The truth is I'm concerned, she should've been back from recovery by now. I don't want Mercy to hear what I say during this phone call in case it's not good news. If I can shield her from whatever report awaits me, I will. I know she didn't die; someone would've called me but that doesn't mean things haven't gone wrong.

I sit in a chair at the nurse's station and place my call to the OR.

"Hi, it's Dr. Lexington. I'd like an update on Ivy Reynolds please."

"Yes, doctor, of course," the nurse says. "She's stable now but there were some complications. Her blood pressure bottomed out after she lost too much blood. She was given two units of blood. Miss Reynolds is on her way to recovery."

"Thank you."

I hang up the receiver, get up, and walk back into Ivy's room.

Mercy stares at me as I sit in the chair beside her.

"She's stable and on her way to recovery."

Crossing her arms she glares at me, "Why are you rubbing your jaw? You do that when you're upset. What aren't you telling me Liam?"

My lips turn up into a smile, she knows me so well. In such a short time she's discovered things about me few people see.

I blow out a deep breath, "I love that you pay so much attention to me that you know my every tell. Although right now, I wish you didn't."

"Liam, tell me the truth."

Reaching out, I stroke her hand. I'm incapable of not touching this woman when she's so close to me.

"She's stable. During surgery her blood pressure bottomed out, and she needed a transfusion."

"Where's her mom? I've been trying to talk to her for weeks," she asks with narrowed eyes.

I shrug, "I don't have a clue. She has not been back since the casket conversation. We, of course, notified her about the changes in Ivy's condition but she hasn't returned a single phone call. I hate to say it, but it might be time for CPS to get involved. Something isn't right with this situation."

"Are you thinking, abuse or neglect?"

I sigh, "Definitely neglect. But there's been a few times that she's flinched when I've gone to touch her for an exam. That concerns me."

"I saw that in her chart but thought maybe she's nervous around doctors."

Shaking my head, I say, "No, she's not nervous around me. That little girl thinks I'm awesome."

That rewards me with a small laugh, fuck I miss that so much. When Mercy laughs her eyes light up with a glow. She doesn't have to say a word to express her feelings, it's all there, in her beautiful eyes.

She glances up at me, "What's going through your mind, doctor?" *You are going through my mind. Every touch, every glance soothes my soul. I need you. Please, give me another chance.*

I shake my head, "Do you want to go to recovery or wait here?"

"I don't think they'll let me in."

"They will if I tell them to." I say with a wink.

This woman is the picture of perfection. She sits in this ordinary off-white hospital chair, her long dark hair hanging down, legs crossed on the chair like a child might do, stunning eyes that draw me in and lock me in place. As she bites down on her lip, I fight every animalistic urge she brings out in me.

I want her, it's not purely physical anymore. Sure, I'm dying to fuck her, I always am. But I envision an entire future with her. I've never wanted this before. She's everything I've ever wanted and more. Somehow, I have to find a way to make her want to give me another chance. I do love her, but how can I make her believe that when my actions told her the exact opposite?

I never meant to hurt her, that's the last thing I'd ever want to do. I'm a fool, I really thought I could get her out of my system and do the right thing. My son's in love with her, and she should be off-limits to me. This is the one girl I never should've touched, yet I've fallen in love with her. It's too late now, I can't go back. Nash will need to find some other girl because mine is not available. And Mercy is mine. I see it in the way she looks at me, how she trembles from my touch. Her gaze travels up and down, stopping at my eyes momentarily before traveling the length of my body. Again, she bites her lip once she spots my swollen cock through my pants.

"Baby girl."

A soft moan escapes from her lips as she closes her eyes for a brief moment.

She reaches her hand up and strokes the side of my face as she leans in, pressing her lips to mine. A nurse wheels Ivy's bed into the room, shitty timing. I walk to the window to allow my body a chance to calm down after the taste of sweet honey that seems to drip from her tongue.

Thirteen

MERCY

SAVED BY THE BELL, or the nurse bringing Ivy back into the room. I'm not sure what got into me, why I kissed him, or why I can't be near this man and not have my hands and mouth on him. He does something to me that makes my mind go to mush. Just one look, and I'm melting into a puddle for him.

Ivy is pale. I sit watching her as Liam reads her chart.

"Fuck," he says.

"What is it?" My gaze quickly snaps to him.

"She's going to need more surgeries and probably skin grafting."

Shit. Skin grafting is really painful, I don't know much about it other than it's agonizing.

"Obviously, the chemo has to stop, right?"

"Yes, for now we don't have a choice."

"Liam, how did she get this infection?"

He shrugs his shoulders and places the chart on the slot at the foot of the bed and places his hand on mine. "We will never have an answer to that question. It would be nothing more than a guess. Everyone has this bacteria on their skin. She could have gotten a nic or it could've even traveled in through her port or IV line. This bacteria only needs the smallest entry way into the skin."

Standing up, he goes to the bedside table and gets two sets of gloves.

"Put these on. If you touch her, you need to not touch yourself. The gloves must be changed before you touch yourself or before touching me."

"In your dreams, doctor," I say as my lips turn into a small smile.

He hovers his mouth over my ear and whispers, "You have no idea what I dream of when it comes to you, baby girl. Your hands are nothing compared to your mouth on every fucking inch of my body. It's what my dreams are made of."

Fuck. Now I'm sitting here in this hospital room with wet panties. And I can tell by the gleam in his eyes that he knows it. He acts like the cat that caught the mouse.

We sit waiting, quietly for what feels like hours for her to wake up. I want her to sleep, it's what her little body needs. But at the same time, I want to hear her voice. I want to tell her it's going to be okay.

She begins to stir lightly, and we both sit up paying close attention like we'll miss something big, earth shattering.

Her eyes open, and her gaze travels from me to Liam and then back to me as her lips curve into the slightest smile.

She whispers, "Dr. L.... Mercy."

I place my gloved hand on her knee. "Hi, sweet girl. How are you feeling?"

"Tired. It hurts, but okay."

I squeeze her knee, "You're such a brave girl. I'm so proud of you."

"How's your throat," Liam asks her.

"It hurts." Her voice is scratchy.

Liam walks to the left side of the bed and presses the call button.

When the nurse answers, he bites, "Water for Ms. Reynolds, STAT."

"Yes, doctor, right away."

The nurse brings the water to give to Ivy, but Liam takes it from her, "That will be all," he says in a dismissive tone. Dr. Grump is in the building.

He puts the straw in Ivy's mouth, telling her, "Sip slowly."

This is beautiful to watch, he strokes her hair as she takes slow sips of her drink. I've never seen this side of Liam. Not a doctor, just a man taking care of someone he clearly has grown fond of.

Once she's had several sips, he puts the cup on the table.

"Dr. L?" Ivy glances up at Liam with questioning eyes. "Did I almost die?"

"What?" he asks, as I gasp.

"I heard the nurses talking. They said they thought I was a goner, which I think means gone. And the other nurse said no way will I live through all the surgeries I need. Do I need more surgeries?"

Liam is furious. I can see it in his furrowed brow and clenched jaw.

He blows out a big breath, "We don't know how many surgeries you will need. But you will live through them regardless how many there are. Do you hear me? Choose to live and you will. Those nurses should not have said that. But you're going to live a long, wonderful life. I will see to it."

Her bottom lip covers her top with the most heartbreaking pout I've ever seen. This would all be too much for an adult but for a child? It's simply too much for a small child to handle.

"I'll be back, I have something to take care of that can't wait."

He glances at me as he rubs the stubble on his jaw, his teeth clenched so tight, I know he's grinding his molars. There's no question for me what Liam needs to take care of. Those nurses are about to get their asses handed to them, rightfully so.

Walking over to me, he whispers in my ear, "Be a good girl for Daddy," and then kisses me on the forehead and leaves.

This man. All it takes is a few words to have my heart pounding like a drum.

Ivy looks at me and giggles.

"Don't you start," I say, with a grin.

"You are his girlfriend!"

"No, Ivy, I'm not."

"He kissed you."

I shake my head, "Ivy one day you'll see, grown-ups are weird and complicated. Do you want to watch a movie? I have my tablet in my purse."

"Yes!"

"Something with princesses?"

A huge grin spreads across her delicate features.

I open up my purse and grab my tablet and download *Disney Plus* where I know I'll find all the princesses.

"Which is your favorite?" I ask.

She puts her finger on her chin, thinking hard. "I want to watch *your* favorite princess movie," she beams at me.

"Well, you're the one who just had surgery," I chuckle, "But my favorite is *Cinderella*."

"Oh, I love *Cinderella*," she exclaims.

I search for *Cinderella*, move my chair closer to the head of her bed, and settle in for a movie. I don't think I've seen it since I was Ivy's age.

Something peculiar happens when the first scene with the evil stepmother plays.

"She's so mean," I say.

"Well, she's not *so* mean," Ivy says in a small voice.

"How is she not mean?"

"She doesn't hit her."

I wince at her words, "What do you know about that?"

"Nothing," she says quickly, focusing her gaze on the movie.

I pause the movie and put the tablet on the bed below her feet.

"Ivy, what do you know about being hit?"

She shakes her head no, and her lips form a tight line.

"You do know you can talk to me about anything, right?"

Turning her head, she avoids looking at me, "I get spanked sometimes, when I'm bad."

"Spanked? On your butt?"

My question rolls over in her mind. She narrows her eyes, "Well sometimes. But it depends on how bad I am."

"Where do you get spanked when you're really bad?"

I spot Liam outside the door, but Ivy doesn't. He moves out of view when he hears our conversation.

"My face, other parts of my body, anywhere, I guess. Sometimes on my neck."

"On your neck?" I ask. What the hell does that even mean?

"Not spanking, squeezing."

She fucking chokes her? It takes everything in me to keep my expression stoic.

I stroke her hair, "That's never okay, Ivy. Your behavior could never be bad enough to deserve that."

"Can we watch the movie? I don't like talking about this."

"Yes, sweet girl," I grab the tablet and press play.

A few minutes later, Liam walks in and casually says, "Can I borrow Mercy for a few minutes? I need her help."

She glances up at Liam, "Can I finish the movie?"

I nod, "Of course, you can. You can watch anything on *Disney* but that's it, no other apps, okay?"

I get up and follow Liam to the on-call room. As we are walking, he chuckles.

"What?" I ask.

"You just don't want her finding your kindle and all the smut books."

I laugh, "Well true, although I don't think she could read them anyway."

"No but the covers."

"What do you know about the covers of smut books, Dr. Lexington?"

"You really like those books, don't you?"

I shrug and speak low, "I'm a smut slut, a total lover of the cliterature, what can I say?"

"Did you just say cliterature?"

I smile, "Why yes, I did, Dr. Lexington."

He growls as we walk into the on-call room. "It makes me crazy when you call me that."

"More than Daddy?" I ask while feigning an innocent expression.

"Fuck, Mercy. Behave, we need to discuss what she told you."

I smile and nod, "Yes, I know. I need to contact CPS, but she's never going to trust me again.

We stand just inside the doorway with the door closed, he places his hands on my shoulders, "Baby girl, it will be okay. She'll be upset at first maybe, but we have to do what's best for her."

I nod, "I know that. But it doesn't make it any easier."

He hands me her chart, and I open it to make the notes I need to make. Then, I do the one thing I don't want to do. I walk over to the phone in the corner and place my call to CPS.

I hang up the phone, and tears run down my face. This poor little girl has been through cancer and chemo twice, abuse, and neglect. The more I find out, the more my heart breaks. So many bad things have happened to her, and still, she's this pure soul with so much love to give. How does that happen? She should be angry and jaded, but she remains this happy, carefree little girl.

Liam comes up behind me, brushing my hair off the side of my neck, and presses his lips to my skin.

"You did the right thing, baby girl. I'm proud of you."

I shiver under his lips.

"Liam," I breathe. It almost sounds like a prayer. "I have to get back to Ivy," I say.

"You have a few minutes," he picks me up, carries me to the bed, and lays beside me.

Continuing his assault on my neck, he moans.

"Liam we shouldn't. It's just going to confuse things."

He puts his hands in my hair on one side and pulls my head, forcing me to meet his gaze, "I'm not confused. I want to make you feel good. Be a good girl and come for Daddy."

When he bites my bottom lip, I forget all of the reasons why I shouldn't let him touch me.

Fourteen

LIAM

I TUG her bottom lip with my teeth, and she moans as she grabs a fistful of my hair and pulls me closer, I release my teeth and press my lips to hers in a devouring kiss.

She pulls me on top of her as she moans, "Please, I need you."

Fucking music to my ears. I'm no fool, I know this doesn't mean we are together. But I'll take whatever I can get from her. While we are in this bed, she's mine.

I reach my hand under her skirt and rub her thigh with a needy, bruising touch as my mouth moves to her neck.

"Yes," she cries out as I bite her hard but not hard enough to break the skin.

"You're so fucking beautiful. Tell me what you need."

"I need you," she cries out, "Touch me, please."

"Spread those beautiful thighs, baby girl." I move her panties to the side and sink two fingers into her wet heat.

"Oh, such a good girl, so wet for me."

I move my fingers in a come-hither motion, followed by my scissor move, knowing it'll make her come quickly.

"Come on my fingers."

"Yes! Oh my God. Daddy, yes!"

There is something this woman does to me. I'm not even worried about getting myself off. I want to spend forever making her feel good. I need to coax every ounce of pleasure from her gorgeous body. It's an all-consuming desire. I'm blinded by my lust for this woman.

She arches her back as she screams my name. I'm sure people can hear her if they walk by the door, she seems to have forgotten we are in a hospital, but I don't even care, there are no patients on this side, it's all on call rooms and offices. Every sound she makes speaks to my soul, calling to me like the sin calls to the sinner.

I move down her body and place my head between her beautiful thighs. Her scent surrounds me, filling me with a feral urgency.

I pull my fingers out, grab her panties, and rip them from her body, and she gasps in surprise.

I slide my fingers back inside her pussy moving them in and out repeatedly as I flatten my tongue and lick her slit. I circle her clit but don't actually touch it.

She cries out, "Please."

"What baby? What do you need?"

"Lick my clit."

I can't stop myself even though I know I should, "Say you're mine."

"I can't. Please, don't punish me for trying to protect myself."

"You don't need to protect yourself from me, baby girl. I won't hurt you again."

I know I will not win this way, so I give her what she wants as my heart breaks. What if this is the last time, I ever taste her? I try to stay present and focus on her exquisite body.

I flick her nub with my tongue, as she arches her back again, I suck it between my teeth.

"Oh my GOD! YES!"

Pulling my fingers out, I suck them clean, "I need to be inside you."

She nods, "Yes, fuck me."

I sit between her legs, undo my belt, unbutton my pants, and unzip them in a flash, pulling them down to my knees.

One thrust into her wet slice of heaven does me in. I've never felt a pussy this good in my life. She is tight and always so warm and welcoming. It's as if she was made for my hungry cock. Wrapping her legs around my waist, she pulls me further into her as she thrusts her hips up to meet mine.

"Always so ravenous for my cock, aren't you, baby?"

"Yes. Fuck me, Dr. Lexington."

I flash her a devious grin. Hovering over her, I place my hands on either side of her on the mattress as I stare into her stunning face. "One rule, baby girl. Keep your eyes open. I want your eyes on me when you come."

"Yes sir," she says as her lips curve into a small smile.

"Good girl."

I slide out of her most of the way and slam back into her.

"You feel so fucking good. The way your beautiful pussy squeezes my cock makes me crazy."

"If you keep talking like that I'm going to come."

I smile as I ghost my lips over hers, "Good girl, come on Daddy's cock."

She grabs my shoulders, digging her nails through my shirt, keeping her eyes open as she comes. Her body tenses before she shudders, crying out. It's the most beautiful thing I've ever seen. To know I do this to her it's an amazing thing. I can't let her go; I can't let this go.

I put her legs over my shoulder and give it to her hard and fast. "I will never understand how you can feel this good, baby. Squeeze me."

Her pussy clenches down on my cock milking every bit of cum from me.

"Yes. Good girl. So perfect."

I lean down and kiss her beautiful lips.

Tears roll down her cheeks, and I'm confused. Why is she crying?

I still inside her and stroke her hair, "Baby, why are you crying?"

"Because I hate you," she says.

I wipe her tears away with my thumb, "No you don't."

"Fine, but I want to," she huffs. I climb off her and lay beside her and pull her into my arms.

"Why are you crying? Talk to me."

She shakes her head.

"Because I'm so fucking in love with you even though I don't want to be."

She sobs into my neck, and it's at this moment I realize how badly I hurt her. I will never forgive myself for doing this to her. I acted like a fucking child. I created this mess. Sure, I had my reasons, but there will never be a reason good enough to cause these tears. How do you comfort someone when it's you that caused the pain?

I pull her tighter and kiss the side of her head, "I'm so sorry. It kills me that I hurt you. I only ever want to make you feel good. Look at me, Mercy."

She moves her head up, looking into my eyes, and the tears on her face fucking gut me.

"I love you, baby girl. I don't care how long it takes; I will prove that to you. Please give me a chance to show you that I won't ever make the same mistake twice."

"I need time, Liam. I need to think about it. I can't decide based on three amazing orgasms."

"I'll give you all the time you need, baby."

"You'll wait? No one else?"

I stroke the side of her face and stare at her with a serious expression on my face. "Baby, I don't throw those three words around. I have never spoken those words to any woman in twenty-three years. If I say it, I mean it. And for you, I would wait a lifetime."

"I need to go home and get panties," she giggles.

"That's your response? Okay, I'll sit with Ivy while you do that."

"I need to call a cab."

I shake my head at her as she climbs off the bed, "No, take my car."

"Are you sure? What if I wreck it?"

"I'd be far more worried about you than I would be, my car. So don't wreck it. I need you back in one piece."

I get off the bed, pull my pants up, and get my keys out of my pocket, then hand them to her.

"Thank you."

"Any time, baby. What's mine is yours."

"Liam," she says with disapproval on her face.

"All the time in the world, baby."

"I'll see you soon. I won't be long. Go make sure she's not looking at the sexy man meat in my Kindle library."

"Yes, dear."

"Bye, doctor. I'll see you soon."

As I walk to the right toward Ivy's room, I shake my head. This woman has my heart in her hands. The only thing that matters in my world is Mercy. She's fucking everything to me.

Fifteen

LIAM

I WALK in and find Ivy fast asleep, but that's not what concerns me. Her other arm is bubbling up. Her entire forearm, from her elbow to wrist, is bubbling up with pus-filled blisters. This is not good. I've never even seen an infection like this.

Sprinting out to the nurse's desk, I practically yell, "Get me Kane on the phone, stat!"

She hands me the phone, "Xander I need you in Ivy Reynold's room. The infection is worse. I don't know how the nurses didn't see this. I went in and it's serious."

He informs me that he's in with a patient but will be here in a few minutes.

I go and sit with Ivy while I wait for him.

When he finally comes in, he glances at her arm, shock displays on his face, his eyes go wide.

"Jesus, Liam. I've never seen a staph infection this bad."

"What are we going to do?" I ask. I'm a fucking doctor, but at this second, I'm at a loss. How are we going to save this little girl? I failed Mercy once with her sister and I can't do that again. If Ivy dies, I'm worried that Mercy's heart will go too. I can't let that happen.

"We are taking her in for another surgery. I also want to run tests. I have a feeling if it looks this bad that it might be in her blood."

"Sepsis?" I gasp. Fuck. This is worse than I even thought. Sepsis? Her organs could shut down and she could die, fast.

"I'm moving her to the burn unit. Everyone that goes in to see her is to be gloved, and gowned up, as well as a mask. No exceptions. Make sure Mercy knows. Do you want to wake her up and tell her? I'm going to have her prepped for surgery immediately."

I shake my head, "Yes."

"Okay get your PPE on."

I grab my supplies and get them on quickly before walking back to Ivy's bedside. I touch her hair, "Sweet girl, wake up for a minute."

She stirs and instantly sobs, "My arm. Ow."

"I know, honey. They need to do another surgery."

"No. I don't want to go to the bottom again." She's referring to her blood pressure.

"It'll be okay. They are more prepared this time. They'll be watching your blood pressure closely; it's going to be okay."

"I want Mercy!"

"Do you want me to call her so you can talk to her on the phone?"

She nods, "I'm scared."

"I know. It's going to be okay. Let's call Mercy."

Pulling out my phone, I find her name and click call.

"Liam, I'm on my way. Your car is just fine."

"I'm sure it is. Listen, Ivy is being taken in for emergency surgery. I'll explain when you get here. But she needs to talk to you."

"Of course, put it on speaker phone."

"Mercy?" Ivy says, between sobs.

"Hi, sweetheart. I know you're scared but it's going to be okay."

"What if I die?"

"That's not an option. You're the strongest girl I've ever met. Besides, we have movies to watch."

"You want to watch another movie?"

"Yes, it's your choice this time."

"Oh! Can we watch Frozen? It's my favorite."

"As soon as you wake up, we'll watch it," Mercy says.

"Dr. Lexington," Mercy says, "Can she eat Jell-O tonight?"

"Well, that's Dr. Kane's call but it should be fine."

"Okay, as long as he says it's okay, I'll get you Jell-O. What's your favorite flavor?"

"Red. Duh. That's everyone's favorite," Ivy giggles.

Mercy laughs, "Oh good, I was worried that you might be one of those weirdos that prefer green Jell-O. Gross!"

And just like that, this little girl that's in so much pain, is giggling.

"I'll be there by the time you are done with your quick surgery, okay?"

It won't be a quick surgery, I know that. But Ivy doesn't need to know how serious this is.

"I can't wait. Bye Mercy."

I take over, "Hey, she's being transferred to the sixth floor. I'll meet you up there."

"Okay, doctor, see you there."

A few minutes later, the nurses come in and preps her for surgery.

"Don't let me go to the bottom," she says to one of the nurses.

It takes her a minute to realize what she's talking about, but she recovers quickly, "Not a chance, honey," she says with a wink.

"You'll be just fine, Ivy. Dr. Kane is an excellent surgeon," I say.

"I wish you would do my surgery."

"No, you don't," I chuckle. "This is his specialty. Mine is cancer, trust me he'll do a much better job than I would."

She shakes her head, "You're the best, you could do anything."

I can't stifle my huge grin, "Oh Ivy, you're such a special girl. The most beautiful princess in the whole world."

She giggles and says, "Nope, Mercy is."

I can't disagree with that, so I just smile, "I'll see you soon, sweet girl."

They wheel her bed out to surgery. I've guaranteed this little girl will live, which I shouldn't have because that is not something I can ever be sure about. It could be a basic surgery, and we can't ensure that a patient will live through it. Several things can go wrong.

I walk out to the nurse's station. "Why hadn't Ivy been checked on while I was gone?"

Nurse Gail glances at me with wide eyes, "We got busy, I'm sorry, doctor."

A newer nurse, Sheila, gapes at me, "You mean while you were taking advantage of a young woman in the on-call room?"

I glare at her while seeing red, "I don't take advantage of anyone. I'm not that kind of man, if you have a problem, I suggest you take it up with Human Resources. Until then, what I do is none of your business. It's not my job to be checking on her consistently, that's your job. Is it not?"

Gail, the charge nurse, glares at her, "Yes, doctor."

"Gail, she's being transferred to the burn unit. I want a Pediatric Infectious Disease Specialist to be in her room by the end of the day."

"Of course, Dr. Lexington. I'll take care of it, personally."

"Thank you. Oh, and Sheila?"

"Yes, Dr. Lexington?"

"You're new here and officially at the very top of my shit list. The last place you want to be. I hope you enjoy catheters."

I won't really put her on catheter duty. This is a children's hospital, and I don't want her to be dealing with my kids when I've pissed her off. Although, the next time she has to put a catheter in, I guarantee she'll think of me and wonder if I'm the reason she was assigned to it.

After throwing away my PPE gear, I make my way to the sixth floor, the burn unit, where Ivy will be for the foreseeable future. I step out of the elevator and immediately grab a new gown, gloves, and a mask.

As I walk away, "Liam," the voice behind me sends shivers down my spine.

"Hey, baby girl," I turn around, and she's so upset. "What's going on?"

"You have to get a mask, gown, and gloves on first."

She nods, sets her purse down, and gets into her PPE gear.

"Follow me, Mercy. We'll go talk."

We stop by the nurses station, "Dr. Lexington and Social Worker Mercy Madison. We're here for Ivy Reynolds. She's in surgery, we'll be in the on-call room taking a nap. I want to be called the second she's out of surgery. And then again when she's out of recovery."

"Of course, doctor. We have four on-call rooms up here; you could have separate rooms."

I roll my eyes, "We're fine. Thank you for your concern," The last thing I want is to be separated from her.

We walk to the room and take off our PPE.

"You need sleep, sweetheart. But first I'll tell you what you want to know. Come lie down with me."

I lock the door and strip down to my boxers, and she laughs.

"How can I sleep with you nearly naked?"

"You'll manage."

I put my arms behind my head, while she takes her shoes off and I enjoy the show. She takes her skirt and top off and places them over the chair, so they don't get wrinkled. Unfastening her bra, she slides it down her arms and puts it on top of her clothes. Standing there staring at me, her lips turn into a seductive smile.

"Talk, Dr. Lexington."

I clear my throat, "I'm not sure I remember how."

"I could put my clothes back on."

"That will not be necessary," I motion with my finger for her to come over to me.

She climbs beside me and lays her head on my chest.

I take a deep breath, "When I went back into her room her right arm was clearly infected. From elbow to wrist, it was pure blisters. It was bubbled, I've honestly never seen anything like that and neither has Xander. I have a Pediatric Infectious Disease expert coming today. This infection is very aggressive. He thinks she may have sepsis."

"Shit," she said. She's quiet for a few minutes, "Liam?"

"Yes, baby."

"Is she going to be, okay?"

Running my fingers through her hair, I contemplate lying to her to protect her heart but realize that isn't what she'd want. It's the truth she's after, regardless of how my words will affect her.

I sigh audibly, "I wish I could tell you, yes, but at this point that would be a lie. I just don't know what the outcome will be. Will she die?

I'm sorry, baby, it's a possibility. If she pulls through, I'm concerned about the cancer spreading. We absolutely cannot give chemo to someone in this state. My only hope is that the treatment was effective at slowing it down. But right now, this infection is the biggest danger for her, not the cancer."

"Thank you for being honest with me," she said.

I kiss the top of her head, "Always, even when it pains me to do so."

She moves her head to my shoulder and gazes at me, so much love behind her stare, it makes me weak.

Running her fingers down my chest, she moans, "You feel so good against my skin. I love feeling you."

I trail my fingertips down her side, "Ditto, baby."

She gets on top of me, straddles me, grinds her pussy on my cock, the only barrier between us is her panties and my underwear.

"Baby girl, no, you need sleep."

"I need you inside me, doctor. Won't you heal my ache?" This woman kills me. I want nothing more than to be inside her, at all times.

"You...Need...Sleep."

Grinding harder, she reaches her hands up and twists both of her nipples.

"Mercy," I whisper. I'm about five seconds from losing any semblance of sanity.

Then she takes one hand off her tit and slips her fingers into her panties. While I can't see through her panties, I know she has her fingers inside her pussy. I'm dying. I want her so bad, but I know she's exhausted.

This girl has my number, she knows me so fucking well. She pulls her hand out of her panties and sucks on her fingers while moaning and closing her eyes, pushing her wet heat down on me. That's it, I've taken all I can take.

I pull her by her hair, so she lands flat on her back. I jump up and get on top of her, "You dirty, fucking girl. Did you enjoy your little game?"

She nods with a pleased grin.

I get up and slowly pull her panties down, trailing them over her hips, and down her legs. It's like unwrapping the most seductive present I've ever seen in my life.

"One other thing you should know baby," I say as I pull my boxers off. "If you think you're not mine you should stop me right now. I'm claiming your fucking pussy, I'm claiming every inch of you. Next time I feel you squeezing my cock, you're mine. And I'll never let go of what's mine. I made that mistake before. I won't make it again."

Sixteen

LIAM

MY DICK IS at her entrance while hovering above her waiting for a response. My gaze locks with hers as she puts both of her hands on my ass and pulls me closer, pushing my cock inside her.

"Liam. Fuck, I love you."

"Mercy, I love you too, so fucking much." I pull back, leaving only the tip in, and slide back into her slowly.

"Yes!" she cries out.

I can't hide my smile, my girl is so fucking responsive. I love it. Making her come is the easiest thing in the world.

Pushing her legs back so her knees are near her ears I tell her, "Hold your legs here."

She flashes me a questioning look.

"I'm going to fuck you so hard they're going to hear your screams in New York City." I notice her swallowing hard, "Oh yes, baby girl," I say.

Placing my hands on her hips, while she holds her legs back, I stop myself for a moment.

"This is fucking beautiful. You baring your beautiful pussy to me is the most erotic thing I've ever seen. Such a fucking good girl. Aren't you? Tell me you're Daddy's, good girl."

"I'm your good girl, Daddy, only yours."

"Fucking right, you are."

I grip her hips tight as I slam into her. She bites her lip, trying to stifle her sounds.

"No, baby girl. You won't ever hold back your sounds from me, I want every single one of them, I don't care where we are."

Her eyes widen as I fuck her harder, her tits bouncing nearly to her face.

She moans so loud, that it makes my cock swell even more.

"Let go of your legs, rub your clit for me, baby."

Barely a touch to her clit, and she's screaming for me, writhing on the bed, grabbing the sheets with her free hand. This right here is the most intoxicating thing in the world. The way she looks, her scent, the way she sounds screaming for me, our sweaty skin touching, this is everything, and I'll never get enough of it. This is how I want to live and die. I've never been surer of anything in my life. She's mine, and no matter how long it takes me to convince her, she'll be my wife.

She's close. I can feel it in the way her pussy clenches my dick.

"Yes, baby girl, come with me."

I thrust faster, a groan escapes from me, and her eyes light up.

"Come for me, Daddy, fill me up."

Jesus, this girl and her words.

She slides her hands from my abs up to my chest, gazing at me. She says, "Eyes on me when you come."

As much as I love being in control, there's something about her turning the tables on me that turns me on so fucking much.

"Daddy, YES!"

That's all it takes until I lose the hold on this orgasm. I can't hold back another second. I fill her with so much cum; it feels like it's been days when it was just earlier today. I swear this woman makes me feel like I'm eighteen again.

I lay on the bed beside her, both of us breathing heavily, when she asks, "Did you go to school for that?"

I chuckle loud, "Are you asking if I went to a school that teaches fucking?"

She giggles, "Maybe."

"No, but I'm glad that I can please you."

"That puts it mildly. I never knew sex could be so good."

I rub the stubble on my jaw.

"What is it, Liam?"

"I'm not sure I really want to know. But did you have sex with a lot of boys your age?"

She laughs, "No."

"They didn't satisfy you?"

"I only fooled around with them, Liam."

I prop my head up on my hand, my elbow on the mattress, as I stare at her questioningly, "What do you mean?"

She can't possibly be saying what I think she is.

"I was a virgin before you Liam, I saved myself for you."

"That's not possible, you were tight, but you never complained of pain."

Then I remember finding a few streaks of blood on the sheets. I thought it was from the anal. "God damn it, Mercy."

I sit up, feeling sick for what I did to her. That was not a fucking first time. That's not how you lose your fucking virginity.

"Why are you upset?"

"Are you fucking kidding me?" I get up and get dressed.

"Liam, don't do this, don't go."

"I'm so pissed at you, if I stay, I might say something that both of us will regret. I'll text you when you can see, Ivy."

She stands in front of me and kneels, "Please, Daddy, please."

"Mercy, don't push my buttons."

She spreads her thighs, places her hands on her legs and stares down at the floor. I'm furious but she's giving me her submission knowing well what that does to me.

"Look at me."

When she gazes up at me with pleading eyes, I crumble. "Why are you so angry?"

I pull her off the floor.

"Baby girl, that was not how your first time should have been. It should have been tender and slow. I must have really hurt you. A hard fuck from a man like me is not what you deserve to have in your memories."

She pulls away from me and starts getting dressed "A man like you?"

"Yes," I bite, "You deserve better."

"Liam, I had wanted you since I was sixteen. That night was the best night of my life, it was everything I ever wanted."

"I told you it wouldn't happen again. I fucked you in your goddamn ass. Jesus, Mercy. And how could you have wanted me so much at sixteen. I don't get it. There was nothing special between us back then."

She rolls her eyes, "Not for you, obviously, you didn't even remember me. For me, the way you looked at me, the way you were present, always maintaining eye contact. You made me feel special, like I mattered. No one had ever done that for me. Let's not forget that you are ridiculously hot, when I saw you in a bathing suit, I was done."

I pull her to the chair and sit down, taking her on my lap, "What made you crawl into my bed?"

She giggles as she runs her fingers across my jaw, "I saw the way you looked at me in the bar. And then when you found me naked in your bathroom, I knew you wanted me."

"That's a very brazen thing for a virgin to do."

"I wanted you so bad, Liam. It was literally all I could think about. Even if I had known it would never happen again, I still would've done it. I wanted you, whether it was love, lust, or some crush. I never would have regretted it."

Sliding my hands into her hair, I pull her lips to mine. My body hums with desire as she slides her tongue into my mouth. She moves to my neck and kisses softly, before trailing her tongue all over.

"Fuck. How does your skin taste so good?"

I chuckle, "I don't have a clue, baby."

She bites me, and in an instant, I'm hard as a rock again.

My phone starts ringing, and she giggles.

I answer, "Dr. Lexington."

Thanks to Mercy's tongue running across every inch of skin she can access, I'm not sure what the nurse actually said. But I know Ivy is out of surgery.

"Baby girl, we have to go see, Ivy. But you're coming home with me tonight."

"Fine, but I'm hungry. I haven't eaten since yesterday. I hope your plans involve food."

"Food and sleep, baby. And tomorrow we have to go to HR."

"Why?" she jumps up.

"We need to tell them about our relationship before more people jump to the conclusion that I'm taking advantage of you. Let's go, we will talk about this more later."

She takes my hand and pulls me to Ivy's room. Finally, she's mine again. I will not make the same mistake again. Nash will find out about us at some point, but he'll have to deal with it. He never had her, I do. She's mine. When I make her my wife, I know he'll struggle, but I won't give up my happiness when she wouldn't want him anyway. Maybe I'm a selfish man, a bad father but I can't let her go.

Seventeen

MERCY

WE PUT on our PPE gear, and I grip Liam's hand tight as we walk into Ivy's room. I'm terrified to see what her surgery was like this time.

Just like last time, I sit beside her while Liam flips through her chart. A few moments later, he comes and sits beside me.

"It went smoother this time. Her blood pressure was stable, and no transfusion was needed."

I breathe a sigh of relief, "I'm so happy."

"She has a long way to go but it's a good sign for future surgeries. Ivy is a fighter."

"What time do you need to be here tomorrow?" she asks.

I run my hand through the back of her hair, "Early. I need to do rounds. I can't make a habit of today."

"I'll take a cab in because there's something I'm going to do tomorrow."

"No. You'll take one of my cars. Also, my housekeeper picked you up some clothes today, they are in my closet."

"Liam, that was unnecessary."

"That's not how I see it. You'll need clothes, baby. I was afraid if you went home-"

"I'm not going to vanish if I leave your sight for a few minutes."

He turns his head away from me, and I can see the walls going up. "What's going on?" I reach out and stroke his back, "Talk to me."

"It's nothing. I'm being ridiculous."

"Tell me anyway."

He sits on the chair in silence, his muscular thighs spread, his elbows on his knees, his head hanging down.

"Liam."

Then Ivy stirs, so he ignores me, rightfully so.

"Hi!" I say with a fake smile pasted onto my face.

"I don't like surgery," she whispers.

I push the hair out of her face, "I know. I don't like it either."

"Did I go to the bottom again?"

"No, sweetheart, you did really well."

"Why does Dr. L look sad?"

He walks to the other side of her bed, "I'm just tired, it's been a long day."

"Do Mommy's come to the hospital when their kids have surgery?"

Liam sighs, "Most of the time, yes."

"Is she coming back?"

"We don't know, sweet girl," Liam says with a clenched jaw.

A tear rolls down her cheek, "I know I'm going to die, it's okay. I hope you remember me."

"Ivy, I need you to stay positive. You're not going to die. Remember, the mind and body are closely connected, positivity is so important. But I can assure you, I could never forget you," he says.

She looks to me to answer the same question, and I'm fighting back tears so hard, I feel like I might explode.

"Ivy, honey you're not going to die because you aren't allowed to. I need you here, okay? For me, will you try to stay positive? And yes, I will never forget you when you get better and go home. I will still think about you every single day."

We sit with her for a while, but we are both so exhausted.

"We're going to go because we are so tired. But I'll be back early tomorrow morning to see you. And Mercy will be in a little later, okay?"

She nods, "I'm tired too."

"I'm leaving my tablet for you, I trust you'll stick to Disney," I say with a serious expression.

"I'll behave, I promise."

"Good girl," I smile at her.

Liam clears his throat. I know exactly where his mind just went.

"See you tomorrow, Ivy."

I turn on Frozen on the tablet for her as I realize I don't need to worry about her watching something she shouldn't be, "You've got two bad arms now. So, you ask the nurses to put something on for you if you need it changed, okay?"

On our way out, after we rid ourselves of our PPE gear, Liam tells the nurses to check on her every hour and to help her with the tablet if she needs it.

"Dr. Scanlon, will be in tomorrow. She is sorry that she couldn't make it today. But she ordered different IV antibiotics after reviewing the chart."

Liam nods, and we walk away.

Walking out to the car, he says, "I'll take you home."

"Liam, what the hell? I'll take a fucking cab!"

"Mercy? Why are you yelling?"

"You wanted me so fucking bad. You get me and now that you have me you don't want me. I'm a fucking game to you. That's it right?"

I spin and walk away from him as the clouds open and rain pours from the sky. It doesn't deter me, I keep walking.

"Mercy," he runs after me.

"No, I'm done."

He puts his hands on my shoulders and spins me around, pushing me against the outside wall of the hospital, out of the rain.

"I want you just as much as I did before. I love you. Nothing has changed. I thought-"

"You thought what, Liam?" I ask breathlessly while my heart pounds.

"Damn it, I thought you wanted to go home. It's been a long fucking day and I didn't want to fight with you about this."

He wraps his hands around my throat, "I fucking love you. This is not a game. I will want you every day, do not doubt me. Don't create fucking issues where there are none. Of course, I still want you."

"I'm sorry."

Ghosting his lips over mine, he whispers, "I need you," and presses his lips to mine as he wraps his hands around large sections of my drenched hair. He kisses me like I'm his entire world.

He moves his face to my neck and licks the rain from my skin.

"Liam. We probably shouldn't be doing this in front of the hospital. There are cameras."

"No, we shouldn't, but I need you. Besides, Javiar will take care of it," he trails his tongue between my breasts.

"Liam lets go. Before I don't have a job. Your job is secure, mine is not."

"Your job is secure. I won't allow anyone to fuck with what's mine," he growls.

He pulls me to the car, and we get in quickly, getting out of the rain or to be alone quicker, I'm not sure which.

"How are you more beautiful, drenched?" He asks as he drives out of the parking lot.

I feign a serious expression, "I think you're a little biased, doctor."

Reaching over, he strokes the inside of my thigh, glancing over at me.

I arch an eyebrow at him, "Eyes on the road, Dr. Lexington."

"Fingers in the pussy, eyes on the road, got it," he says with a chuckle.

I laugh, "That's not exactly what I said."

"It's what you meant; I know you."

He skates his fingers on the outside of my panties, rubbing my clit through the thin material.

"Do you remember the first time I finger fucked you in this car?"

"I remember," I say, my cheeks flushed.

"Do you want to come, baby?"

"Yes."

"Ask me, properly and I'll make you come."

"Please make me come, Daddy."

"Good girl."

He slides his hand inside my panties and presses hard on my clit, rubbing it exactly the way I like.

"How does that feel?"

"So, fucking good, Daddy. So good. Oh God, I'm gonna come."

"Yes, baby girl, come for me."

My body jerks as my orgasm absorbs me.

He takes his hand out of my panties and licks my arousal off his fingers. I'm still not sure why, but that is so sexy. But everything he does arouses me. Every glance, touch, and sound is all as if it was manufactured only for me.

We pull into the garage, and he opens my door for me, always the gentleman.

"I'm going to make you something to eat." He walks into the kitchen, and I stand at the island watching him.

"What are your plans tomorrow?" he asks.

"I'm getting a tattoo."

"Absolutely not. No fucking way, Mercy."

"I was not asking for permission, Liam."

"I said no. I meant it."

I grab the counter with a death grip, my irritation growing by the second. "This is not your choice."

He sighs audibly, "Baby, if you want a tattoo, you can get a tattoo but not right now. If you get one now you cannot go into Ivy's room until it's completely healed. It's dangerous. I won't risk losing you."

"What?"

He rubs his fingers across his jaw, "It's not about the tattoo. Ivy's infection is very contagious. If there's an opening in your skin, you could get it. So please don't fight me on this."

Well now I feel like an idiot.

"Oh, I didn't know a tattoo could cause infection. Maybe next time you could lead with that."

After he serves the beef stir fry, onto two plates he brings them to the table.

"Thank you," I say as I sit down.

I take a bite of food, and it's delicious. Is there anything this man can't do?

We sit eating mostly in silence because we are both so exhausted.

He takes the plates and cleans up the kitchen, I stare at him, my mouth watering.

"Don't look at me like that, we aren't having sex."

I pout, "Why?"

"You need sleep, that's why."

Standing behind him in the kitchen, I run my nails down his back, he shivers. "Temptation is my specialty, doctor."

Turning so he's facing me, his tongue darts out, sliding against his bottom lip, "You tempt me every fucking day. There is never a second I don't want to be inside your beautiful cunt. But my need to take care of you, outweighs my need to fuck you. Be a good girl and do what Daddy says. Good girls always get rewarded. Bad girls get punished. Do you want to be rewarded, baby girl? Or do you want me to bend you over and spank you until your skin is blood red?"

His words take every ounce of breath from my lungs. I nod and whisper, "I'll be good."

"Good girl," he says, and every inch of my body is like a live wire. Two fucking words, that's all it takes.

I follow him to his bedroom, and he gets a t-shirt from his drawer, "Put this on. I can't have your naked body pressed against me and not fuck you."

We both get ready for bed and after I brush my teeth, I come out and find him already lying on the mattress looking like a fucking king. He's wearing nothing but gray boxers and he looks delicious.

Good girls get rewarded.

I don't know what the reward is, but I do know that I want it. So, I crawl into bed beside him, pressing my face into his neck, and I kiss him softly, "Goodnight, Daddy."

He groans, "Goodnight, baby girl."

Eighteen

MERCY

EIGHT WEEKS LATER...

It's been a difficult two months to say the very least. Ivy went through twelve surgeries in three weeks. Then the skin grafts. I could hear her screams in the hallway. It was the most emotional pain I've been through since my sister died. Everything in me wanted to run in and make them stop hurting this precious child, but of course, that was not an option. Sometimes, I have nightmares about it, but I always wake up to Liam soothing me in some way. Then there was the CPS visit which Ivy was less than pleased about. She was upset but after a few weeks she returned to her former self, sweet little Ivy. Her mother still hasn't tried to see her.

Other than the fact that Ivy is in the hospital, my life is perfect. I have a job I love, and the man of my dreams in my bed. Everything between us is simply amazing.

The sex of course is hot as hell, and he treats me like gold. He hasn't asked me to move in with him, but he hasn't asked me to leave either. I spend every night in his bed which is exactly how I want it. I'm not sure if I could even fall asleep without him at this point.

Today I sit with Ivy in her room waiting for Liam to come in with her PET Scan results. She went months without cancer treatment, so the results might be devastating. We've watched nearly every princess movie on *Disney Plus* at this point. So, we are rewatching *Frozen,* as we wait.

"I love this part," she beams and quotes, *"That's no blizzard, that's my sister,"* she giggles. This little girl's giggle is everything good in this world. It makes my heart full when I hear it.

Liam walks in the room and winks at me, my heart fucking gallops.

"Dr. L," Ivy screams.

"Hi, Princess, may I sit?" She balls her hands into fists as if she's bracing for the impact of his words and nods at him.

He takes a seat, holding her chart in his hands and both of our hearts.

"WELL?" she says loudly.

He chuckles, "Well, your treatment was quite effective. I'm so pleased with the results. But we still need to do another round of treatment."

"I'm not going to die?" she asks.

Shaking his head at her he states, "Nope. Not a chance, not on my watch."

"Mercy, check your text messages, please."

I nod, "I was busy watching a movie."

I fetch my purse and pull out my phone and see a text message from Liam.

Daddy: Ivy's mother lost custody.

A shocked expression crosses my face as he nods and then turns to Ivy.

"I was thinking, Princess, how would you like to get out of the hospital for the day?"

"Really?" she asks.

"Really."

"Will Mercy take me?"

He grins, "Well, of course, but I was hoping you might let me tag along," he states with an enormous smile.

Ivy gazes down at her lap, sadness appears to suddenly consume her.

"What is it?" I ask.

"I don't have anything to wear. I only have a hospital gown."

Liam narrows his eyes at her, "Did you think I wouldn't be prepared?" He gets up and walks out of the room when he returns Ivy's face lights up like a damn Christmas tree.

"Every Princess needs a dress," he says.

She absolutely gleams as she takes it in.

It's a light blue dress with a sheer overlay that has sparkles all over it. It reminds me of *Frozen*, and I know it reminds Ivy of it too.

He even got her matching slip-on light blue shoes, the softest shoe I've ever seen. They look like ballet slippers.

"Mercy, can you help her get dressed?"

I nod, "Yes, doctor, of course."

He winks at me again, and I melt.

After I help her get dressed, we walk into the hall and Liam says, "Alright, let's go."

As we walk down the hall to go outside, I ask, "Are you going to get into trouble for this?"

He shrugs his shoulders, "I don't think so, but I really don't care. It's better to ask forgiveness than to ask for permission."

"I'll have to remember that sir."

"Sure. Just remember for you forgiveness only comes after punishment. Good girls get rewarded, bad girls get punished."

I sigh, his words get me every single time. Every time he says that to me, I get a tingle that runs straight to my core.

We step outside, and Ivy spins around, "Oh my God. I'm outside," a tear rolls down her cheek.

"Today, we forget about cancer and treatment, the hospital, everything. We will celebrate your birthday; you were too sick to celebrate. You will have to go back tonight and start treatment tomorrow, but we won't think about that today, okay?" He said with a serious expression.

She wraps her arms around him, squeezing him tight, "Thank you, Dr. L!"

"Let's go have lunch and then we will figure out where else we will go."

We get into the vehicle and Liam drives us to a restaurant with an outdoor patio.

"I thought eating outside might be nice since she's been cooped up inside for so long," he says.

"So thoughtful, Dr. Lexington."

We park and get out of the vehicle and walk up to the hostess stand as we wait for our table. Liam hands Ivy a mask and she rewards him with a scowl.

"Put it on Ivy, now. I won't risk you getting sick. It only comes off when you're eating."

"Fine," she huffs and puts it on.

After we are seated, Liam orders a bottle of wine and a Shirley Temple for Ivy, when the waitress brings it, Ivy beams.

Finally, our meals arrive, and we start to eat. I got a steak salad; Liam got his favorite steak and Ivy got an adult-sized hamburger and French fries.

She eats a few of her fries, then all of a sudden asks, "What's going to happen to me?"

Both of us glance at her unsure what the question is.

"I mean if my mom never comes back. When I get out of the hospital, where will I go?"

I turn to her and take her hand in mine, "You won't be going home with your mom. You'll be going to a foster home."

"Why?"

"A judge decided that is what's best for you. He doesn't think it's a good idea for you to live with your mom."

"What's a fosters home?" she asks.

"It's a family that takes in kids that need a home. There will probably be other kids there for you to play with."

I'm trying really hard to spin this positively for her, but I know the reality of foster homes. I know what could very well happen to her in one. She might get bounced from home to home. It's rare for a child to stay in the same foster home the entire time. It's almost unheard of. And then there's the abuse. Not every foster home is like that, but it does happen. That's the thought that has my chest constricting. Irony at its finest, take a child from an abusive home to put them in another one. In college I worked on a case as an intern for CPS involving a four-year-old boy. He was murdered by his foster mother while his biological mother was in drug treatment doing everything, she needed to get him back.

"I'll miss you," she says taking me from my dark thoughts.

"Well, you aren't ready to be discharged yet. You're stuck with us for a while. We have many more movies to watch!" I say.

After we finish eating, the waitress comes to the table with a chocolate cake with six candles. We sing happy birthday to Ivy and she glows. I hand Liam a wrapped gift, he nods and passes it to Ivy, "Happy Birthday, Princess."

She stares at him, no gawks at him.

"Open it!" He says with much anticipation. I'm not sure who is more excited for her to get the gift.

Ripping open the paper she yells, "It's a tablet!"

"A kid one, so we will know that you aren't anywhere that you shouldn't be."

"Thank you, Dr. L and Mercy!"

She has an ear-to-ear grin plastered on her face. Unshed tears fill my eyes as I try to reign my emotions in. I love this little girl with my whole heart.

"Next up, I'm taking you where you've always wanted to go," Liam says.

"Where?" she asks.

He piles the plates together as he states, "When you had your first blood draw this time and were so scared, I asked you where you wanted to go if you could go anywhere in the world. You told me about the butterfly place."

She starts bouncing up and down with excitement, "That's where we are going?"

"Yes, we're going to the Butterfly Conservatory, if you'd like to."

"Are you ready?" He smiles at her.

"YES!" She squeals.

Liam leaves money on the table for the bill and tip. We walk together back to the car. It isn't lost on me that, to observing eyes, we look like a happy family. But the truth is that after this little girl finishes treatment and is cancer free, I'll never see her again. Liam probably will for the occasional check-up but she'll be out of my life permanently. As we drive down the road, I stare out the window, looking at nothing, trapped in my emotions.

"Are you okay?" Liam asks me.

I nod. Ivy is in the back seat playing on her new tablet. Liam already set it up and charged it, so it was ready to go.

Biting my lip, I try to suppress the emotions that threaten to bubble over.

"Baby, what is it?"

"Nothing. Now's not the time, I'm fine, just thinking," I ramble.

"Have you been here before?"

"No, but I've always wanted to see it. I love butterflies."

"It's amazing. If you're still sometimes they'll land on you. They sell nectar as well so you can feed them."

I paste a fake smile on my face, "She'll love that."

We get out of the car and Ivy is feeling one thing, pure excitement. It oozes from her; it's overflowing and beautiful to watch.

Nineteen

LIAM

AS WE WALK UP to the entrance of the Butterfly Conservatory, I can't keep my eyes off Mercy. Something is wrong with my girl, and I don't like it one bit. She seems sad, and not at all what I'm used to. The last couple of months she's been so happy other than when Ivy had surgery. Smiling and laughing have become a constant that I have grown fond of. It's got to be about the conversation with Ivy regarding where she would be going.

After I pay, we walk in, Ivy's in the middle between Mercy and me, holding both our hands. If this were a few years down the road I'd want to adopt Ivy, in a heartbeat. But it's too soon, Mercy isn't even quite twenty-four yet. While I'm ready for more, I know she's not. Her career has only just started, she's too young. As much as I want to, I cannot ask her to do something like that. So, I clear the thought from my mind.

As we stand in the Butterfly Conservatory, a Blue Morpho lands on Ivy's hand. She freezes so she doesn't scare it away. Mercy takes out her phone and takes a picture—one close-up of her hand and one showing her sparkling face. If you had to define happiness by showing only a picture, this would do it. It'll be short-lived, but this is a memory I'll cherish.

Before long, Ivy is covered with butterflies. There are six on her head, covering her short hair that has begun growing since she's been out of chemo for a few months. We spend hours here and I'm so glad I did this. It's bittersweet however, I know this is the only day we'll ever have like this.

"They have a rose garden here too, should we go see it?"

Both my girls are excited by this idea, "YES!" They shout in unison.

I chuckle, "This way, ladies."

We walk to the enclosure outside, and we're surrounded by roses. There must be thousands here.

Mercy walks to the lavender-colored roses and gets close, inhaling their scent.

I commit this to memory, I want to buy her those exact roses because I want to see this look on her face again, this peaceful, content expression is one I want to see repeatedly.

Walking up behind Mercy, I whisper in her ear, "I love you, baby girl."

She lays her head back on my shoulder, "Thank you for this."

While Ivy wanders around smelling every color of rose, I take a moment and kiss my girl's neck.

A smile spreads across her beautiful face.

We walk back through the butterfly portion and head out of the building. Everyone is quiet, knowing Ivy has to get back to the hospital.

Climbing into the vehicle Ivy says, "I'm going to stay up and watch movies all night long."

Shaking my head I say, "Your tablet is on a timer, sweetheart. At seven, it won't work until seven the next morning."

She groans loudly.

I love the fire she still has after everything she's been through. But when we get back to the hospital, the fire I admired not so long ago is annoying to say the least.

She sits in the back of the car, arms folded across her chest, "I'm not going in."

"Ivy, get out of the car please," I stand against the open door.

"I can't want to."

"IVY!"

Mercy comes up behind me, "Liam don't."

She reaches her hand into the car towards Ivy, "Come on, baby. You can do this."

I tried to get her out for fifteen minutes and nothing. Mercy tries for thirty seconds, and she gets out of the car in an instant.

She puts her hand in Mercy's, "Can we draw butterflies tomorrow?"

"I'd like that a lot," Mercy gushes.

We walk back into the hospital, and I'm hit with the realization that Mercy is going to be an amazing mother one day. But me, I've pretty much struck out in the parent department. Would it be different with Mercy being there? I take a deep breath to calm myself down. I'm clearly getting way ahead of myself here.

After we get her settled in her room, we leave with the promise of butterfly pictures for my girls tomorrow. I'd much rather be involved with that than be the person responsible for the poison that will be put into her body. It's not a choice, this is the only treatment that will be effective for her cancer. We both say our goodbyes and Mercy kisses her on the forehead.

* * *

Once we get back to my house, I sit Mercy down in the living room. "Talk to me, baby. What made you so upset?"

"I don't want to talk about it."

Pulling her into my arms, I run my hand through her hair as I kiss the top of her head, "Please talk to me."

"I'm going to miss her. Once she's cancer free, she'll leave the hospital and go God knows where. You'll see her for check-ups but I won't. I'll never see her again, Liam. She'll just be...gone."

"I know, this is the hard part of the job, baby."

"No. This isn't just my job. We both know we are attached to her in a different way than any other patient."

She climbs onto my lap, straddling me, "Kiss me. I need you to take away my pain."

Not giving me a chance to respond she slams her lips to mine, and her tongue aggressively enters my mouth. When she moans into my mouth I react with need. I fist both of my hands in her hair pulling her head back, I bite her neck, kissing where I bit. She cries out as my hands touch her ass.

"Clothes off, now," I demand.

She gets up and I watch her take her clothes off, she's so sexy.

With a furrowed brow she demands, "You take your clothes off too or I'll put more on."

I chuckle, "Yes, Ma'am."

Once we are both naked, I sit on the couch again, "Ride my dick, baby."

She bites her lip and then smiles a seductive smile.

Climbing on top of me, she lines her entrance with my cock, and slides down taking my length inside her ravenous pussy. She leans forward slightly, placing her hands on my shoulders, while she bounces up and down on me. When her tits hit me in the face, I'm a happy man, I grab one and suck on her pink bud. There's a mirror on the wall across the room, and I watch her ass as she fucks me, it jiggles with perfection, her head is back, and her long hair flows down, touching the top of her ass. Watching her use my cock for her pleasure is so erotic.

"What are you looking at?" she asks, clearly annoyed.

"You. I'm always looking at you, baby girl. Get up for a minute, I'll show you."

She climbs off me, and I put her in front of the mirror, "Get on all fours."

I get behind her and thrust into her, pulling her hair so she's staring at us in the mirror.

"Look how beautiful you are when I fuck you, baby girl. So fucking exquisite."

Grabbing her hips, I slam into her again and again, "Keep your eyes on us, baby girl."

She does as she's told and watches me from the mirror.

"Daddy, YES!"

"Who owns this pussy?"

"YOU DO!" she yells as she digs her hands into the carpet.

I smack her ass, "That's right, baby. You're mine. All of you."

"Hit me harder," she cries.

Jesus, this girl, my girl, is everything I've ever wanted."

I hit her as hard as I can with an open hand, "Fuck, Mercy...You... Are...Fucking...Perfect."

"Daddy, I'm going to come. Can I come?"

"Yes, baby girl," I reach my hand around and grab her throat, squeezing, her eyes go wide, she's so close, I release her throat and a strangled cry escapes from her beautiful lips. I've never heard her like this before. It only takes two more pumps before I fill her.

I pull out and she turns around, and I wrap her in my arms, "Let's go take a shower, baby."

Standing with her cradled in my arms, I walk to my ensuite bathroom, turn the water on, and once it's the right temperature, I put her inside. I step in moving behind her, she turns to face me. I take her face in my hands, holding her head back in the shower stream.

She moans as I lather her hair with shampoo and massage her scalp. After I rinse the soap, she wraps her arms around me and presses her face to my chest.

"I don't want this to end," she whispers.

It's so low that I'm not sure I'm meant to hear it, "It won't."

She gazes up at me, "It will eventually."

"It won't," I repeat.

Shaking her head, she sighs.

"I'm going to marry you. I'm never letting you go," I confess.

She gasps, "Liam, don't say things like that. Don't make promises you can't keep."

I cup her cheeks, tilting her head back so she's looking at me, "Baby girl, I don't make promises I can't keep. I will marry you, the second you're ready."

A giggle escapes her lips, "I think that will need to wait. You're just going to blurt out to your son, by the way, here's your stepmom."

"We will figure it out, I'm never letting you go. This is it, you're my future, and I'm yours."

I kiss her deeply before taking her again in the shower.

Twenty

LIAM

WAKING up to this gorgeous woman wrapped around me is the best way to greet the morning. The sun gleams through the curtains shining on her head like a halo on her crown. Her hair spreads across the pillow, her hand on my chest, a creamy thigh stretched across my pelvis, and gazing down at her, a smile spreads across my face. This is it, and I never knew I wanted this, but I do. This is my forever, she will be my wife, and have my children. At forty, I never thought about having more children. But Mercy has changed it all for me. Watching her with Ivy showed me she needs to be a mother. I can't wait to put my baby in her belly and watch her grow.

I'm not trying to wake her up, but I can't have her this close to me and not touch her. My fingers stroke her back lightly. She arches her back and moans, my cock twitches under her leg. Her lips curve up into a soft smile before she opens her eyes. I turn my head toward her face and my lips find hers. Parting her mouth, she slides her tongue against mine.

Pulling back from our kiss I stare at her as her beautiful stare meets mine.

"Good morning, beautiful."

She bites her lip before responding, "Good morning, doctor."

"It's six a.m., baby girl. I have to get ready for work."

A groan escapes her lips as she rubs her leg against my cock, "Daddy, don't you want to fuck me?"

I shake my head, "Yes, I always want to fuck you. Unfortunately, I have to wait until later tonight."

Kissing her neck one last time, I rise out of bed, although it's the last thing I want to do. I really want to stay here all day fucking her until she screams my name so many times her voice becomes hoarse. As always, responsibility wins.

"I'm going to take a shower."

"Fine!" she huffs, my good girl is being awfully bratty this morning. She may need that perfect ass spanked tonight.

I walk into the kitchen after getting ready and she stands there holding my mug in her hand reaching out to me, "Coffee, Daddy?"

"Such a good girl," I say as I take the cup from her.

"Good girls get rewarded, don't they?" she says and then bites her lip.

"Yes, they do, baby girl. What is it that you want?"

"I have a fantasy," she stares down at the floor as if she's nervous.

"Please don't say you want a threesome. I will not share you."

She giggles, "No. I want to watch you."

"You want to watch me do what, baby girl?"

Yes, I'm going to make her say it. I want to hear the words; fuck I need to hear them.

"Never mind, it was stupid," she turns to the counter ending our little conversation.

"Oh no, baby," I walk up behind her and press my cock into the crack of her ass. I'm hard just from thinking about fulfilling any of her fantasies.

"Tell me, baby girl. You know I'll give you anything you want. Tell Daddy what you want."

"Do you remember when you got mad at me for watching you in the shower?"

I groan, "Yes, I remember."

I was so pissed when I got caught jerking off thinking of her perfect mouth. It was not my finest moment.

She arches her back, pushing her ass against my throbbing cock, "I want to watch you stroke yourself until you come. I want you to come all over my body."

Grabbing her hair, I yank her head back, and run my mouth down her neck, biting her gently.

"How did I get so fucking lucky? My perfect, dirty girl. I'll be home late tonight but when I get home, I will give you your fantasy."

She moans before asking, "Why are you going to be late? Do you have a date?"

I chuckle, "Never baby. There's no point when I have everything, I've ever wanted waiting at home for me. I'm meeting Nash for a drink. I haven't seen him in a while."

"Okay."

Placing my hands on her shoulders, I turn her around and slam my lips to hers. I try to pull back so I can leave, but she bites my bottom lip sending me into a frenzy. I kiss her hard, giving her exactly what she needs. This time she is the one to pull away, dropping to her knees, she gazes up at me with a pleading stare. Fuck I need to go, but I can't tell her no. It looks like my rounds will be a little late this morning.

"Ten minutes, that's all I've got, baby girl."

"Yes, Daddy."

I undo my belt and pants, dropping them to the floor, pull my underwear down to my knees and watching her lick her lips has my cock jumping with joy.

She takes me into her hand stroking me with a touch I've never known before her. Running her tongue from base to tip, "I love your dick, Daddy."

She circles her tongue around the head and my God she feels so good. Then she takes my cock into her mouth inch by inch as she moans down my length. I love watching my dick disappear into her mouth.

I grab her hair and move her up and down, slamming myself into her throat. Tears well in her eyes but I know she loves this, so I don't stop.

"Fuck yes, baby. You suck my cock so good, baby girl."

Her mouth is like heaven, and I never want this to end. I can't hold back much longer, "Are you going to drink Daddy's cum?"

She hums her agreement, and it pushes me over the edge.

"Fuck yes, such a good girl. My good girl," I slam into her throat one last time as I shoot my seed into her beautiful mouth.

I pull out of her mouth and pull my pants up as I watch her swallow me down, she leans back on her feet, a pleased smile on her face.

"You are perfect, baby girl. So, fucking perfect. I hate to come and run but I have to get to work."

She stands up and wraps her arms around me. I kiss her head, "I'll see you at the hospital later."

Placing her hand on my chest over my heart, she stares up at my face, her eyes meet mine, and there's so much emotion in her gaze. Unshed tears fill her eyes, "Liam, I love you, so much."

My heart pounds for her, "I love you more."

Her lips tug into a sexy smile, "Go to work, I'm tired of looking at your handsome face. It's stupid that anyone should be this gorgeous."

I chuckle, "Be a good girl. No orgasms without Daddy. You know the rules."

Walking out the door with this gorgeous woman in my house is a challenge, it always is but I do anyway. I have patients that need me. I take one last look at her and then walk through the doorway to my car.

As I drive to work my mind is on seeing my son tonight. I'm not looking forward to it, something has been off with him as of late. While I haven't seen him, we've spoken on the phone a few times. His behavior has seemed bizarre and when he's brought up Mercy, I don't like how he talks about her. He has always spoken highly of her but now he's bitter about her shooting him down. I know he'd never hurt her, but I don't like hearing anyone talk about my girl like that. Of course, I can't say much because he doesn't know about us. Eventually, I'll need to tell him because this isn't just a fling, not anymore anyway. But not tonight because I need to find out what the hell is going on with him and how he plans to deal with all this anger that he's got bottled up. Tonight, is about making sure my son is okay, not causing him to go off the rails even further.

I pull into my parking spot as I try to mentally prepare for the day. I've got many kids going through chemo, so I have a busy day ahead of me as I walk through the door my cell phone chimes.

Mercy: I miss you, Daddy.

Me: I miss you too, baby girl. What are you doing? Are you being a good girl?

Mercy: I'm just thinking.

Me: About?

Mercy: You tying me to your bed, standing over me, stroking your delicious cock while you stare at my naked body.

Me: Baby girl, I can't read these types of messages before going into kids hospital rooms.

Mercy: Are you hard for me, Dr. Lexington?

Me: Always, you dirty girl.

Mercy: Good. I love your hard cock.

Me: I said I'd give you your fantasy tonight and I will. But not before I spank your naughty ass.

Mercy: Promises, promises...

Me: I have to work now, but please remember that I have never broken a promise to you. Your ass will be red tonight, a delicious shade of red.

Mercy: I look forward to it, Dr. Lexington.

Mercy: I mean, no, please God, no.

I chuckle, this woman is everything to me, but she drives me insane in the best possible way.

Twenty-One

LIAM

I SPEND most of the day checking on patients, and luckily, it's boring. That's the way I prefer it, no excitement is a good thing. I have a feeling my evening will be exciting enough.

After stopping by the nurse's station, I head into Ivy's room. She's doing well, I'm thrilled that she hasn't been as sick as I expected this time. Although, that could change in an instant. I've seen it many times before. The small amount of hair she grew back, started to thin again, so I expect it'll fall out completely, which is difficult for any girl.

"Dr. L!" She yells as she moves trying to look behind me.

"She's not with me, Ivy. You're driving the nurse crazy, you know? I'm told you have asked seven times when she's coming in?"

Tears roll down her cheeks as she gazes down at her lap, rubbing the material of her hospital gown, "I'm sorry."

I sit beside her bed, "Talk to me, Ivy. Why are you crying?"

She intakes a shaky breath, "None of you know what this is like. It's lonely here. I don't have anyone anymore. Only Mercy. When she visits me..."

"Tell me, Princess."

"I forget I have cancer. She makes everything better. I forget about my mom. I forget about the fosters. It's the only time I can be happy."

Taking her hand in mine, I give myself a moment to get my emotions under control. But I get it, I understand exactly what she's saying. Mercy does the same thing to me; she makes me forget every bad thing. She's a bright light in my dark world.

"That's a special talent of hers, she makes everything better, doesn't she?"

Swiping at her tears with her other hand, "I wish she was my mom."

This little girl gets to my heart like no other patient has before.

I hear a gasp behind me and turn to see Mercy standing there.

She obviously heard what Ivy said to me. I get out of the chair and motion for her to sit in my place.

"Someone has been dying to see you."

Ivy giggles, "I don't think you're supposed to say dying in a hospital, Dr. L."

As soon as she spotted Mercy, the tears stopped and were replaced with a beaming smile.

"I'll see you beautiful ladies a little later," I say as I give Mercy a wink.

I love the way she melts when I wink at her. It makes me want to do it again and again. Instead, I smile as I walk away, leaving them to have one-on-one time.

Before I leave for the day, I stop at the nurse's station to talk to Gloria about Ivy. "Do we have any volunteers that could spend some time with Ivy?"

Gloria laughs, and I arch an eyebrow at her in irritation. What's funny about this?

"Doctor, we have tried, there's been four volunteers that have come to see her. They've brought books, toys, art supplies, we even had Cheyanne Cash here."

"The country singer?" I ask.

She nods, "Yeah, she was doing a radio event and came in to see the kids. But Ivy had zero interest."

I rub the stubble on my jaw, "Mercy would've killed to be here, I swear that woman's music is on repeat in my house. I wonder why Ivy is so uninterested in people coming to visit with her."

Gloria files away some charts and laughs, "Isn't it obvious doctor?

None of them are Mercy. That's all she wants to be honest. Her life revolves around seeing her. Every day it's what she looks forward to. The only time we see her smile is when Mercy is in the room with her. We've tried, there's nothing we can do. Maria thinks it might be best to pull Mercy off her case to force her to spend time with other people."

Maria is the head of social work, but she doesn't know what she's talking about. My girl will still see Ivy regardless of whether it's in a professional capacity or not. Nothing will keep her from Ivy. Honestly, they could fire her, and she'd still be here. There aren't many things in life that I'm certain of, but this is one of them.

"That's pointless," I state matter-of-factly.

As she walks over to the board, she wipes off the name of a recently released patient, "Clearly. That girl would walk over hot coals to see Ivy."

"Indeed," I say, and then add, "Thank you for trying. I was hoping to ease some of her loneliness but if you've tried then there's nothing else you can do."

I turn to walk away, but she stops me, "Doctor?"

"Yes?"

Her gaze is contemplative, as if she's not sure she should say what she's thinking. "We all know that you're with Mercy. It's not a well-kept secret."

I glare at her, "It's not a secret. You keep secrets when you are ashamed, which I am not." I run a hand through my hair, becoming irritated at this topic.

"Right, well it's none of our business, I like Mercy a lot. Anyway, I wanted to let you know that Cheyanne Cash is performing in New York City. She really wants to go; it's been mentioned several times. Apparently, her best friend hates country music. So, she won't go because she doesn't want to go alone. It happens to fall on her birthday."

I flash her a warm smile, "Thank you. I don't know if I'll be able to get tickets though. Her birthday is in a week."

A patient buzzes in, asking for a drink.

"Thanks Gloria, I'll see you tomorrow."

I call my assistant and have her look into getting two tickets for the show regardless of the cost. But it has to be close to the stage. If I take her, I want it to be the best experience for her. I text Mercy requesting that she meet me at my car for a moment.

I stand at my car waiting patiently when she comes out, my breath catches. Her smile is the first thing I notice. It warms me from the inside out.

"Doctor, is everything okay?" She asks as she gets closer to me, and her scent surrounds me. God, she smells so fucking good, like roses and honey surrounding me.

"It is now, I wanted to see you before I leave."

Placing her hands on both sides of my neck she pulls me down to her face, "Don't be long. I'm not sure what I'll do with myself in your absence."

A groan rumbles through my chest as I pull her into my arms and kiss her. This woman's mouth drives me insane. I could kiss her for days and never get bored.

"You're hard again, sir," she says as she pulls back and gazes at me.

I pull her hair and bite her lip, "I am beginning to think my naughty little slut, likes me constantly hard."

"Mmmm," she moans as she grabs my dick.

She lets go of me and flashes me an innocent look, "Hurry home, I can't wait to watch you cum all over me, Daddy."

Turning around she walks back to the door and leaves me standing with my mouth open and my cock stiff. She turns her head back to me and winks at me before walking back through the door. I watch her disappear and shake my head as I walk around to the driver's side and get in, preparing to see my son.

* * *

I walk into the On-Call Room, and Xander comes over to me as I walk through the door.

"Don't you have anywhere else to drink?" He smirks at me.

"I should find another place, this bar is owned by an asshole."

He laughs and slaps me on the back, "What can I get you?"

"Whatever is on tap is fine. I'll grab a table, I'm meeting Nash here but he's always late."

"I'll send my waitress over shortly."

Walking past the hostess stand I find an empty booth and take a seat.

A redhead walks over and hands me my beer, "Your beer, doctor," she drawls seductively as she sits the glass on the table. "Can I get you anything else?" she asks.

"No, my son can order when he gets here."

She nods and touches my hand, "If there's anything you need, please let me know."

"All of my other needs are provided to me by my girlfriend, thank you," I say as I retract my hand from hers.

"Of course," she says as she walks away.

I wait for about ten minutes before Nash walks through the door looking like absolute hell on legs.

Twenty-Two

LIAM

HIS HAIR IS DISHEVELED, he hasn't shaved in at least a week, and he's shaky as he sits in the booth across from me.

"Nash, what the fuck?"

He averts his gaze; he won't even look at me.

The waitress comes over and he looks her up and down like she's a slab of meat.

"What can I get you?" She smiles at him.

"I'm in the mood for a redheaded slut. Know of any?"

"Jesus, Nash. Just get him a beer," I say with a bite.

He taps his fingers on the table as if he's nervous.

"What's wrong with you?"

"I need money, dad."

I swear, that's all he wants to see me for anymore. "For what?"

He rubs his face with both hands, "Stuff."

I pull out my wallet, it's business as usual with this kid, "How much this time?"

Rubbing his finger on the table he says, "Five thousand."

"FIVE THOUSAND DOLLARS?" I yell far louder than I intend, attracting attention from the other patrons.

I intake a sharp breath trying to calm myself down, "What do you need five thousand dollars for, Nash? What have you gotten yourself into?"

Leaning forward, I put my wallet back in my pocket, I definitely don't have that kind of cash on me.

He bounces his leg as if he's about to jump out of his skin. "I owe some people money."

Drugs, he's on fucking drugs, why didn't I see it the second he walked in the door. The way he fidgets, he looks sick, it should have not taken me this long to figure it out. "What kind of drugs are you on, Nash?"

He looks up at me for the first time, flashing me a glare.

"Your mother would be so disappointed."

He cackles, "I never even met her. I don't give a shit what she would think because she never fucking mattered to me. She's dead, Dad. Get over it. I have. I wish she would've had an abortion."

"She gave her life for yours. And you act like that means nothing."

I grip the edges of the seat trying to contain my rage.

"It doesn't. Are you giving me the money or not?"

"No," I spit through a clenched jaw.

"Maybe I'll just kill myself like you want. Walk out in front of a train, then you won't have to deal with me ever again. Obviously, I mean nothing to you!"

A guilt trip. Lovely. I honestly don't even know how to respond. How the hell did this even happen?

He gets up and storms off, and I notice his balance is off, he nearly falls three times before he's out of my sight. Fuck!

I leave money on the table for both of our drinks even though Nash never even got his. I head out to my car. As I get to my vehicle, I see a long key mark along the driver's side door. He keyed my fucking car! What the absolute hell is wrong with him? Sliding into my vehicle I'm at such a loss.

My hands grab the steering wheel with a death grip as I drive home to see my girl. I'm so furious with my son, the blood is pumping in my ears. Pulling into my driveway I park and go to the front door and it's open. My heart stops. He wouldn't hurt her I'm sure of it. No, I'm not sure of anything with him anymore. If he found her in my house, I'm not sure what he would do—panic claws at my chest as I run in to find her.

"MERCY!"

I'm frantic when I reach the bedroom and she turns to me in purple lingerie.

"I missed you, Daddy." she whispers.

Casting her eyes up to my face she sees my face and rushes over to me wrapping her arms around me.

"Mercy. Why is the front door open?" I ask calmer than I feel at this moment.

"I left it open for you."

Cupping her face, "Don't do that again. The door stays locked even if you think it's me. You do not open the door for anyone."

"Liam, what's going on?"

I run my hand through my hair as I sit on the bed.

She comes over and sits beside me, running her hand down my back. In an instant my rage diminishes, her calming affect washes over me.

"I need you to stay away from Nash baby girl. Promise me."

Crossing her arms over her chest she glares at me, "He's my best friend, Liam."

Flashing her a glare, "This is not open for discussion. You will stay away from him, Mercy. He's on drugs. He keyed my fucking car, he's angry. I do not trust him with you."

She stands and gasps as she jerks her head back, staring at me with wide eyes, "Nash does not do drugs, Liam."

I take a deep breath and pull her closer. "Maybe not before Mercy, but he is now. He asked me for five-thousand dollars to pay a drug debt. I've never seen him like this. He's not the same Nash as he was before. The drugs have taken over."

"Liam, we have to help him," she says as tears stream down her cheeks.

"No. You are going to stay away from him. I will help him."

She nods, and I breathe a sigh of relief.

"Come here, baby girl. I need you."

Straddling me she pushes me, so I land with my back on the mattress, hovering over me her lips ghost mine.

"Tell me what you need, baby. I'll give you anything you desire," she whispers.

What do I need? I don't have a clue, other than her in my arms, that's what I need more than anything, always. But she said anything I wanted.

"Anything?"

She sits up on top of me, "Liam Lexington, don't you know by now? I will give you anything you want. Whatever you wish, it will be granted."

I'm terrified to utter the words that run around in my mind.

"Jesus, Liam you're scaring me. Would you just say it?"

I grab her hips, "I want you to marry me."

Her eyes go wide, her mouth forms an 'O' but her words are silent. This is definitely not the 'yes', I hoped for. Minutes go by, and she doesn't move, her expression now stoic. I don't know what to do with this.

Fuck. It's too soon—you idiot.

"Baby girl, I'm sorry. I shouldn't have said that. Can we just forget I said that?"

She gets off me and stands beside the bed, arms across her chest, glowering at me. "So, you didn't mean it? Why would you say something like that if you didn't mean it? That's mean, Liam."

"I meant it," I say quietly.

She puts her hands on her hips, she's so fucking adorable when she's angry, "Then why take it back?"

"Were you going to say yes?"

Shaking her head she says, "No."

"There you go."

Rolling her eyes at me, she explains, "Maybe, it's all the damn princess movies I've been exposed to recently. But I want more Liam, and I think I deserve more than a bedroom proposal with your hard cock pressing into me."

I get off the bed and pull her against my chest, "I'll do better, baby girl. You deserve everything. Come take a shower with me."

"I thought you'd never ask," she says with a grin.

"Baby girl, I wasn't asking. Get naked."

Walking away I get undressed and turn the shower on.

She comes into the bathroom and runs her nails down my back.

"Get in and stand with your back against the wall."

I climb in the shower standing under the spray facing her, "On your knees, beautiful."

"That day you caught me in the shower do you know what I was thinking about?"

She bites her lip and shakes her head no.

"This right here. The second I saw you in my bathroom, I've never had another fantasy about anyone other than you. Even when I knew I couldn't have you, you were still there every single time I stroked my cock, baby. It's always you."

I take my cock into my hand, and she moans, I stroke myself slowly only inches from her face. When she reaches between her legs and rubs her clit, I fight myself from doing what I want which is to take her and slam into her beautiful cunt. But this is what she wants.

"I'm giving you what you wanted, baby girl. After I come all over you, I'll fuck you, hard."

She casts her eyes up at me as she licks her lips, "Yes. God yes."

Her gaze travels back to my cock as I stroke faster, my breathing getting heavier.

"Fuck, baby girl. I'm going to come all over you."

Moaning loudly, she begs, "Yes, Daddy. Come for me, all over me."

This stunning woman in front of me brings me to my knees all the time. But it's the way she sounds begging for me to desecrate her body with my cum that brings me to the edge. Then she runs her hands up both of my thighs and I can't hold on. One single touch makes me lose control.

"Tilt your head back."

She does and my cum squirts all over her beautiful tits, running down to her belly. Fuck it's the most beautiful sight in the world. I watch her as she hangs her tongue out of her mouth, she reaches down and scoops up the cum from her tits and spreads it on her tongue. Covering her tongue with my seed she swallows it down while staring into my eyes. Fuck, she's the dirtiest woman I've ever been with. It's like she has a direct line to my fucking cock. And with that I'm ready to go again. So much for recovery time.

"Stand."

"You're such a dirty slut, aren't you?"

"Yes," she squeaks.

I push her against the wall holding her by her throat, "Are you this dirty with all the boys? Sometimes, it seems like you're not so innocent, maybe you've done this before."

"No, Daddy. Only for you."

"Good girl, you're my slut. Nobody else's."

"Only yours," she whispers.

I grab onto her waist and lift her onto my cock, and she wraps her legs around my waist.

We both moan together as I thrust into her fully. "Hold on baby."

She grabs onto my shoulders as I fuck her hard, fast.

Every single push into this woman makes me lose myself a little bit more. I dig my fingers into her hips as I slide her up and down my length. With no warning she screams for me, digging her nails into my flesh, her body shaking uncontrollably.

"Fuck, Mercy, baby girl, FUCK!" I shoot deep inside her pussy.

I pull her off me, set her down, and clean the cum from our bodies.

Twenty-Three

MERCY

WE DRY off and get changed into dry clothes. As I pull a t-shirt and shorts on Liam looks at me, "Baby girl, don't make any plans this weekend.

"Why?" I ask.

"Because I said so?"

I glare at him, "Just because I call you Daddy does not mean you get to use that line."

He chuckles, and I roll my eyes. His comment annoyed me slightly, but that laugh is worth all the annoyance in the world.

Smacking my ass, he smiles, "Because you have plans with me."

"Jessica wanted to go out for my birthday on Saturday."

"Too bad. You can go out with her on Friday. We leave first thing on Saturday morning."

I glance at him while I brush my wet hair, "Where are we going?"

He grips my chin lightly with his thumb and forefinger, tilting my head up, "That's for me to know and for you to find out," he kisses my lips quickly and leaves the bedroom.

What is he up to? I have no idea, but I'm enjoying his light-hearted mood after everything with Nash today.

What the hell is going on with Nash? Why would he suddenly start using drugs? It makes no sense to me whatsoever. How does someone with a good upbringing decide to start using drugs all of a sudden?

I know that Liam asked me to stay away from him, but I can't, so I text him.

Me: Can we have coffee in the morning?

Nash: Yes. I can't wait to see you.

Me: Good. How about the Moonshine Coffee on Crescent Peak Blvd?

Nash: I'll be there. What time?

Me: Eight. I have to go to work afterward.

Nash: See you then, Merce. God, I've missed you.

I don't reply to the last message for fear of sending him mixed signals.

I wander into the kitchen to find Liam making dinner. "You're making dinner?"

He chuckles, "Don't get too excited. My chef made it earlier today, I'm simply reheating it."

"That's fine but it's almost nine. Isn't it kind of late for dinner?"

Turning to me, he arches his eyebrow, "Have you eaten?"

I shake my head no.

"Well, then you need to eat, so no it's not late."

He brings a salad to the table and sets it down, "Is there anything I can help you with?"

"Pick a bottle of wine," something to go with lasagna.

I grab a bottle of Leroy Domaine d'Auvenay Mazis-Chambertin Grand Cru and set it on the table. Liam smirks at me, and I give him a questioning look.

"Do you not like this one?" I ask as he opens the bottle.

"I like it just fine baby, otherwise I wouldn't have bought it."

I sigh, "Then why the look?"

He laughs, "I was only realizing that my girl has expensive taste, baby. That's a ten-thousand-dollar bottle of wine."

I gasp, "Why the hell did you spend that much on wine?"

He shrugs his shoulders, "It's only money, baby."

How much fucking money does this man have? I sit at the table and pour myself a glass of expensive wine.

"Do you have a job other than a doctor? I mean, I know doctors can make good money but to spend so much on a bottle of wine and say it's only money."

"Are you asking me how much money is in my bank account?"

I shake my head, "No, of course not, I would never," I stammer.

He laughs, "I have made several well thought out investments, all legal. I bought my first house when I was twenty-two. I have been smart with my money, and it's paid off tremendously. I'm a wealthy man, Mercy. But also, I don't throw it around needlessly. However, I like to enjoy the finer things in life, like wine."

I nod, "Okay."

Picking up my glass, I sip the wine, "Wow, this is really good."

We eat our food mostly in silence, probably because of me. I'm preoccupied with tomorrow's coffee I have with Nash, and I'm feeling a little guilty about not telling Liam. But I know if I tell him, he will try to stop me. I need to know that I've done everything possible to help Nash. I understand Liam's concern. But how could I possibly not try to help him and keep a clear conscience? I can't. This is non-negotiable, I have to do this.

"Is everything okay, baby girl?"

I nod, "Yeah, everything is fine," I flash him a smile that I expect him to realize is fake. But he doesn't say anything, so I'm relieved.

"Mercy, I need a promise from you that Nash won't be there on Friday."

"Friday?" I say, trying to buy time to think.

"You said, Jessica wanted to take you for drinks. Does this involve Nash?"

I shake my head, "Nash won't be there, Liam. I'll make sure Jessica knows not to invite him; I promise you."

"Thank you. I'm trusting you, baby girl."

I swallow the lump in my throat. Fuck, I feel like shit right now. If he ever finds out about tomorrow, he's going to hate me. But I have to do what I think is right. I hate lying to Liam, but I have to try to help my friend.

I get up and start clearing the dishes from the table. Liam comes up behind me and wraps his hands around my waist. "I'm not trying to control you, Mercy. I only want to keep you safe and right now he's not safe. It's not that I don't want you to be friends with him, but it can't happen until he gets help. Please understand, baby girl."

"I do," I say, but this is breaking my heart. Nash has been my friend since kindergarten. Honestly, it kind of pisses me off that Liam thinks I'll just stand back as my best friends life fucking detonates.

"There's a few work-related things I need to do in my office. I'll be in bed with you shortly."

"Okay," I say, as I fight the tears threatening to fall.

He squeezes me tighter, "I'm sorry. I love you; I can't risk anything happening to you."

Kissing my neck softly, he sighs and walks away.

After I finish cleaning the kitchen, I head to the bedroom, and for the first time ever, I'm glad Liam isn't here with me. I can't stand the guilt; I try to brush it aside as I get undressed and climb into bed.

I fall asleep quickly and I don't know when he came to bed but he's here now. I pretend to be still sleeping so I don't have to talk to him. I'm terrified he'll do what he always does and read me like a book and know something is going on. He kisses my cheek and whispers, "I love you so much, baby girl. I'll see you at work."

He leaves and I let out a breath once I hear the front door close. I climb out of bed and get ready to meet Nash before going to work.

* * *

I take my car because, of course, Nash probably knows all of Liam's cars and I don't want him to ask questions I'm not prepared to answer.

When I pull up, he's sitting at a patio table outside, which is strange. In all the years I've known him, he is never the first one there, he's always late. He claims it's called being fashionably late, but he's just late. There's nothing fashionable about it, it's flat out annoying.

I park my car and get out, and as I get close to him, I gasp, "Nash, what's wrong? You look terrible."

He fidgets with a sugar packet in his hand as he bounces his leg repeatedly. I sit down and he stares at me, "Thanks, Merce. You look beautiful as always."

"I got you a coffee," he pushes it toward me.

"Thank you," I smile politely.

"I have missed you," he says.

I push my hair behind my ear unsure of what to say, "Are you okay?" I ask.

"I am now. Come spend the night with me tonight, Merce."

My head jerks up, I stare at him wide eyed, "What?"

I take a sip of my coffee as I look away from him. It's hard to see him so unraveled.

"That's why you sent me a text right? You changed your mind?"

I shake my head, "No, Nash I have not changed my mind. I'm seeing someone anyway. But I definitely would never want you like this."

"Like what?"

"You're obviously on drugs, Nash."

He laughs, "It doesn't mean I can't fuck the hell out of you."

Gross.

"Don't talk like that, I'll leave," I sip my coffee while he continues to fidget with the same damn sugar packet.

"So, why did you want to see me then?" He sits staring at my breasts, and it makes me uncomfortable.

"I wanted to see you. You're still my best friend, aren't you? Now, I see that you're on drugs and I want to help you. I can help you get into a rehab."

His eyes flash. It's like watching Bruce Banner turn into the Incredible Hulk. It happens in an instant.

Rising from my seat I say, "I'm going to go," I run, literally run, to my car, but it's too late. He comes up behind me and grabs me by the back of my hair spinning me around like a rag doll. Knocking me against the car he lets go of my hair and puts his hand on my throat, squeezing hard, and slams my head against the car window.

"You fucking cock tease."

My eyes are wide, and panic rises through my body. I have no idea how to get away from him. Liam was right, I should have listened to him. Nash is going to kill me right in front of a coffee shop. He doesn't care, the boy I knew, is gone.

"You walked around at my dad's house in those skimpy little bikini's and then act surprised when I want to fuck you? Hell, my dad probably wanted to fuck you. But you wouldn't do that would you? You're just a tease that toys with men, just stringing them along."

He grinds his hard cock into my pelvis. Tears flow down my cheeks, my best friend, and I've never been more terrified in my life.

"Oh, don't be a cry baby you fucking bitch. You said you wanted to help me well this is what I need help with. You've given me blue balls, now fix it."

He lets go of my throat as he says, "Come on."

"Nash, you need help. I'm leaving. Don't contact me until you go to rehab or whatever."

Anger flows through him like a live wire, "So that's fucking it? Eighteen years and you're just done with me?"

"This isn't you. I can't be friends with whoever the hell this is."

He makes a closed fist, I know I should run, but I'm frozen in place as he punches me in the face. "Fucking cunt."

Grabbing my throat again he squeezes with more force than the first time, I can't fucking breathe. I get lightheaded as I spot flashing lights. But will they get here in time or is it too late? Everything goes black.

Twenty-Four

LIAM

IT'S NOON, and still no trace of Mercy. She doesn't have to be in at a certain time as long as she sees her patients. It's rare for her, however, not to be here by ten. Xander walks up to me as I stand in the hallway glancing at my unanswered text to Mercy.

"Hey man, I need to talk to you. On-call room, it's private."

I follow him, he looks worried, but if it's private it can't be about a patient, so he has me nervous. I hope Isabella is okay.

We both step into the room, and he states, "Close the door, Liam."

"Look, I can't answer the questions that you'll have because it will violate HIPPA."

What the hell is he talking about? I scowl at him getting impatient with his theatrics.

"As your best friend, I'm telling you to go home and see Mercy."

"What the hell is going on Xander?"

I run my hand through my hair. What the fuck has happened?

"I can't tell you more. She's okay, I'll tell you that, but she's been through a lot today, so when you get home, you need to keep your cool. Mercy doesn't need you blowing up at her. Honestly, I'm not sure she could take it. Did you know she's afraid of you?"

"Why would she be afraid of me?" What the fuck is happening right now? The panic travels through my body threatening to bring me to my knees. Something is wrong with Mercy. I have to get to her.

He puts his hands in his pockets and shakes his head, "I don't know man but when I mentioned calling you, she freaked out. She started shaking, sobbing, and begged me not to."

"Fuck, I have to go."

If he's worried about violating HIPPA, she must have been at the General Hospital because Xander has privileges there.

On my way out, I tell Gloria to not call me but to call the on-call doctor instead. I get out to my car and race home. I pull out into traffic with my mind reeling. He said she's okay, still I'm wrecked with concern.

How could she be afraid of me? I don't understand that. I love her and I'd never hurt her. I have spanked her but there is no doubt that it was consensual. Finally, I pull into my driveway.

Walking in, I find Mercy applying makeup to her neck in the bathroom.

"Wash it off."

She jumps as she gasps, "Liam."

I know she wasn't expecting me home for several hours. Backing away slowly, until there's nowhere to go, she puts her head down, trying to hide her neck.

"Don't hide from me, I've already seen it. The make-up isn't working."

Gently I touch the side of her face lifting her head up to look at me.

"Who did this to you, baby girl? Tell me his name and then I'm going to fucking kill him with my bare hands."

Tears roll down her cheeks, "I'm sorry, Liam. I'm so sorry. You were right."

"Right about what? Who fucking did this to you?"

She whispers, "Nash."

This is what Xander was talking about. This is where I don't explode, but I fucking told her to stay away from him. I fucking told her, and she promised.

I keep my voice as controlled as possible, "Why? You promised, Mercy. You lied to me."

"I promised you about Friday."

Raising my voice, I say, "You lied by omission. I don't play games. When you tell me you'll do something or not do something, I trust you. You fucking lied to me. That's one of the two things I can't tolerate."

I walk away from her because I need space. But then I hear her body crash to the floor, howling in pain like a wounded animal, "LIAM!" it crushes something so deep within me that I can't walk away, not even for a minute.

Bending down, I lift her into my arms and carry her to the bed. I take my shirt off and crawl in beside her and pull her tight against me while I stroke her hair.

"Shh baby girl, it's okay. I've got you. You're safe now."

For the longest time she sobs into my chest as she struggles to catch her breath.

"Baby girl, please calm down, you're scaring me. Deep breaths."

"I'm sorry, please don't leave me, Liam."

Honestly, I'm not really sure how to even respond to that. Is that why she's fucking crying? "Look at me."

With hesitation she tilts her head and looks into my eyes.

"Baby girl, I will never leave you. I'm not happy about what you did, mostly because you got hurt. I need to keep you safe. You put yourself in danger by seeing him. You went to see him, right? He didn't come here?"

She shakes her head, "I went to have coffee with him. I thought I could help him."

Kissing her on the forehead, I take a deep breath before asking, "What did he do to you?"

Her voice is shaky, "He wanted me to have sex with him. He said I'm a tease because I walked around your house in my bikini. I've never seen him like that with so much anger. He grabbed my throat, and bashed my head into the window, punched me, and then choked me again. I don't remember anything else because I blacked out."

"Please tell me he didn't-"

"No. He pushed up against me but that's it, Liam."

I breathe a sigh of relief, "Good."

"Baby girl, you are not to see him again."

Reaching up she touches the side of my face, "Never, Liam. I will never trust him again."

"I have one other question."

She nods.

"Why does Xander have the impression that you're afraid of me?"

"I don't know," she says simply.

Rubbing her arm slowly I ask, "Are you afraid of me?"

"No."

She leans forward and kisses my neck. I know her all too well; she's trying to avoid this difficult conversation and her mouth feels so fucking good.

"Mercy, stop."

A wounded look in her eyes reflects back at me.

"I need to know."

"Damn it, Liam, I'm not afraid of you. I was afraid at the hospital of everything. My best friend attacked me and maybe tried to kill me. Then, I was so terrified that you'd be so angry with me that I would lose you. That's what scares me more than your son beating the shit out of me."

"Silly girl, you couldn't lose me if you tried," I press my lips to hers as she wraps her hands around my neck.

She moans while her hands slide from my neck into my hair. Tilting her head back, she whispers my name, "Daddy."

As much as I always want to be inside her, it's not happening tonight. When she exposes her neck to me, it physically makes me sick, but I swallow it down for her. Gently, I press soft kisses on the fingerprint indentations my son left on her beautiful neck.

He will be dealt with, Nash being my son will not prevent that from happening. My fucking son could've killed my girl. And that will not be tolerated. This won't happen again, because if it does, I am afraid of what I might do.

"Come baby, let's watch a movie."

She groans, "I need you."

"Not tonight, baby girl. Your body needs rest."

Rolling her eyes at me she sighs, "My body needs you."

I tap her ass lightly, "Doctors orders, beautiful."

Standing beside the bed, I hold back a laugh while she glares at me. I pick her up in my arms to carry her to the living room, "You know, baby, you're fucking adorable with this cute little scowl on your face."

She slaps my chest lightly, "You're being mean."

"I'm doing what's best for you. A good man takes care of his baby girl, placing her needs above his own."

I set her down on the couch and hand her the remote, "Find something on Netflix. Do you want anything to drink?"

She licks her lips as she stares at my crotch, and I can't help but laugh again.

"Such a dirty girl. A drink from the kitchen, is there anything I can get you?"

"No," she pouts.

I sit in the corner of the sectional, one leg stretched out on the couch, my other on the floor. I leave space between us since she's mad. But she quickly scoots over to me and crawls between my legs, laying on her side with her head on my chest while the movie starts.

Running my hands through her hair, I find myself watching her, instead of the movie. I love having my hands in her hair or on her body, anywhere really.

It takes about thirty minutes until she's asleep, she moved to her stomach and has her arms around my waist. I knew she had to be exhausted after what she went through today.

Carefully, I pull her into my arms and lift her up, carrying her to the bedroom. I lay her down and get undressed. I remove her skirt, and then unbutton her blouse, trying to get her comfortable without waking her. When I remove her bra, I see red all over again. She has three bruises on her breast. She never mentioned anything about him touching her here.

I climb into bed beside her and kiss the bruises and whisper, "I'm sorry, baby girl." This somehow feels like it's my fault. Where did I go so wrong with my son that he could do this to any woman, even more so, a woman he claims to love? I gave too much, I let him get away with shit I shouldn't have. When he asked for money in his adult years, I gave it to him because I had it. I never dreamed that this is how he would spend my money. And now, Mercy has paid the price for it. I'm certain if it weren't for the drugs, he never would've done this. My son is a stranger to me, this is not the child I raised.

Twenty-Five

MERCY

IT'S BEEN a few days since the incident with Nash and I can finally cover my bruises with make-up so today I'm at work. I'm excited to see Ivy, I know she's been upset that I couldn't come see her. But I couldn't let her see me with bruises on my face and an actual handprint on my neck.

When I walk through her door, I feel like a million bucks. She sits up, her eyes flash excitement, "MERCY!"

"Hi, sweet girl!" I go and sit beside her bed, "I missed you."

"I missed you too," she beams at me.

"What have you been doing to keep yourself out of trouble, missy?"

She covers her mouth with her hand and giggles, "Abby took me to the playroom so I could paint you a picture. It's on my table," I'm not allowed out of bed. I've been weak, so Dr. L says I have to stay in bed for now."

Rising out of my chair, I walk over to the table, and it's a canvas.

"This one?" I ask as I pick it up.

"Yes," she smiles.

I stare at it and tears run down my face, it's so beautiful. It's a long strand of gorgeous ivy with three lavender purple roses threaded through it.

"Honey, this is the most stunning picture. I'm going to hang this at home, so I see it every single day. This means so much to me, thank you."

"There's a rose for me, for you, and Dr. L."

I set the picture down on the table and ask her, "Would it be okay if I hug you? It's okay if you say no."

"Yes."

Walking over to her, I hug her, my heart is so full. It's at this moment, I decide even though I shouldn't be making decisions like this without Liam. I want to adopt her. I sit down and we talk about the movies she's been watching and a game she found. Apparently, a game where you can dress up princesses and do their make-up is about the best thing in the world.

Suddenly I know he's here, I don't know how I know but I know. I feel him before I see him. I turn as Liam walks in with two cupcakes, one with a candle in it.

He lights the candle, "Help me sing to Mercy, it's her birthday tomorrow."

Ivy claps her hands excitedly, "HAPPY BIRTHDAY MERCY!"

Liam starts singing and Ivy joins in. If you want to see the happiest moment of my life up to now, this might just be it. Liam hands me my cupcake, "Make a wish."

I wish to adopt this little girl which all of a sudden is what I want more than anything. I blow out my candle and Liam asks, "What did you wish for?"

Ivy screams, "NO! DON'T TELL HIM! IF YOU TELL YOUR WISH, IT DOESN'T COME TRUE!"

I laugh, "I won't tell him. Boys think they need to know everything," I wink at her.

Liam hands Ivy her cupcake, "Just a little bit, okay? I don't want you to get sick."

We spend the afternoon watching movies and talking about girl stuff after Liam heads back to work. She was a little disappointed that I'd be out of town this weekend for my birthday, but she'll be okay.

I'm getting ready to go with my painting in my hand, when she says words that stop me in my tracks.

"Mercy, I wish you were my mom."

Glancing at her, I attempt to keep my emotions stuffed down, "I know it's hard with the way things are. But you're going to find a family that sees what I see. They will get to know you and want to adopt you."

I want to adopt her but I'm not telling her that because I don't know what the outcome will be. And I really owe it to Liam to have this conversation with him.

"What's adopt?" she asks.

"When a family decides they want you to be part of their family forever, that's adoption."

She wipes tears that have fallen on her cheeks, "Oh."

I know this is a lot for a little girl. I can't imagine being in her shoes. She's got to be terrified. Every child deserves to know where they will live. This cloud of uncertainty hanging around her has got to be devastating. Her mom is not a good mother but she's all she has ever known. If I get my way, we will adopt her. When we do, I'm going to love this little girl with everything I've got.

Liam comes in, "Are you ready to go?"

I nod, "Yeah."

I give Ivy a quick hug and whisper, "It's going to be okay, sweet girl. I promise."

We walk out to his car, and I ask, "What's going on?"

"What do you mean exactly?"

I slide into his vehicle, "Why am I in your car?"

He closes my door and gets in on the driver's side, "You didn't think you'd be going alone tonight after-?"

"Liam, it's a girls night. He won't be there."

Shaking his head he says, "I am going. That's not open for discussion but I won't sit with you. I'll just be there to make sure you're okay."

"And if he comes in then what? You're going to beat your son up?"

I glance over at him as he pulls out of his parking spot, he grips the steering wheel tightly, his knuckles turning white, "If I have to, I will. I won't let him hurt you. No one will hurt you."

"I hate this."

"I'm going to tell him about us next week. He needs to find out from me rather than someone else. It's only a matter of time before someone says something. We haven't kept it a secret. And the sooner I tell him the sooner he'll adapt," he says as he turns down the street to the bar.

I exhale a deep sigh as he pulls into a parking spot at the back of the bar, "He's not going to take it well."

"I know."

"Let's go celebrate you, baby girl."

I nod, but I'm hardly in the mood to celebrate with the thoughts running around in my brain. Ivy. Nash. Liam. It's all a little bit much so I do the only thing I can do in this situation. I plan to get drunk; tequila will be my poison tonight.

We walk in and Jessica already has a table. She brought some other friends with her and I hate it when she does that. Jess thinks that it's about the number of people at a so-called party, but I think it's quality over quantity. So, now I have people here that I really don't even know. I've met Marissa, Michelle, Denise, Iris, and Giada before, but I don't really know them. In fact, I could almost guarantee that they don't even know what I do for a living, nor do they care. They know nothing about me other than the fact that I'm friends with Jessica. But here we are celebrating my birthday with strangers.

"The birthday girl sits beside me," a drunk Jessica squeals. I slide in beside her and she giggles.

"I've got something for you to wear tonight."

I turn to her confused as she reaches into her purse and pulls out a penis tiara and places it on my head. I'm likely ten shades of red right now, "It's not my bachelorette party."

She laughs, "Your birthday is a good enough excuse for a bunch of dicks on your head."

I glance over at Liam who is sitting at the bar watching us like he's, my bodyguard. He shrugs his shoulders and shakes his head.

Pointing to the table I ask, "What's with the insane number of shots sitting here?"

"Twenty-four shots of tequila in honor of you."

I gasp loudly, "I'm not drinking twenty-four shots."

Jessica laughs, "They are for the entire table. You take what you want but I think you need to start now. Bitch, you need to loosen up."

Six shots later, and we're dancing to the music. There's no dance floor so we make our own. I turn around as we're dancing, sweat dripping down my neck, and I catch Liam's gaze. He stares at me with a dark look that is deadlocked on me. Never taking my eyes off him, I tell Jessica that I'll be back. I walk over to him, ignoring the giggles behind me.

"Mercy, what are you doing?"

I arch an eyebrow at him, "It's my birthday. Should I not get whatever I want?"

He runs his tongue along his bottom lip, "You should always get what you want."

"Dance with me, Daddy," I whisper in his ear.

Shaking his head, he says, "I don't dance. Ever."

Hanging my head down in disappointment, I say, "Oh."

"You should go spend time with your friends."

I nod and walk away feeling deflated.

Taking my seat at the table, I sit by myself, feeling alone in this crowded room. Jessica and the other girls are still dancing. I hope whatever he has planned this weekend is better than this, because so far, this birthday fucking blows.

Twenty-Six

LIAM

I'VE NEVER BEEN the guy to dance anywhere, not in a bar trying to score, not even in the privacy of my home. It makes me uncomfortable. But as I sit here watching her seated at a booth by herself, at her fucking birthday party, while all of her friends ignore her, it motivates me. I can't leave her looking miserable.

Walking up to her, I extend my hand, "Would you care to dance?"

Her gaze stops on my hand before moving up to my face, "You don't have to, it's okay."

"Baby girl, I'm out of my comfort zone here, please don't make me ask again. I don't like repeating myself." Leaning in closer, "Be a good girl for Daddy."

She rises out of her seat, taking my hand, and we walk to the makeshift dance floor for the night. I pull her into my arms and place my hands just above her ass.

I whisper in her ear, "You're so fucking beautiful."

Resting her face against my chest, I spin her around, and she wraps her arms around my waist. I'm surprised because I don't hate this. Although, any activity which leads to me touching her, would probably be something I'd like. She's the cure for everything that ails me. One touch, and the entire world disappears.

I stop moving and cradle her face in my hands, tilting her head back slightly, and touch my lips to hers. She snakes her tongue into my mouth, making me hard as a rock.

Our kiss is slow and full of love until she pulls back and bites my lip. I kiss her again in a frenzy, craving more delicious friction. I grind my cock into her, completely forgetting where we are. I whisper in her ear, "I can't wait to fuck that gorgeous cunt of yours. Are you going to let Daddy make you scream, baby girl?"

She swallows hard and nods, "Yes."

Moving back to her ear I whisper, "Such a fucking good girl." She takes my hand and pulls me from the dance floor back to the table.

Grabbing her purse she says, "Let's go. I'm ready."

I wait for her as she says goodbye to her friends. I notice that Jessica is the only one she hugs. She doesn't seem very comfortable around the other girls.

When she comes back, I put my hand on the small of her back, and we walk out to my car.

She's quiet on the drive to my house. After I park, and open her door, I ask, "Is everything okay?"

Her lips turn up into a soft smile, "Yes."

"Let's get you to bed, we have to leave early."

As much as I wanted to fuck her, she does not seem like she's in the mood for it now. There's sadness around my girl, so I'll just hold her tonight. If she wants more, she'll let me know.

We get ready for bed, and she climbs in beside me.

Kissing my chest she says, "No matter what Liam, know that I love you."

Glancing down at her, I ask, "What is that supposed to mean?"

She kisses me again softly, "It means I love you."

I run a hand through my hair, "I love you too."

There's something hidden in her words as if we have some kind of fucking expiration date. And that I cannot even begin to deal with. My heart pounds painfully as I try to decode her words, but I come up empty.

* * *

I had trouble sleeping all night long, replaying her words repeatedly in my mind. Climbing out of bed, I gaze at her, and sigh. Maybe I'm reading too much into what she said last night. After I get ready for this weekend, I walk up to sleeping beauty and kiss her neck.

"It's time to wake up, baby girl," I say softly.

She stretches, it's the sexiest thing, as she arches her back, her breasts peeking out of the sheets.

I'm greeted with a sweet smile, "Go take a shower, I'll make coffee."

Walking to the kitchen, I can't stifle the grin on my face. I'm excited to give her an amazing weekend. I scoop the coffee into the filter and take our mugs out while it brews.

I pour our coffee and place the mugs on the counter, after putting just the right amount of hazelnut cream in hers, just as she likes it.

She comes up behind me and wraps her arms around my waist. I turn to her and smile. You look beautiful."

There's a gleam in her eyes that settles my nerves about last night's conversation. My girl always looks beautiful, but today even more so. She's wearing a short black skirt with a light blue sweater with a V cut, showing off her perfect cleavage. There's no make-up on her face, which is exactly how I prefer it. I'll never tell her, but I hate it when she covers up her flawless skin with that fake crap.

I hand her mug to her, "Thank you, baby."

Arching an eyebrow at her I say, "Baby?"

"Sorry," she says with a sad expression.

"Don't be. I think I like it," I sip the last of my coffee, we rinse out our mugs, and put them in the sink. Turning to her, I pull her into my arms, "Happy birthday, baby girl."

She smiles, "Thank you, Daddy."

Kissing her quickly on the lips I say, "Let's go."

I walk into the bedroom, grab our overnight bag, and go to the car. I put the bag in the back of my vehicle before getting in.

As I pull out of the garage, she asks, "You're really not going to tell me where we are going?"

"Well, that wouldn't make for a very good surprise, now would it?"

I slide my sunglasses on as I grin at her.

I'm listening to 80's music when my girl gets brave. She turns my radio station to country.

"Excuse me?"

She laughs, "I don't want to listen to that old shit."

"Are you calling me old, baby girl?"

Shrugging, she says, "Well, I called your music old. But if the shoe fits..."

"I may be old, but my hand is still very capable of spanking your sassy ass."

Her lips form an 'O', "Should I pretend I don't like it?" She smiles as I arch an eyebrow at her and turn it back to my station.

We're about an hour into our drive, and she yells, "Oh my God! Are we going to New York?"

I smile at her, "Maybe."

"Cheyanne Cash is performing there tonight! Oh my God, Liam are we...?"

I feign a sad expression, "I didn't know that. Why didn't you tell me? I would have taken you."

"Oh," she says trying to mask her disappointment, "It's not a big deal. I probably wouldn't like a concert anyway. Besides, if we are together, I'm sure this weekend will be amazing."

Extending my arm, I squeeze her leg, "You're amazing. Next time, tell me what you want before it's too late, okay?"

She bites her lip, appearing lost in thought.

"What is it?" I ask.

"Nothing. You wouldn't want to. It's fine."

I run a hand through my hair, it annoys me when she won't just speak her damn mind, but I don't want to snap at her this weekend.

"Mercy, tell me. If it's something I don't want to do, I'll tell you. I need you to communicate with me. Come on, you're a social worker, you know how important it is."

She stares out the passenger window as she speaking low, "It's just that my parents live in New York, and I haven't seen them in a while. They couldn't make it to my graduation. But it's too much to ask."

"Baby girl, if you want to see your parents, then you will see your parents."

Shaking her head, she says quietly, "I want *us* to see my parents. I want you to meet them, Liam."

I swallow hard, obviously at some point, she'd want me to meet her parents. But I hadn't thought about it until now. I can't imagine her parents will be pleased to meet me.

"Does your father own any guns?"

"He's a detective with the NYPD, of course he does."

I shake my head, "Fantastic."

She takes my hand, "It'll be okay, baby."

Sighing, I ask, "Can it at least wait until Monday, so the rest of our plans aren't ruined?"

Giggling, she nods, "Yes, sir."

As we arrive in New York City, the traffic slows to a crawl. I hate this fucking place so much. I will never understand the fascination.

"Were you born here?"

She smiles, "No. I was born in Manhattan, but we moved to the Poconos before I started school. After I left for college, my parents moved to the city full time."

Finally, we get to our hotel, and her excitement is palpable. "Oh my God, Liam this is amazing!" She shouts, "Oh doctor, you do know how to show a girl a good time."

I get out and scowl as the valet gawks at my girl, looking her up and down, but I don't say anything. There's no way I'm ruining her mood.

As we walk into the hotel she stops, "Our bag!"

I laugh, "They will bring it up."

Holding her close to me, we walk inside and to the front desk.

Twenty-Seven

MERCY

I STAND with him at the guest check-in counter as he argues with the front desk attendant.

"I need our stay extended; we'll be checking out on Tuesday instead of Monday."

"Dr. Lexington, I'm sorry but it's booked."

Although I know it'll probably upset Liam, I speak up, "You don't have any room available for Monday?"

She clears her throat, "Your father booked a penthouse. I do have regular rooms but not a penthouse for Monday."

Liam grips the counter, "I suggest you don't assume you know the relationship of your guests. I want the best room that you have available."

"Of course, Dr. Lexington."

She hands Liam the keycards and points us toward the elevator. We step inside, and I run my hand down his chest.

"Don't be grumpy, baby, it's fine."

He glares at me, "I'm not grumpy."

"Then why are you rubbing your face? Something is wrong."

A laugh rumbles through his chest, "I just want to make you happy, baby girl. I want everything to be perfect for you."

I take his hand as the door opens, "I don't need a penthouse to make me happy, Liam. You make me happy we could stay in a tent, and I'd be thrilled."

"Do not ever expect me to go camping." He says with a scowl.

I cover my face trying to hide my laughter. Liam Lexington camping would be entertaining.

He opens the room, we walk in, and I cover my mouth in shock. "This is amazing, Liam."

I stand in one place, glancing around the room. Right in front of me is the living room area, with a massive white sectional sofa, a glass table in front of it, and the biggest TV on the wall I think I've ever seen, outside of a movie theater. But what takes my breath away is the enormous ceiling to floor window spanning the entire room facing the New York City Skyline. I run to the window, and my God, I spot the Empire State Building.

I gasp, "I've always wanted to go there."

"You lived in New York and never went to the Empire State Building?"

I laugh, "No. I wasn't allowed. We used to come back to Manhattan for the summers and I snuck to the city when I was fifteen to see a play, I wanted to see badly. When my dad found out, it was explosive."

"What play?"

"Phantom," I smile at the memory. It was worth what I went through with my dad.

Liam comes from behind, presses against me, pushing my hair off my shoulder, and kisses my neck.

Running his hands up the sides of my thighs makes me lean my head back on his shoulder as I moan.

He growls when someone knocks at the door. I giggle as he moves to answer it, but I keep looking out at the impressive view in front of me. The door closes and he's behind me in an instant, I can feel his breath on my neck.

"Hands on the window," he says in a husky erotic voice.

"Liam," I whisper.

"Now Mercy. And did you forget my fucking name?"

"Daddy."

I place my hands on the window, and I hear his belt buckle clink together as he undoes his pants. Excitement courses through my body, my heart pounds, and my clit throbs. Whatever he does to me will be extreme pleasure.

Reaching under my skirt, he grabs the sides of my panties with his thumb and finger, then pulls them down quickly.

"My baby girl, is so fucking beautiful."

He digs his fingers into my hips with a bruising grip and plunges into me hard and fast. His mouth finds my neck while he slides in and out of me.

"Fuck. You feel so good. Your pussy was made to take my cock."

He bites my neck as he reaches around and rubs my nub. His thrusts are hard and slow. Moving his hands to my hips he pounds into me at an accelerated pace. Our breaths are heavy, mine is nearly a pant. The sound of our perspiring skin slapping together is the only sound in the room other than our moans of pleasure.

"Yes, Daddy. Yes. I'm going to come!"

I feel him swell inside me, and it takes me over the edge. I scream out my orgasm as I push on the glass. He slams into me one last time as he grunts the sexiest sound I'll ever hear.

He pulls out of me, puts his pants back on and lifts me into his arms, carrying me down the hallway. I wrap my arms around his neck. He walks into the bedroom, and he lays me on the king-size bed with a beautiful white cover.

"Lift up," he says, and I do as he yanks the blankets to the foot of the bed.

I flash him a questioning look, "Are we going to bed at three o'clock?"

"No. Can I hold my beautiful girlfriend?" He lays on his back, and I climb on top of him, putting my face to his neck, "I love you."

Running his fingers through my hair, he whispers, "I love you too, baby." He kisses me on the forehead and whispers, "Don't fall asleep. You have to get ready in an hour. We have dinner reservations and plans after dinner."

"You should know that this is already the best birthday I've ever had."

He doesn't say anything but wraps his arms around me and pulls me tighter to him. Not a word needs to be said, he easily conveys every emotion he feels for me. For a long time, I planned to get him in bed. I wanted to fuck him more than I wanted anything. What we have now, far exceeded my expectations. After the first time we had sex, I never imagined he had a soft side like this. But I'm glad I found it. I love that he has this part of him that's only for me. I'm in my happy fucking bubble when my insecurity shows her ugly face. I know I should keep my fears to myself. I've told myself more than once to keep my mouth closed before I lose him. But it's like a train-wreck. I know it's going to happen but there's nothing I can do to stop it.

"Wait. You knew where the bedroom was as if you'd been here before."

He kisses my cheek, "Yes, baby. I've stayed here before."

I jump up and sit at the edge of the bed, and he stares at me like you might an animal ready to attack.

"What the hell just happened?"

"You've brought the others here."

"Mercy, you are not the first woman I've been with."

I sigh, "I shouldn't have said anything. I'm going to go get ready."

Grabbing my wrists, he says, "No. We are talking about this. Why do you seem like you're ready to jump? What's going on? I thought you were happy."

"I am," I say, my voice low.

I shake my head, "What happens when I get older, Liam?"

"What the hell does that mean?"

"I'm going to age. When I'm thirty, then what? You'll leave me for a younger woman. I don't think I can handle that."

He gets off the bed and paces, "Is this what you fucking think of me? I just go after the young pussy and throw them away when I've had my fill? That's the man you think I am?"

"No. I don't know," I stammer.

He glares at me, pain reflecting on his face, "Just so you know, you are the first woman in her twenties I've been with since I was in *my* fucking twenties. This is not a habit or some kink of mine. Let's remember who chased who here, little girl. I tried to get you to leave me alone, but you wouldn't."

His hands are balled into fists. I haven't seen him angry at me, and I'm unsure how to undo what I've done. I'm such a bitch.

"I'm going to take a shower," he walks into the bathroom and slams the door. I don't move from where I'm sitting. I just wait.

He comes out wearing nothing but a towel, "It's all yours."

"Liam, I'm sorry. I shouldn't have said that. It wasn't fair. You've treated me so well, I'm sorry. I guess I'm scared."

I should really stop talking. I have a feeling I'm making things worse with every word that comes out of my mouth.

His gaze softens, "Scared of what? I told you I'd never hurt you."

I shrug my shoulders, "I'm afraid of losing you."

"Then stop talking nonsense. You aren't going to lose me, baby. It's not even possible. If I wanted other women, I could have them. I don't. I'm so fucking in love with you. I can honestly tell you, there will never be another woman for me. You're my future."

I gasp at his words. He motions me over to him with his finger.

He cups my face in his hands, "Only you, baby girl, forever," and kisses me quickly.

"Go get ready."

Twenty-Eight

LIAM

WELL, fuck. After her little meltdown, I'm not honestly too sure where I stand, and tonight, might just blow up in my goddamn face. Where did that even come from? It's as if she's trying to find reasons to end the best thing that has ever happened to me. I try to show her every fucking day, how much she means to me. What more can I possibly do? At this point, I'm not sure what she wants from me. Anything she wants, I give her. This girl is going to fucking destroy me, I just know it. Still, I'm all in. I won't turn back now. I'll keep giving her my all, and if she blows up my life then so be it.

I pour myself a drink because God knows I need it. I grab the whiskey from the fully stocked bar, and a glass, pouring myself two fingers. I gulp it down when I hear her heels clicking on the Italian tile.

I turn to her, and fuck she takes my breath away. She's wearing a pearl-colored dress that falls to above her knee, covered with a sheer material over what appears to be satin. I'm a big fan of the plunging neckline, it makes my mouth water.

"Do I look okay?" She spins around showing me the back as well.

"Okay? No. You look stunning, as the kids say, you're a snack."

When she throws her head back and laughs a hearty laugh, every worry melts away. Walking over to me, she runs her finger down my chest, "You're not so bad yourself, Doctor Lexington, quite the snack."

And just like that my dick is hard as steel, "Let's go before I change my mind and keep you here all night."

I take her hand in mine and we leave the room, taking the elevator to the lobby. I've arranged for a driver because I'd rather sit in a car staring at her, than to have to deal with the traffic here.

We walk out to the car, and I open the back door for her.

"You're not driving?"

"Not tonight, gorgeous."

She slides in, and I close the door. I go to the other side and sit beside her.

"You look very handsome in a three-piece suit, doctor."

I grin at her, "Thank you."

We arrive at the restaurant and get out of the vehicle. Her eyes travel up the tall glass building.

"Manhatta?" she asks. Shit has she been here already?

"You've been?" I ask as we walk to the elevator and get in.

She shakes her head, "No. Jessica told me about it."

"The restaurant is on the sixtieth floor, it's stunning."

We walk in and the hostess smiles, "Dr. Lexington?"

I nod.

"Follow me, please," she says.

She takes us to a table next to the wall of windows that provide an impressive panoramic view of the city. When I saw her reaction to the view in the hotel, I knew I had made the right choice when I booked the restaurant for tonight.

Our table is circular with a white tablecloth, a dark purple overlay is on top, and our wine is already waiting for us. It's her new favorite wine. It's expensive, especially in a restaurant where prices are increased but I'd buy her anything she wants.

I pull out a chair for her, she takes a seat, with a smile on her face.

Walking to the other side, I sit across from her gazing at her while she sips her wine.

I nod to the waitress.

"Why is no one else here, Liam?"

"I wanted to be alone with you."

Two violinists come out and start playing, I get up and walk over to Mercy, extending my hand, "Dance with me, baby girl?"

She bites her lip, and nods as she rises from her chair. I take her to the middle of the room, take her into my arms, and dance with her, holding her close to my body.

I spin her around as she grips her hands on my shoulders. She looks like an angel, smiling at me, she's happy. We dance until the music stops, the musicians leave after one song, as they were instructed. Standing back from her, I hold her hands, staring at her a little too long.

"Liam?"

I clear my throat, "Mercy. When I found you in my bathroom, I swore I'd never do anything with you. But your beauty made it impossible for me to stay away. When I saw your tenacious personality, your infectious spirit, I knew I needed you. The day I saw you with Ivy for the first time, I understood your heart. I never planned on falling madly in love with you, but I'm glad I did."

I kneel in front of her and see the tears in her hazel eyes.

"Baby girl, I love you so fucking much. I can't imagine a life without you, and I don't want to. I promise to love you and take care of you forever. Will you marry me?"

I take the box out of my suit jacket and open it, holding it out to her.

"Oh my God, Liam."

She drops to her knees as she shakes and wraps her arms around my neck and slams her lips to mine. Our tongues tangle with each other and she runs her hands through my hair, but I pull back quicker than I'd like to.

"Baby, I'm dying here. Please give me an answer."

She laughs, "Yes, Liam. I'll marry you."

I slide the ring on her finger, and she laughs, "This is huge, Liam. I would've been fine with a ring that didn't cost as much as a mansion."

I put the empty box back in my jacket and stand, holding my hand down to help her up off the floor, "Let's eat."

We go to the table, and our food is waiting there already.

"You really thought of everything didn't you?"

I grin, "I tried."

"We have to be at our next stop at seven."

She puts a piece of salmon in her mouth and nods.

I ordered salmon for her, because it's her favorite, and I got steak and it's 'melt in your mouth' tender.

"The food is excellent. I hope it was worth the cost."

"You're worth every penny, baby."

When she's done, I leave money on the table for the tip. I paid in advance for our meal. The wine was so expensive, they wanted it paid for before uncorking it. I can't say that I blame them. When Mercy first chose that wine at the house, I was concerned that she wouldn't like it and it would go to waste.

We finish off the wine and she strokes my hand, "Thank you for a wonderful night, Liam."

"It's just getting started, baby girl. Are you ready?"

We walk to the elevator and make our way back outside to the chilly New York weather. After we get into the vehicle she straddles me, which I was not expecting but I am not complaining.

"Let's just go home, Daddy. I need you to fuck me."

I arch an eyebrow, "Not a chance, baby girl."

She grinds her pussy on my cock, and I want to say that we'll go to the hotel so I can fuck her senseless, but that's not part of the plan.

"Patience. I'll make you come after this next surprise."

Leaning forward she whispers in my ear, "Daddy. I need you. Fuck me."

"You and your impatient, greedy pussy."

I lay her down on the backseat and pull her panties to the side and thrust three fingers into her.

"Is this what you want, dirty girl? You want me to make that pussy come all over my fingers?"

"Yes, Daddy," she squeaks.

I move my fingers back and forth the way I know she likes it. She breathes heavily, moaning for me. Then I slam into her over and over, she's panting, and her pussy clamps onto my fingers with a tight grip.

I pull out of her and shove my digits into her mouth, "Fucking dirty slut, my dirty slut, taste what I do to you."

She sucks my fingers and moans.

I pull out of her mouth, and slam my lips to hers, kissing her with all the passion I feel for her. This woman drives me fucking crazy.

"Sir, we are here."

Sitting up I glance at Mercy as she giggles, "Busted."

I laugh, "Let's go, naughty girl."

We get out and she realizes we are at Madison Square Garden. Her gaze casts up to the huge sign that reads, 'Cheyanne Cash One Night Only Sold Out'

"Oh my God, Liam."

I can't stifle the huge grin on my face and the satisfaction in my heart. I live to make her happy.

"How? I just told you and it's sold out."

I chuckle as we walk towards the door, "Gloria told me a week ago that you wanted to go but wouldn't go by yourself."

She shakes her head in disbelief as I open the door and we walk through.

Twenty-Nine

MERCY

WE WALK in and he smirks at me, "I need to wash my hands. I'll be right back."

I'm still blushing when he comes back out and winks at me.

He hands our tickets to the usher, and he takes us to our seats, all the way in the front row, center. We sit down and I glare at him.

"You have spent entirely too much money on me tonight."

Locking his fingers with mine, he stares at me with a heated gaze, "Baby girl, you are worth every cent."

I probably look really stupid with how much smiling I've done tonight, but it's really been a magical night that I never expected.

A man comes to the stage, "Ladies and Gentlemen, please welcome Black Cash recording artist, Cheyanne Cash!"

She comes on stage, and I say in Liam's ear, "Wow! She's really pregnant. I hope she doesn't have that baby tonight."

He laughs, "She is about ready to pop."

Everybody is standing, so I stand, guessing that is what I'm supposed to do. Liam pulls me into his arms, my back to his front, and we sway to the music.

I'm amazed at how good she is performing live. Her voice sounds as perfect as it does on her CD.

During a break between songs, she grabs a stool and sits down. Liam says, "Something is wrong. She's pale, something is wrong."

Just then she grabs her stomach as she falls to the stage floor. It all seems to happen in slow motion, I don't know this woman, but my heart breaks for her. I hope that she and her baby will be okay.

A gorgeous dark-haired man runs on the stage yelling, "Cheyanne! No! I NEED A DOCTOR! IS THERE A DOCTOR IN THE HOUSE?"

Liam steps forward, "I'm a doctor."

"Are you an Obstetrician?

"I'm a Pediatric Oncologist, but I've delivered babies. I did a rotation in Obstetrics."

The panicked man glances around and says, "Fine, come around." He motions to security to let us through.

Liam takes my hand and pulls me with him.

The man carries Cheyanne in his arms, and we follow security to the backstage area, and into what I assume is a dressing room. He lays her on a blue couch.

"I assume there's no bed?" Liam asks.

"No."

"Answer my questions quickly. Time is of the essence," Liam says.

"Are you the father?"

"Yes, I'm her husband. Asher Black."

"Is this her first pregnancy?"

"No. It's the third live pregnancy. We've had a few losses."

"Take her underwear off, I'm going to examine her."

Liam walks to the sink in the room and washes his hands.

"You better be a fucking doctor," Asher says, but he does as he's told.

Liam is annoyed to say the least, "Mercy, get my wallet and show him my ID."

"Cheyanne, look at me," Liam says.

She does as tears fall down her face, "You have to save my baby."

"That's the plan, sweetheart. How far along are you?"

"Thirty-four weeks," she sobs out.

I hand Asher Liam's ID, and he relaxes a little bit. But he's still a mess, pacing back and forth.

Liam says, "Asher, come hold her hand."

He comes over to her head, takes her hand and kisses her face.

"I'm here, baby. It's going to be okay," he says.

"Can I help?" I ask.

"Yes, hold her right leg back."

Liam looks between her legs and looks up at Cheyanne's face, "Your baby is coming. It's crowning right now. Asher, I need towels, heavy string, and scissors. Fast."

Asher calls someone to bring the supplies, "I'm not leaving her."

Why he needs string at this moment I'm really not sure but now is clearly not the time to ask him questions.

Liam tries to keep her calm, "Is it a boy or a girl?"

"We don't know. This is our last one and we have a boy and a girl, so we wanted to be surprised."

Asher gazes at her like she hung the moon, "You wanted to be surprised. I wanted to know."

"Well, you're about to find out."

A man comes in with the towels and Asher runs to him and takes them, "Now get out!"

I bite my lip to suppress my smile. It's funny to see a man as possessive as Liam. Asher gives Liam the towels and goes back to Cheyanne, kneeling beside her.

"Okay, Cheyanne. With the next contraction I need you to push while Mercy counts to ten."

Asher brushes the sweaty hair off her face as he whispers to her.

"A couch is not great for delivering a baby, so I need you to hold your left leg back, Cheyanne. There you go. That's good."

He has his hand on her stomach, "Okay, you're having a contraction, push really hard while Mercy counts."

I count 1-2-3-4-5-6-7-8 and she stops pushing.

"I can't," she cries, "It hurts so bad."

I take her hand, "You can do this, Cheyanne."

"Okay. Contraction, push Cheyanne. Good girl," he says, and I look at him and he smirks.

"One more push, and the baby's head should be out."

"This fucking burns like hell!"

Liam glances up at her face, "Yes it does. They don't call it the ring of fire for nothing. But you're doing great."

"Contraction. Push," Liam says.

I resume my counting as Cheyanne stares in my face while she pushes.

"Oh, what a beautiful little face. You're doing great Cheyanne, once the shoulders are out the rest is a piece of cake."

"Easy for you to say," she nearly yells.

Liam chuckles, "Yes, it is."

Asher speaks to her in a low, gravelly voice, overcome with emotion, "You're doing so great, baby. I love you."

He kisses her on the forehead as she replies, "I love you too. But this really fucking hurts."

"Contraction. Push. Let's get this baby out."

I count for her again, and she cries, "I can't."

"Come on Cheyanne, you've got this!" I say.

She screams and bears down with all of her might; I can see it in her scrunched up face.

"Shoulders out. Good job."

"Mercy come hold this towel," he says, he has his hands under the baby's head and back.

I let go of her hand and walk to Liam and hold the towel open for Liam to put the baby in it.

"Support the neck and hand the baby to Mom."

"Congratulations, it's a girl!" I say as I place the baby on her stomach.

"Is she okay?"

Just then the baby cries and everyone smiles.

"I need you to push a few more times. We have to get this placenta out."

Once the placenta is out, he wraps it in a towel. He takes the string and cuts off two pieces and ties them around the umbilical cord in two spots.

"Ok, Dad, do you want to cut the cord?"

Asher smiles as a tear runs down his face. With shaky hands he takes the scissors from Liam.

"Make a cut between where I've tied the string," Liam says.

After he cuts the cord, he sets the scissors on the edge of the sink and goes back to Cheyanne, kissing the baby on the forehead and then her.

"Thank you," he says, "You made me a father again. Thank you."

She smiles with tears running down her face, it's a beautiful thing to witness.

Paramedics run in and Liam glares at them, "Did you stop for dinner? What the hell took you so long?"

Cheyanne looks at us with tears flowing, "Thank you so much. Free tickets to any show for life. Asher, give him your card." Asher hands me his card while Liam washes his hands.

"If you want tickets contact Asher," She smiles.

The paramedics lift her and the baby onto a stretcher and Asher follows them out of the room.

He comes over to me, "Let's go back to the hotel so I can shower."

As we walk, I say, "Yeah and then you can pay penance for calling another woman, good girl."

"Penance?"

"Yes, you will be punished, Dr. Lexington."

He laughs, "You can try, tomorrow. But tonight, I have it planned out. Your penance will have to wait."

* * *

We get back to the hotel and Liam seems a little out of sorts, like he is worried about something.

"I'm going to take a shower," he kisses me on the cheek and walks to the bathroom as he sighs.

I walk over to the bar to get a drink. I can't believe how well stocked it is. Decisions, decisions. I opt for wine as usual. Maybe it's boring but I like what I like.

A few minutes later, Liam comes out in nothing more than a towel.

My God this man is gorgeous. His well-defined abs and that perfect 'V' that all women love, have me drooling. But those dark green eyes get me every single time. He stares at me with wonder in his eyes, like I'm the most precious diamond he's searched the world for.

He comes over to me and runs his fingers down my arm from shoulder to hand.

"Baby, I've never done what I'm going to do tonight with any woman. But I want to give it to you because you deserve it."

I swallow hard, what the hell is he planning to do to me?

"You've never done what?"

Softly he kisses my neck, "I've never been gentle. It's not in my nature, I think you know that. But for you, I'll do anything."

I moan into his kisses but ask, "What makes you think that's what I want?"

When his mouth moves to my ear I melt, "Baby, I ripped your virginity away from you like a monster. I can't take it back, but I can try to give you a different memory, a gentle one."

"Liam, that's not-" he silences me with a slow, tortuous kiss.

After he takes my clothes off, in the slowest fashion I've ever seen, he lifts me into his arms and carries me to the bedroom. He gently lays me on the bed and gazes at me with adoring eyes.

"Mercy, you're so beautiful."

He climbs on the bed and runs his hands and mouth all over my entire body, leaving me a quivering mess. Hovering over me, his hands on the mattress on either side of me, he slides into me slowly, gently. I know he thinks this is what I need, but it isn't.

"Fuck me."

His lips ghost over mine, "I love you," he continues his slow, gentle torture.

"Liam, you're killing me. Fuck me, already."

A confused expression washes over his face, "I'm trying, Mercy."

I cup his face, "I've never asked you to be gentle. It's not what I want. I don't regret my first time and you shouldn't either. I love every time we are together. I enjoy it when you take control of my body."

Thirty

LIAM

WE GET BACK to the hotel and Liam seems a little out of sorts, like he is worried about something.

"I'm going to take a shower," he kisses me on the cheek and walks to the bathroom as he sighs.

I walk over to the bar to get a drink. I can't believe how well stocked it is. Decisions, decisions. I opt for wine as usual. Maybe it's boring but I like what I like.

A few minutes later, Liam comes out in nothing more than a towel. My God this man is gorgeous. His well-defined abs and that perfect 'V' that all women love, have me drooling. But those dark green eyes get me every single time. He stares at me with wonder in his eyes, like I'm the most precious diamond he's searched the world for.

He comes over to me and runs his fingers down my arm from shoulder to hand.

"Baby, I've never done what I'm going to do tonight with any woman. But I want to give it to you because you deserve it."

I swallow hard, what the hell is he planning to do to me?

"You've never done what?"

Softly he kisses my neck, "I've never been gentle. It's not in my nature, I think you know that. But for you, I'll do anything."

I moan into his kisses but ask, "What makes you think that's what I want?"

When his mouth moves to my ear I melt, "Baby, I ripped your virginity away from you like a monster. I can't take it back, but I can try to give you a different memory, a gentle one."

"Liam, that's not-" he silences me with a slow, tortuous kiss.

After he takes my clothes off, in the slowest fashion I've ever seen, he lifts me into his arms and carries me to the bedroom. He gently lays me on the bed and gazes at me with adoring eyes.

"Mercy, you're so beautiful."

He climbs on the bed and runs his hands and mouth all over my entire body, leaving me a quivering mess. Hovering over me, his hands on the mattress on either side of me, he slides into me slowly, gently. I know he thinks this is what I need, but it isn't.

"Fuck me."

His lips ghost over mine, "I love you," he continues his slow, gentle torture.

"Liam, you're killing me. Fuck me, already."

A confused expression washes over his face, "I'm trying, Mercy."

I cup his face, "I've never asked you to be gentle. It's not what I want. I don't regret my first time and you shouldn't either. I love every time we are together. I enjoy it when you take control of my body."

* * *

We spent the last two days touring New York. I took her to see a few Broadway plays which she loved. But now, we are on our way to see her parents, which I'm not looking forward to. The age difference is going to be a problem. How could it not be? If I had a daughter, and she were dating a man nearly two decades older than her, I would have a problem with it. I'd probably beat the hell out of him.

As we pull into the driveway, even Mercy suddenly appears nervous. Great.

"My dad's kind of rough, just try not to hit him, okay?"

Her unease fills me with more apprehension than I had a few minutes ago.

"It'll be fine. What father wouldn't appreciate a forty-one-year-old man fucking his twenty-four year old daughter?"

A woman, who I assume is her mother, runs out to the car, pulling open the passenger door.

"Get out here and hug your mom!"

Mercy gets out and her mom pulls her into a tight hug.

She looks over at me, "Well aren't you just the yummiest thing I've ever seen?"

I laugh uncomfortably as Mercy says, "Sorry, I should have warned you that my mom says whatever comes into her mind. She has zero filter."

"Mom, this is Dr. Liam Lexington, Liam this is my mom, Sophia."

She walks around the car and throws her arms around me and whispers to me, "How old are you?"

I answer, "Forty-one."

"Oh shit. Good luck. I don't care, but my forty-five-year-old husband will not be pleased."

"I assumed."

She stands back and looks at me, "As long as my daughter is happy, I'm happy. But Gilbert won't see it the same way. I hope you have your bullet proof vest on," she laughs.

"Yeah, I don't have one of those."

"I'm kidding, he won't shoot you. Probably not anyway." Sighing she says, "Let's go get this over with, so we can have a nice visit."

Mercy takes my hand, gripping it hard, as we walk through the front door. What happens if he won't accept our relationship? Is she the type to end things if her parents don't approve? That scares me far more than getting shot.

We walk in and he's sitting in a recliner reading a paper and holding a glass of what appears to be scotch.

Looking up from his paper, he arches an eyebrow at me.

"You're the boyfriend?"

"Yes, sir. Well, fiancé I suppose. I asked Mercy to marry me, and she said yes." I hoped that the fact that I was serious about her might soften him. No such luck.

"I don't think so," he says before downing his drink.

"Sir?"

"How old are you?"

My hands are sweating, I don't get intimidated by anyone, but I am right now. It feels like he holds my future in his hands and he's about to crush it.

"Forty-One."

He laughs, "Four years younger than I am, and you're fucking a little girl, my little girl. You have quite the nerve to step into my home."

Tears run down her face.

"This is how this will go. You're going to stay away from my daughter. If you don't, I guarantee you, I will make your life hell."

I rub the stubble on my jaw, this is going far worse than I had even thought it would go, "I'm sorry to have upset you, but I can't stay away from Mercy."

He sits his empty glass on the small table beside him, "Very well, then you have brought this on yourself."

Mercy takes my hand, "Come on Liam, let's go. This was obviously a terrible idea."

Her mom gets upset, "No, don't go. Gilbert stop this! She's the only child I have left!"

Mercy pulls on my hand, urging me to the door, as I hear his final words, "Don't come back to my house until you're done with this rebellious stage. No daughter of mine would act like such a whore. Now leave."

Every muscle in my body tenses. My jaw is clenched so tight that it clicks.

"Liam, no. Let's go," Mercy pleads.

We get into the car and leave, heading home since we had already checked out of the hotel. It's a long two-hour drive with my girl crying most of the way. Once we pull into the driveway, I'm relieved. I want to take her in my arms and make her feel better. Walking inside, I try to do just that. But she steps back from me, "No!"

What the hell?

She runs to the bedroom, and I go in to find her packing clothes.

"Baby girl, what's going on?"

"It's over, Liam. I'm leaving."

I stand frozen, watching her pack, watching my heart crumble before me, "No, baby girl, please don't do this. You said you'd be my wife."

She swings her bag over her shoulder, "Liam, he will destroy everything. Your career will be left in ashes. I won't do that to you, I love you too much," she sobs.

"I don't want a life without you. I don't care about my career, Mercy. Please, baby girl, don't go."

She shakes her head, "Those kids need you and I think you need them too."

Putting her ring in my hand, she kisses my lips softly and leaves me with her parting words, "I love you, Liam. I always will. Thank you for the best time of my life. I'll never forget you. But this is how it has to be. I'm sorry."

Placing her hand on my chest, more tears roll down her cheeks as she whispers, "Goodbye, Liam," then she turns and walks away.

Standing frozen I just watch her leave my life. I run both of my hands through my hair. How can I go on without her? I can't. I'm wrecked. There's no me anymore without her. I sit drinking because I don't know what else to do with myself. Fuck. My chest aches, and it's only been an hour. How the hell am I going to get through this?

I send a few drunk texts to her, begging her to change her mind but they all go ignored.

Thirty-One

MERCY

IT'S BEEN a week since I ended things with Liam, and my heart is still broken. I'm not sure how I'll ever get through this. Seeing him at the hospital is the worst torture I've ever been through. The pain is evident every time he looks at me. I hate that I'm responsible for breaking his heart. But I know my dad and what he's capable of. He has connections that he will not hesitate to use. When he threatened Liam, I knew he was serious, and I've seen firsthand what he'll do if someone didn't heed the warning. Liam would be lucky to not go to prison and simply lose his medical license.

Dad, of course, has connections in the police department, the FBI, and also criminals. You would think that a police officer who vows to serve and protect, would be a good man. He's not a good man, quite the opposite. He skirts the line between legal and illegal. More often than not, he's on the illegal side. Gilbert Madison is what they call a dirty cop. No one will ever bring him down because he's got too many powerful men in his pocket. He joined the force at twenty-one and made detective at twenty-three after rescuing twenty-six women from a human trafficking ring. It's ridiculous that he's been involved with the very thing that made his career.

I'm not an idiot, and I knew my dad wouldn't be happy with Liam being so much older than me. But I didn't expect this, and I really thought he'd be pissed, yell and scream, and eventually get over it.

I'm sitting in Ivy's room when Liam comes in and flips through her chart.

"Miss Madison," he nods at me as my heart breaks even more.

He takes a deep breath and looks at Ivy, "How are you feeling, Princess?"

"Okay," she says, adding, "I'm tired of throwing up."

"Let's try some new medication for your tummy, okay?"

He leaves, and I can finally breathe again.

Perceptive little Ivy asks, "Don't be sad, Mercy."

I paste on a smile just for her, "I'm not. How can I be sad when I'm here with my favorite girl? Let's watch a movie!"

She smiles brightly, I grab her tablet and put *Snow White* on.

I stare at the screen, but I'm not really watching it because all I can think about is Liam. After she falls asleep, I put the tablet beside her and go so she can rest. I walk towards the break room when I'm stopped in my tracks. I spot Liam with a nurse standing pressed against him, her finger trailing down his chest. He gazes down at her with a heated stare. Bile rises in my throat as I turn to run out of the hospital.

"Mercy!" he shouts, but I keep running until I'm outside. I get in my car, and Liam rushes over banging on my window. I drive away because I don't know what else to do. My emotions are overwhelming me. I told him it was over; I had no right to be upset about seeing him with another woman. My brain understands this, but my heart does not. It's as if it's been ripped open. As I drive home, my phone rings, and it's Liam. I dismiss the call because there's nothing to say that hasn't been said. Again, my phone rings and I answer it because it's not Liam. It's my doctor's office.

"Hello?"

"Miss Madison, it's Dr. Shein's office."

"Yes, how can I help you?"

"We need you to come in to see the doctor. Can you come in today?"

As I drive down the road, I wonder why they need me to come in today. But I answer, "Yes, I am free for the remainder of the day."

We agree that I'll come in now. This is bizarre, I went in for a routine pap and to get more birth control because I thought I'd be having sex. I turn around and go in the other direction towards my doctor's office.

I park and walk in to see what's going on. I'm taken back to the examination room quickly.

Dr. Shein comes in and sits next to me.

"Your pap smear came back abnormal. Normally we just repeat it but due to your family history I want to be quick. I'd like to run some tests."

"Okay," I respond.

"We'll do several tests including a colposcopy and cervical biopsy."

"Do you think I have cancer?"

"I certainly hope not. But with your family history, I don't want to wait to make sure. Abnormal paps happen all the time. It's normally not cancer, but again, with your family history, I want to be certain."

I nod, "Okay, whatever you need to do is fine."

"The nurse will schedule everything and call you."

She leaves me with my racing thoughts. Of course, I first want to call Liam, but I don't, because that's no longer an option.

I go home and call my mom because it feels like she's all I have now. Just like I knew she would, she asked me to come home. But I tell her let's wait for the results because we don't even know yet.

One week later...

I'm in Dr. Shein's office waiting for my results, and I tap my fingers on the desk. My anxiety is through the roof. If you could jump out of your skin, I just might. When she comes in, she smiles weakly, "I'm sorry, to keep you waiting for so long. I'm a little behind schedule today." She takes a seat and gazes at me softly.

"I'm so sorry, Mercy. You have cervical cancer as well as ovarian cancer."

When I hear those words, I think I leave my body. Just like my grandmother who died from ovarian cancer. Somewhere in the distance,

I hear the words, "The good news is that we can get rid of it. I am recommending a hysterectomy."

I shake my head, "No. I won't do that. I want children."

"You need to do this, Mercy. Maybe you can adopt but if you don't have the surgery you will die from cancer. Right now, it's contained in your reproductive organs but if you wait, it will be too late."

I grip the desk, trying to ground myself, "Maybe if I go to a donor and get pregnant right away it will be alright."

"Even if you were pregnant now, nine months is a long time for cancer to spread. Mercy, don't be foolish."

I stand to leave, "No. I won't do this."

Walking out of the building, I'm determined, I'm not going to lose my chance of becoming a mother. I go to the hospital to resign and stop to see Ivy on my way out.

"Hi, Princess."

She beams, "Mercy, I'm happy you're here."

"Can I see your tablet?"

Giving me a strange look, she hands it to me.

"I have to leave for a while. But I want to still be able to talk to you, so I'm adding myself to your kids messenger. We can video chat."

"Where are you going?" Tears form in her beautiful eyes.

"New York with my family, but I don't want Dr. L to know, okay?"

I know that asking a child to keep secrets is wrong. But I can't just leave her without a word.

"Will I see you again?"

"Definitely," I smile.

I show her how to call me and how to accept my calls. Liam walks in, and I stare at him a little too long and touch Ivy's hand, "I'll talk to you soon, sweet girl."

Liam watches me leave, and it's almost as if I can physically feel his pain. But even if the shit with my dad hadn't happened, I wouldn't drag him through this. Cancer has taken so many people from him. I couldn't do that to him, even if things were different besides, they aren't.

Thirty-Two

LIAM

THREE WEEKS LATER...

It's been three fucking weeks since she's been here. I ask Gloria about it, but she doesn't know much other than, "Mercy doesn't work here anymore."

I found out from HR that she resigned, but they are tight-lipped as to why. Maybe they don't even know why. It's not like you have to give a reason, but I feel sick in my gut.

I call my buddy, Javiar, a computer genius.

"Javvy, you've got to help me find her."

"It's only been three hours since you called me asking for help. It's gonna take a little time, Doc."

"So, you have nothing?"

I pace back and forth. I'm losing my fucking mind. Somehow, I know that something is wrong, very wrong. Where the fuck is she? I checked with her apartment building, but they said she moved, and of course, they have no forwarding address.

"Not yet, no. I called Jeff to get his help."

Jeff is a private investigator that we both know.

"Fine. Call me when you know something, I don't care what time it is."

"You got it, doc."

I hang up the call. Where the fuck are you, Mercy?

I text her for the millionth time.

Me: Baby girl, please respond. I just need to know that you're okay.

I try to work, but I'm having trouble focusing when all I do is worry about Mercy.

Gloria stops me on my way out of the building, "Doctor, Gilbert Madison has called six times to talk to you. He's here now, he wants to see you."

"Why?"

"He wouldn't say, but said it was urgent."

I nod, "That's Mercy's dad. Set him up in the consultation room, I'll be there in a moment."

"Yes, doctor. I hope everything is okay."

"Me too," I say as I run a hand through my hair.

I try to compose myself and then walk into the room where the man who hates me most waits for me.

Opening the door, I walk through, "Sir."

"Doctor, thank you for seeing me."

"If this is about more threats, you should know that Mercy ended things like you wanted, so there's no point. I haven't even seen her for three weeks."

"Sit down. I have difficult news for you."

My heart drops, "Is this about Mercy?"

He nods.

I take a seat across from him.

"You're the last person I wanted to come to for help. But you may be the only one that can help at this point."

He takes a shaky breath, "Mercy has cancer."

While I sit with a stoic expression on my face, inside, I'm screaming, *NO NO NO NOT HER!* I have lost so many to cancer. God please, not again. Not Mercy. I don't know everything. But I do know I will not live through her death.

"What kind?" I ask, dragging my hand down my face.

"Cervical and ovarian."

"Stage?" I ask.

"One."

I breathe a sigh of relief, "Oh, well if there's a cancer to have, that's it. She'll be fine, they can do a hysterectomy and get rid of it. You scared the hell out of me."

He shakes his head, "Yes, that's what was recommended."

"Good. Is that all?" This man makes me uncomfortable and honestly angry. I don't want to be in his presence longer than necessary.

I stand, and he glares at me, "No that's not all. Sit down."

Lowering back into the chair, I stare at him, waiting for whatever else he says.

"She has refused surgery, because it'll make it so she can't have children."

"What? She can't do that. It's not elective surgery."

"That's why I need your help. She loves you. You're the only person that she'll listen to."

I shake my head, "Maybe that was true. But she won't even speak to me anymore."

"My daughter's feelings for you have not changed."

"That's hard to believe, since she won't even respond to a text message."

The irony is not lost on me. It wasn't that long ago that it was me that wouldn't respond to her. Maybe this is exactly what I deserve.

"Look, I know I'm responsible for her not talking to you. But I'm asking you to help me save my little girl. My wife cannot lose another child to cancer."

"I'll do anything for Mercy. Just don't expect too much. Where is she?"

He breathes a sigh of relief, "New York, at my house."

"Very well, I'll clear my schedule and I'll leave."

"Thank you," he stands and extends his hand for me to shake.

"I'll see you at your house."

I walk out of the room, and thoughts race through my head. What the hell is she thinking? You can't get cancer and decide not to treat it.

Dead women can't have fucking babies. I love her, but boy, does she piss me off. Patients like Ivy would love the option to have surgery and be done with it. Mercy is being a spoiled little brat. You don't choose to die to save the idea of becoming a mother. I will not go through this again.

After clearing my schedule, I head out, but Gloria stops me. "When will you be back, doctor?"

"I'm not sure."

If I can somehow talk her into having this surgery, there is no way I'll leave her side. She'll be coming home with me so that I can take care of her. My heart pounds from the mere thought of seeing her again. Fuck, I miss her so much. I'm torn between beating her ass for being so stupid and kissing her.

Thirty-Three

MERCY

I'M GETTING tired of my dad yelling at me for being stupid and reckless. Although, that's easier to take than my mom's constant crying as if I'm already dead. I've gone to a few fertility clinics to try and get pregnant. They've all turned me down because it's irresponsible to get a woman with cancer pregnant. I stopped taking my pills, and my next plan was to find a random guy to fuck and get pregnant. I want a baby. I know it sounds insane, but I want this so much. The thought of having sex with any man other than Liam makes me physically ill. There will need to be a lot of alcohol involved for me to go through with it. I need children.

I call Ivy because, damn I miss her. Her little smiling face greets me, making my heart smile.

"Can you come back now?"

"I wish I could, sweet girl. I will as soon as I can, okay?"

She blows me a kiss, and my heart skips a beat before I blow one back.

"I have to go, Abby is here."

I smile, "Okay sweetheart."

I'm sitting in bed reading a book when I hear his heavy steps on the stairs. My dad is coming to scream some more as if it will do any good. He knocks on the door, which is odd. My dad never knocks.

"Come in."

The door opens, and it's not my dad.

"Liam," I say, as my hand goes to my heart which is now beating rapidly, I think it might burst.

There's a softness in his gaze, but it vanishes almost as quickly as it appeared.

He walks over to me and sits on the edge of my bed.

"You should go. My dad will be back anytime. He'll kill you if he sees you."

He rubs his jaw, he's stressed, "Baby girl, tell me what I should do with you, I'm torn."

"What?"

His fingers grip my thigh painfully, "I can't decide, should I kiss those beautiful lips or spank your ass until it bleeds for being so fucking stupid."

He knows. Oh my God, how?

I look down at my book because I can't look at him.

Grabbing my chin with his thumb and forefinger, he tilts my head back, "You will look at me when I'm speaking to you. Now tell me, baby girl, what should I do?"

"Liam, I think you should go."

He growls and pulls my face to his, kissing me with a bruising kiss.

When he pulls back, we're both out of breath, "Now, would you prefer to have the surgery at home or in New York?"

I glare at him and huff, "I'm not having the surgery, Liam."

He bites, "Yes you are. You're having the fucking surgery, Mercy."

I clench my fists, "I'm not having it. You do not get a say, we are not together anymore. I don't know why you're here, but you need to go now."

"You don't know why I'm here?"

I shake my head, "No, but it doesn't matter."

"I'm here, because I fucking love you, because I've lost so many people to cancer and I can't bear the thought of losing you. I'm here for myself, for your parents, for fucking Ivy. I will not allow you to make the same choice that Nash's mom made. I will not let you choose death. Suicide by cancer is not a fucking option."

My heart aches for what I can't have and what he wants but can't have. I'm also growing very tired of people telling me what to do. What happened to 'my body, my choice'?

"This is my body, it's my decision, Liam, I'm not having the surgery until after..."

"After what?"

I sigh, "When I have a baby, then I'll have the operation."

He laughs, "No clinic will touch you."

"There are other ways to get pregnant, Liam," I blurt out, which I immediately regret.

He turns red, and I've never been afraid of him, but I've never seen him like this, "If you think I'm going to let you fuck someone else to get pregnant, so you can commit suicide, you've lost your goddamned mind."

"I'm sorry but I'm not yours anymore."

"Oh, the fuck you aren't, baby girl. Any man who touches what's mine, will fucking die. I'm a doctor. I know how to kill a man and make it look like a fucking heart attack."

He pushes me back and climbs on top of me, holding me down by my throat, "Have you already let another man touch what's mine?"

"No," I whisper.

"Good girl."

He kisses me harder this time while his hands travel frantically all over my body. I should push him away, but I can't. Every touch is like heaven. When he growls into my mouth, my pussy pulses with need.

"Do you have lube?"

"In the drawer," I squeak, "But why?"

"I'm taking what's mine, baby girl. Do you have a problem with that?"

I shake my head. But lube, we've never used lube. That can only mean one thing.

He gets the lube and yanks my pants and panties off me. Taking his pants off, I stare at his cock, my God, it's fucking beautiful, thick, swollen a deep vein running down the underside.

"Did you miss me, baby girl?"

I bite my lip and nod.

He gets between my legs as he applies the lube to himself by stroking his length. "I'm not going to be gentle with you. I fucking hope it hurts like hell."

I swallow hard.

Lifting my ass with both hands, he thrusts into my ass, and I cry out, it does hurt.

He shoots me a warning glare, "Do you want your mother to hear you cry?" Pounding into my ass, he says, "Does it hurt, baby girl?" His voice is husky and sexy as hell.

"Yes," I answer.

"I bet it doesn't hurt nearly as bad as what you're doing to me. Choosing to die instead of living a life with me."

Sobs wrack my body, the pain is too much, not the physical but the emotional. I do what I have never done before, "MERCY MERCY MERCY!"

"Please stop," I sob.

He stops, pulls out of me, and puts his pants back on. He climbs onto the bed with me and pulls me into his arms.

"I'm sorry. Fuck, I'm sorry."

I wrap my arms around him. I sob into his chest. He strokes my hair, "Baby girl, I'm sorry."

"It wasn't the physical pain, Liam," I pull my arms tighter around him.

He pulls back to look at me, "Baby girl, I'm begging you, please have the surgery. We'll adopt as many babies as you want."

"Liam, I can't."

Tears roll down his cheeks, "Please. I need you. The last month has been fucking hell. Don't sentence me to a life without you, baby, please. I'll give you anything."

I reach up and wipe his tears, "I want a baby, Liam."

"We'll adopt one. No, we'll adopt two. A baby and Ivy."

I can't contain my shock, "Liam, you would do that?"

He shakes his head, tears forming in his eyes, "When are you going to learn, baby girl? I would do anything for you. Your happiness is mine. If you want children, I want to give them to you, but I won't lose you in the process. You are playing a dangerous game. Have the fucking surgery, Mercy. Have the surgery, marry me, raise our children with me, live a life with me. Don't choose the idea of a baby over me. I need you."

I nod.

"What does that mean?"

"I'll have the surgery."

More tears roll down his cheeks as he pulls me into his arms, "Thank you. God, fucking thank you."

"I'd like to have it at home."

He kisses my forehead, "Good girl. Such a fucking good girl, now call your doctor and schedule it."

I grab my phone and call Dr. Shein's office to schedule my surgery. After I hang up, he stares at me expectantly.

"In two days."

"Pack whatever you need, baby. We are going home, where I can fuck my girl senseless before I can't for four to six weeks. "He pulls me off the bed and into his arms, tight against his chest. He lets out a deep breath, "Thank you." I can physically feel his relief running through his body as he relaxes against me.

He kisses me on the forehead and releases me. I start throwing things in a bag but then find myself giggling.

He wipes a tear from his cheek, "What are you laughing about?"

"Oh, not much, doctor. I'm just wondering if you can last four weeks without sex let alone six weeks."

With an amused expression, he says, "Oh it's you, I feel bad for baby. Maybe not right away, but I know you'll want to suck my cock."

He walks over to me and rubs my bottom lip, "Isn't that right, baby girl? Do you love sucking Daddy's dick? Are you thinking about it now...hitting the back of your throat, do you love tasting my cum on your tongue?"

"Yes," I say in a whisper, he makes me breathless with just his words.

"Such a good girl," he kisses my forehead, "Let's go tell your mom."

He takes my bag from me as we walk downstairs.

"Dad," I say with a shaky voice.

"I'm going back to have the surgery."

My mom cries out in relief.

My dad walks up to Liam, and my heart pounds.

He extends his hand to him and says, "Thank you, I owe you. Should you ever need a favor remember, I am in your debt."

Thirty-Four

LIAM

I HOLD her hand or leg the entire drive home from New York. I'm so happy to have my girl back where she belongs, with me.

"I need to go to the hospital first, to see Ivy."

I groan, "You're killing me. I need to be buried in that beautiful pussy of yours."

She takes my hand and puts it between her legs outside her panties.

"Fuck, you're so wet, baby girl."

A moan slips out of her sweet lips, "I do have to ask you something before I can let you have this pussy."

I glance at her before turning my eyes back to the road.

"Did you fuck that nurse I saw you with?"

I move my hand back to her leg, "Is that what you think?"

She crosses her arms around her chest, "Yeah it is."

I chuckle, "You clearly have no idea how strong your hold is on me."

"The fact that you aren't even answering my question tells me that you did fuck her."

Alright, now I'm getting annoyed with her accusations.

"Mercy. Let me make this abundantly clear for you. I did not fuck that nurse or anyone else. The last cunt I was in, was yours. And before you ask, no I did not do anything else with any other woman either."

"I'm sorry, I'm on edge. I shouldn't take it out on you."

I lock my fingers with hers, "It's okay, baby."

We drive to the hospital first so that she can see Ivy. When we walk into Ivy's room, I stand back and watch, taking in the bond that these two people share. Life that Ivy hasn't had in her since Mercy has been gone, comes rushing back to her. Happy is not a strong enough word to describe how she looks, when Mercy rushes over to her. She doesn't even greet me as she normally would. They're in a little bubble, just the two of them. I count myself a lucky man, to see this.

"Ivy, I need to talk to you," Mercy says as she sits in the chair beside her bed.

She continues, "It's time for another grown up conversation, it might be upsetting but I'll answer every question you have."

Ivy nods, "Okay."

"I am having surgery the day after tomorrow."

"Why?" Ivy asks with a shaky voice.

Mercy responds, "I have a little bit of cancer."

Obviously, she's trying to cushion the blow because there's no such thing as a little bit of cancer. You either have cancer, or you don't.

A tear runs down Ivy's cheek, and Mercy shakes her head.

"It's not like yours, sweet girl. They'll do the surgery and then it'll be gone."

"No chemo?" She appears shocked as if she didn't realize you could have cancer and not go through chemo. Honestly, I'm sure this is news to her.

Mercy smiles, "No chemo."

Ivy relaxes.

"It's going to be a little while before I can come see you though, I have to heal from the surgery before I can come back."

Ivy glances at me, then to her tablet, and back to me before her gaze settles back to Mercy.

Mercy giggles, "Yes, you can still call me."

Damn, all of a sudden, it hits me, Ivy could have reached her when I had no clue where she was. Of course, she wouldn't leave without a word to Ivy.

When Mercy is ready to go, she hugs Ivy quickly and walks over to me.

I hate that the one thing Mercy wants most is being taken from her, and I can't give it to her. She wants to be a mother, and she wants to carry the babies. I want to give her everything she desires, but I can't do anything about this. It's completely out of my control.

I need to remember she's going through a lot emotionally. This will be a challenge, and I don't know if she's even been told what it all means. As we get out to the car, I am afraid to ask the burning question in my mind, but I have to. I need to make sure my girl isn't blindsided.

"Baby, did your doctor tell you what to expect?"

"Yeah, of course," she shrugs, "I'll go home somewhere between one and four days and recover for four to six weeks."

"Did she mention menopause?"

"No," she responds as she pulls her hand away and stares out the window.

I grip the steering wheel as I turn off the highway. I choose to leave her alone for a few minutes. This is a lot for such a young woman to process, and I know she's struggling. It's not going to get easier for a while.

She doesn't speak another word the rest of the drive. When we finally get back to my house, she doesn't wait for me to open her door. She gets out, walks up to the door, enters the code, and goes inside. I take a deep breath and grab her bag from the back of the car. I need to be here for her, but I feel like I'm preparing to walk into a lion's den. When I walk in, she's nowhere in sight. I take my wallet and keys and set them on the coffee table. She's not in the living room, the kitchen, I walk to the bedroom, and she's not there either. What the hell? She couldn't have simply disappeared. I head down the other hall that leads to the guest bedrooms. The sobs echo from outside the door of the bedroom she stayed in when she was here with Nash.

I open the door and walk in slowly, and I'm honestly terrified right now. Will giving her this information make her change her mind about the surgery?

She's on the floor between the bed and end table, knees are drawn to her chest, arms draped over her legs, she looks so small and broken like this.

I sit on the floor in front of her, and without touching her, I just stare at her. I'm trying to give her time, but I can't let this go on all night.

"Baby girl, tell me what you need right now."

"I hate you."

Her words fucking sting, even though I know, it's a complete lie.

"Why?"

"If it weren't for you, I wouldn't even know I had cancer. I only went to the doctor to get more birth control, so I could keep having sex with you without getting pregnant and now I'll never get pregnant because you're making me have the surgery."

I rub my hands over my face to conceal the laughter that's threatening to bubble up. My beautiful girl is being ridiculous.

"Should I also be credited with saving your life then?"

"I hate you."

Shaking my head, I say, "Come here, baby girl."

"No," she looks down at her knees.

"It wasn't a request. Get over here, now."

She lets go of her knees, crawls over to me, and I pull her into my arms.

"Good girl," I kiss her on the forehead.

"You're going to break up with me."

I sigh, "Why would you even think that? What's going on in that beautiful head of yours?"

"The sex is going to be horrible with me after the surgery, Liam. You love how wet I am for you, all the time, and I'll be dry as a fucking bone."

She's not wrong, and I will miss it. But I won't leave her, I will never leave her.

"Baby girl, I love having sex with you. But there is more to us than sex. I will never leave you. I'll buy a fucking lubricant company, if I have to."

Laying her head against my chest, she shivers with the after-effects of her sobs, "What else will happen? I don't know much about menopause."

"You're going to be emotional for a while, but we're going to find you the very best doctor to help you manage your hormones. There's a doctor I met at a conference that specializes in bio-identical hormones which are closer to the hormones you have now than the synthetic garbage. I'll talk to him."

"What else?" she asks, wrapping her arms around me.

"Hot flashes, mood swings, insomnia, fatigue, night sweats. That's all I can think of, but I'm not a gynecologist, baby."

"I know it might sound stupid to you, but I'm really scared."

I cup her face with my hands and pull her head back to see into her eyes, "Baby girl, no. I don't think you're stupid. You are entitled to feel scared or any other emotion."

She closes her eyes and then opens them again, "I don't hate you," she whispers.

I can't stop laughing, "Oh baby girl, I know that." Pulling back from her slightly, I say, "Why don't you go get a glass of wine while I take a shower."

She looks at me with her splotchy red face, "I need to wash my face if that's okay."

Kissing her on the top of her head, I say, "Of course, let's go."

We stand up, and I squeeze her ass, "Even with tears on your cheeks, you're still the most beautiful woman I've ever seen."

That gets me a bright smile that warms me from the inside out. I love her smile.

She goes into the bathroom to clean her tear-stained face, and I walk into the kitchen to pour my girl a glass of wine. I leave it on the table in the living room for her.

I nearly collide with her as she comes out of the bathroom, I grab onto her waist, "Go drink your wine, it's in the living room. I'll be out in a few minutes."

She pulls my shirt out of my pants and runs her fingers up my chest, inside my shirt, "Don't take long, doctor. I need you."

Running my hands through her hair, my lips turn into a slight smile, "While I shower, think about what you want. Whatever it is, it's yours."

Biting her lip, she turns and walks away.

After I finish my quick shower, I dry off and pull on a pair of boxer shorts. I walk out to the living room and am stopped in my tracks.

She's naked and on her knees, legs parted, gazing at me through hooded eyes.

"Baby, what are you doing?"

Her lips turn into a half smile, "Submitting to you, sir. Good girls get rewarded."

If my cock could get any harder than it is right now, it'd be a fucking miracle. "Did you decide what you wanted?"

She bites her lip and says, "I want you to use me for your pleasure, sir. Dominate me. I don't care if I come, I want you to lose yourself in me."

This girl is a fucking wet dream. I can't believe that she's mine. This dirty girl belongs to me.

"Go in the bedroom, get on the bed, on your back. I'll be right there."

She wants me to dominate her, and I am more than up to the challenge. I get undressed in the living room, leaving my boxers on the couch. My dick is hard as a rock, and I walk into the bedroom with the thoughts of what I'm going to do to her. But when I see her lying there, all the air escapes from my lungs. I've never seen such a stunning woman as the one on my bed, spread out for me. I grab my leather straps from the closet and turn to her.

Thirty-Five

LIAM

"ARE YOU SURE YOU WANT THIS?"

She's already breathing heavily as she answers, "Yes, Daddy. I'm sure."

"What's your safe word?"

Giggling, she responds, "Mercy."

"Good girl. I'm going to do what I've wanted to do since I found you naked in my bathroom. But if you need me to stop, you'll need to use your safe word. Do you understand?"

"Yes, sir," she squeaks.

I grab the restraints out of the closet I bought just for her months ago.

Walking over to the head of the bed, I take her wrist and close the leather strap around before connecting the hook to the headboard of my bed. Moving to the other side, I do the same with the other wrist. I stare at her before fastening the ones for her feet, thinking. A grin spreads across my face as I put the last two restraints back in the closet and grab the spreader bar.

"Oh my God, what's that?"

I attach her ankles to the cuffs and adjust the rod, winking at her,

"It's a spreader bar, baby girl. It's going to keep you wide open to me. You will not be able to close your legs."

Standing back a few feet, I admire how she looks like this, "You will be at my...mercy. Your pussy will be mine, and there's nothing you can do about it, unless of course, you use your safe word."

When she swallows hard as she processes my words, it makes me fucking crazy. The way her throat moves, makes me want to fuck that gorgeous mouth.

Sliding my hands under her back, I move her up slightly. I climb between her legs and stare at the best pussy I've ever seen, wet, pink and perfect, less than an inch from my face. Already she tries to squirm, "I haven't even touched you yet."

"Daddy, please."

I slide two fingers up her slit, "Look how perfect you are for Daddy. Such a fucking good girl, so responsive."

Placing two fingers on each side of her clit, I pull up, and she yelps.

Ghosting my lips over her little nub, "Is this what you want baby? Do you want me to kiss your pretty pussy?"

She cries out, "YES! DADDY!"

I flatten my tongue and lick up her slit and then circle her bundle of nerves while watching her face as she moans in pleasure. I take her clit between my lips and suck as I thrust two fingers inside her, and she screams for me. Her back arches, as she clenches down on my fingers. But I don't stop, and I finger fuck her harder as I flick her clit fast with the tip of my tongue.

"Daddy! No, stop."

I glance up at her as she writhes beneath my mouth.

"You have a safe word," I say before I bite her clit. She screams in pleasure, "DADDY!"

She pulls on the wrist restraints as she crumbles from another orgasm.

I undo her wrist restraints, "I'm not removing the spreader bar."

Placing my hands under her ass I pull her to the edge of the bed as I shake my head.

"What," she asks.

"You're so fucking perfect. Sometimes I can't believe that you're mine."

Her pussy is drenched, so I slide in with ease. I love this spreader bar. Her pussy bared to me is my new favorite thing. I grab the bar spreading her even more, and fuck her hard, while she runs her nails down my chest.

I'm fucking her harder than I ever have. Her tits bounce all over the place as she lets out a guttural scream.

She stares at the door, shock in her expression as she says, "Liam, stop."

It's not her safe word but I stop, pull out of her, and turn to see my son standing in the doorway. FUCK! I cover her with the blanket, grab a pair of boxers from my drawer, and put them on.

Nash stands there, glowering at her.

"This is why you don't want to fuck me? Because you're fucking my dad? You fucking whore!"

He charges at her, and she flinches. I grab his arm he has cocked, ready to hit her.

Motioning to the spreader bar, he says, "This is how you like to be treated? You let him do this shit to you?"

I shove him against the wall, "That's awfully rich coming from the man that beat the hell out of her."

"Why dad?" he says with a shaky voice, "Why her? How could you do this to me? Of all the pussy in the world, you had to fuck her?"

His words gut me, and I can't even look at him. I back away from him but continue to stand between him and Mercy. I won't let him hurt her.

"You disgust me!" He turns and walks out of the room.

"Are you okay, baby?"

She nods but remains quiet.

"I'm going to go talk to him, I'll be back. Stay here. Your hands are free, you can take the cuffs off your ankles."

Stepping out of the bedroom, I walk down the hallway to the living room, but he's not there. I look all over and can't find him then I see my wallet, open on the table. "FUCK!"

I pick it up, and my credit cards and cash are gone. My own fucking son robbed me.

"Liam?"

"Come on out, baby girl, he's gone."

I turn to her, and she's shaking like a leaf. Yet she looks beautiful in the white silk bathrobe she put on.

Throwing my wallet down, I walk over to her, and hold her tight against me, "It's okay, baby. I've got you. I've always got you."

She put her arms around me, "Now he really wants to kill me."

"I won't let him."

Her arms hold onto me so tightly, as if she's hanging on for dear life, "He just left?"

"Pretty much. After he robbed me."

She glances up at me, "He what?"

"He stole my credit cards and cash."

"Liam, you have to call your credit card companies now before he uses them."

"I know," I say as I grab my phone from my pants pocket.

I spend the next hour calling all the companies and my bank. The police came out and took a statement. I told them I didn't want to press charges. I mean, he's my fucking son. How do you have your own son thrown in jail? Besides, would he have done it had he not found Mercy and me together? I sigh, yeah, he probably would've. The Nash he is today would have. The kid I raised could always be trusted. But now, I've cut him off financially, and this drug addiction is strong, it's stronger than my love for him.

I sit on the couch, feeling devastated about how this all went down. Mercy sits beside me and pulls me down so my head is on her lap. She runs her fingers through my hair and calms me instantly.

Nobody has ever loved me the way she does. It's in every touch, every kiss, and every look. Everything she does, is done with love.

"I have a pre-op appointment tomorrow. I know you have work; I'm just telling you."

I kiss her leg, "I'll be working from home until you're able to take care of yourself."

"Liam, you can't do that."

"I can do anything I want to."

She sighs, "I can try to get my apartment back and stay there. I'll be fine."

"You must be out of your sexy mind if you think I'm leaving you alone."

Lifting my head, I move her robe to the side and kiss the inside of each thigh. The way she moans when she feels my lips, makes me crazy. I get off the couch and I kneel in front of her.

"Show me your pussy, baby girl, let me see it."

She spreads her legs, and I stare at her with desire.

"Open your robe."

Biting her lip, she stares down at me as she unties her robe and pushes it open.

I intake a sharp breath, "You're so beautiful. Every fucking inch of you is exquisite."

Wrapping my arms under her thighs, I pull her toward me, "I'm going to taste this beautiful cunt."

She pulls my face to the apex of her thighs and bucks her hips into me.

I pull away, "Let's do this in the bedroom."

She giggles as I stand and pick her up. I throw her over my shoulder, walk to the bedroom, while she squirms, and I spank her ass. I set her down and strip naked, as she stares at me with a heated gaze.

I lay down on the bed, "Take your robe off and ride my face, baby girl."

Taking her robe off, she appears nervous. She admits, "I've never done that."

I smile, "Good girl."

Thirty-Six

Mercy

I climb onto the bed and move up to his face placing a leg on each side of his head.

"Fuck you smell so good, baby girl. Hold onto the headboard. Daddy is going to eat your pussy so good; I don't want you to fall."

Wrapping my hands on the frame, I lower down on his face. He inhales deeply and it's so damn dirty, but it turns me on at the same time. His hands slide up my thighs and squeeze my ass, and he growls as he plunges his tongue inside me. I rock my hips back and forth as he moves his tongue around. Pulling his tongue out, he says, "Fucking delicious."

He slides his tongue up my slit and circles my clit before sucking it between his lips. Reaching behind me, he thrusts three fingers inside me, and I cry out in pleasure. When he moans, it sends me into a powerful orgasm crashing down on me in waves.

"DADDY!"

He flicks my clit with his tongue fast, while his hands slide up the front of my body until he reaches my tits, and cups them before pinching my nipples.

Sliding his hands down my sides, he grabs my hips and lifts me off him.

"Ride my dick, baby. I need to be inside you."

I climb off the bed, walk around the foot, and spread his legs as I lick my lips. I crawl between his legs and stare into his eyes.

Running my fingers up his cock, it jerks when I take it in my hand. I lick the underside of his length before I lower my mouth on him.

"Jesus...Mercy...Fuck."

He slides his hands into my hair, moves my head up and down, while he moans, "Take me baby, you make Daddy so proud."

Lifting his head, he watches his cock appear and disappear into my throat. He groans and all of a sudden pulls me off him.

"I need to be inside you. I don't want to come in your mouth tonight."

I put my knees on both sides of him and rub his dick between my folds.

"You want this pussy right here?"

He growls, "Yes. You're killing me, baby girl."

I line him up with my entrance and sink onto him.

"Finally," he groans.

I move up and down slowly, as I run my fingers down his chest.

"Oh, Dr. Lexington, I knew I would get you. I knew you'd love this fucking pussy. I knew you'd get addicted to it. You're addicted to it now, aren't you?"

He flips us over, grabs my wrists with one hand, and pins them above my head.

"Am I addicted to this pussy?" His thrusts are hard and punishing.

"You're damn right I am. It's mine now, you're mine. I think I knew if I fucked you, I'd never get you out of my system. Now you'll be my wife, so I'll get to fuck this beautiful pussy forever."

He lets go of my wrists, pins my legs back beside my head, and fucks me even harder, faster.

"Daddy, I'm going to come!" I dig my nails into his shoulders.

Reaching up, he presses his hand against my throat, "Come for me, my fucking dirty slut."

He removes his hand, my back arches, and I come undone, screaming for him. He slows for a moment before returning to his hard thrusts, "Fuck that's the sexiest thing in the world, watching my beautiful girl come for me."

I run my hands from his shoulders to his chest.

"Mercy...God...baby girl." He grunts as his muscles tighten; he shoots his cum in my pussy.

Once he's soft and slips out, he lays beside me.

His breathing is heavy, and it's sexy, so sexy.

"Fuck, that was amazing."

I roll over to him and press my face into his neck, "I love you."

"Marry me, tomorrow."

"What?"

"I'm so in love with you. I want you to be my wife."

"Liam, are you afraid I'm going to die?"

He pulls me closer to him, "No baby girl, you're going to be just fine."

I run my fingers through his hair, "Then there's no rush. I want a wedding, it doesn't have to be big, but I do want one."

"What my girl wants, my girl gets," he says.

"Thank you."

We spent the rest of the night having so much sex that I think he was trying to make up for all the sex he was about to miss out on. I've heard that men in their forties have a slower libido, but I'm certainly not seeing any signs of Liam slowing down. That is not a complaint, and I love that he wants me all the time.

* * *

Liam

Surgery Day...

I told her that I wasn't worried about her dying. As a physician, we tell our patients that while there are risks, they are minimal and rarely happen. That's the truth, but it's different when it's someone we love. My head knows she'll be fine, but my heart is in meltdown mode. What if she has trouble with the anesthesia? What if they fuck up and nic something they shouldn't? What if she develops an infection?

I sit beside her, holding her hand, pretending to be calm. She knows every single one of my tells, and I hold her hand in both of my hands, so she can't see the stress. My girl knows me very well.

"So, if something happens-"

"No. Stop it. We aren't having this conversation."

She squeezes my hand, "Please don't make me do this without telling you what I need to tell you. Liam, please."

A tear falls from her eyes, and it kills me.

"Fine. Nothing is going to happen but tell me."

She takes a deep breath, "If something happens, I'd like you to adopt Ivy, but if you don't want to, I understand."

I nod, "I'll adopt her, if they let me."

Continuing, she says, "I want you to be happy, Liam. You have to find someone to share your life with. If I'm gone, I want you to move on. Promise me, baby."

The emotion bubbles over, "Why are you doing this to me? You can't ask me to promise something like that."

"I am asking, Liam."

Clenching my jaw, I spit out, "You're asking too fucking much of me, Mercy. No. If I were to lose you, I'd live my life for Ivy. I will never love again; I don't want to. I will not fucking promise you something so preposterous, so you better get this death shit out of your head. God, you piss me off."

Standing, I take her face in my hands, "I fucking love you. And I do not love easily, so you do not get to talk like I'm going to lose you. I think I would die. I can't live without you, baby girl. So please stop. Please," I plead with her.

She puts her arm without the IV around me, "I'm sorry. I won't say anymore. I love you, Liam."

"I love you too Mercy, so goddamn much," I kiss her. My worst fear is this is our last kiss ever.

A clearing of a throat interrupts us, and I turn to see a Nurse standing there.

"We're ready."

I turn back to Mercy one last time, "Positive thoughts only. I mean it, it's important."

She nods, "I love you, Liam," she cries as they start to wheel her away.

"I love you too, baby girl. I'll see you soon."

Before they've even started the surgery, I'm a nervous wreck. With her death talk, this girl has gotten so deep into my head. And all I can think about is how I've lost her in my pursuit to keep her.

It's a routine surgery, done every day, and the fatality rate is low. It's a ninety percent five-year survival rate. There is nothing to be worried about.

I know this, but that ten percent is what has me concerned. That and I have always believed the mind and body are closely linked. It's why I tell all my patients' parent's they have to stay positive. Personally, I think if someone goes into surgery, sure that they will die, that the chances are far higher they will. I know a patient's highest risk is not during surgery, but after they go home. Still, I can't get the what ifs out of my head. My mind races right along with my heart that nearly pounds out of my chest. I can't lose her.

Thirty-Seven

LIAM

I HAVE BEEN PACING in the surgical waiting room for what feels like hours, even though I know it hasn't been that long. A hand on my shoulder stops me from pacing again. I turn to see Xander, and he points to a chair, "Sit."

"I'm fine."

He chuckles, "I don't think you are. Regardless, you're making these other people nervous."

I sigh and sit down, and he sits in the chair beside me.

"Liam, she's going to be fine. It's-"

"Routine surgery, I know. She went into surgery, thinking she was going to die. You know my thoughts on that, Xander. Can you fucking believe that she wanted me to promise I'd find someone else if she dies?"

He laughs, "You do realize that most people worry they will die before going into surgery? I've never agreed with you on this. And your girl was just being emotional. It's normal."

"I can't live without her," I say under my breath.

"Jesus Liam, who the fuck are you?"

I simply shrug.

"If something happened to her you would go on without her. You wouldn't want to, but you would, the same as she would, if something happened to you."

He shakes his head, "I still can't believe she turned you into this big sap."

"Shut up, asshole."

Putting his hand on my shoulder, "There he is."

"Seriously, she's going to be okay."

I sigh, "She wants to adopt one of my patients."

He chuckles, "That sounds like Mercy."

"I sometimes forget that you know her."

"Yeah, I know her well. She did work for me. I had to dock her pay more than once for sneaking free dessert to kids when she worked the day shift." He laughs, "I'm honestly surprised she never caught your eye before that night."

I lean forward, resting my elbows on my knees, "I don't remember ever seeing her in the bar before that night. Fuck, she took my breath away."

"When she's better, Isabella wants you to bring her over to the house for dinner."

I smile, "She'd like that. Have they met?"

"Briefly."

"Take a deep breath, Liam."

I do, but it doesn't help.

"Do you want me to call and get an update? I have privileges here, so I'll be more likely to get information."

I nod, "Please."

"I'll be back," he gets up and walks away.

This is stupid. I know she's going to be fine. This girl has me going crazy, that's what it is. Have I gotten that soft? I never thought I had, but Xander has seen a change in me.

He comes back, "She's fine, stable. They aren't done with the surgery but she's okay."

I nod, "Thanks. Hey, can I ask you something?"

"Sure," he sits, "Ask away."

"Do you really think I've changed?"

"Yes, you've changed."

I rub my jaw, "I see."

"Liam, man it's not a bad thing. Fuck, you were so closed off before her. You're happy now. Do you think I'm not soft and mushy with Isabella? Of course, I am, she's the only one I'm like that with."

"I asked her to marry me."

"Well, holy shit. Doc Delicious getting married. The nurses will be distraught."

I can't help but laugh, "You enjoy that nickname a little too much."

"Dr. Lexington?"

I stand when Mercy's doctor is in front of me, "Yes."

"Everything went fine, she's in recovery now. Would you like to see her?"

"He can't spend five minutes without that woman, yes he wants to see her," Xander blurts out.

She smiles, "I don't blame you; Mercy is one of my favorite patients when she isn't being impossibly stubborn. I'll have a nurse come out for you in a few minutes."

I nod, "Thank you, Dr. Shein."

"Are you gonna make it now, jackass?"

I laugh, "Yeah."

He pats my shoulder, "Good, cause I fucking hate hospitals. I'm out. But call me if you need anything."

"You're a doctor, how can you hate hospitals?"

He shrugs and walks away.

The nurse comes in a few minutes later, "Dr. Lexington, this way."

I follow her to the recovery room and put on the PPE gear after she instructs me to.

"She's very emotional just so you know."

"Hormones?"

"Oh, it could be that or it could be the anesthesia, and it could simply be the gravity of it all. It's not easy for such a young woman to go through this and have her body change so much in a few short hours."

I nod, "Okay, thank you."

She points, "First bed on the right."

Taking a deep breath, I walk over to her bed, she's asleep. I shake my head, she just had surgery, and she's still so beautiful.

I kiss her on top of her head, and she opens her eyes.

"I'm sorry, I didn't mean to wake you."

Tears fall down her face, "I will never carry your children," she has a Kleenex clutched in her fist.

"I know, baby, but it's going to be okay."

Kissing her cheek, she cries harder.

"Mercy, stop, you're going to make the pain worse."

"I bet the nurse could give you children, you should go be with her."

Emotional doesn't begin to describe this fucking nonsense.

"I love you. If we adopt children, it will be for you. I can live with or without children. So stop. I only want to be with you." Then I kiss her lips softly and she softens.

"I'm sorry."

"How are you feeling physically?" I ask while I rub her arm.

She sighs, "Fine. They have me on something."

"Probably Percocet. Go to sleep, baby girl. I'll be right here. You need rest."

Closing her eyes, she drifts off to sleep quickly. It's amazing, she can listen. I sit on the chair beside her bed and watch her, grateful that she's okay but dreading the next few months. It's not going to be easy.

The nurse informs me that they're ready to move her to a room. So, I follow behind as the nurse wheels her bed around.

On route, Mercy wakes up, and she yells, "Liam!"

I go to her side and walk next to the bed while holding her hand, "I'm right here."

We get into the room, and the nurse gets her situated and puts the call button where she can reach it, and leaves. I pull the chair that's in here closer to the bed and sit beside her.

Her eyes find mine, and there's profound sadness behind her hazel orbs.

"I thought you left."

My lips curve into a small smile, "Not a chance, baby, not a chance."

Taking her hand in mine, I kiss every finger, and she smiles down at me.

"I want to go home."

The fact that she considers my home, her home, fills me with joy, "Soon, baby."

"Liam, I need to tell you something."

I squeeze her hand, "Okay, baby girl. Tell me."

"When I was in New York, all I could think about was having a baby. I was pretty sure I'd never have the surgery. But I went to a fertility clinic and had some eggs frozen. We weren't together, so I didn't talk to you about it beforehand."

I smile, "Good girl, I'm glad. That means that we can still have a child together."

"We need to give Ivy a sibling."

"Can we wait until you recover a little bit before starting that process? I'm thinking I'll have my lawyer come to the house in a week."

She smiles brightly, "That sounds perfect."

"My doctor friend I told you about, is going to come see you tomorrow morning. The sooner we get your hormone levels right the sooner you'll feel like yourself."

A serious expression crosses her face, stroking her fingers down my wrist to my knuckles, "I think I might die if you don't kiss me right now."

Fuck, how can she be so sexy in a hospital bed?

Arching an eyebrow, I say, "Well, I guess I better kiss you then. I'm a doctor, I need to save lives," I lean forward and press my lips to hers. I had planned a short peck on the lips, but she grabs my head, holding me in place as she slid her tongue into my mouth, deepening our kiss. Moving her hand from my head to the side of my face, she moans, "Doctor, I love your lips. Your mouth is heaven."

"You're not going to make the next month easy for me, are you?"

She giggles, "Do I ever make anything easy?"

"On very rare occasions."

Thirty-Eight

MERCY

I'M RELIEVED to finally be home. I was only in the hospital for a few days, but it felt like forever. Poor Ivy, being in the hospital for months must be torturous, especially for a young child. I started on the bio-identical hormones while I was in the hospital. I was told they would take a few weeks before I start feeling better, but it'll be months before they take full effect. My emotions have been up and down like a damn roller coaster. While I expected Liam to lose it with me, he's managed to stay calm and help me through every mood swing. He reminds me every day how much he loves me. He has waited on me hand and foot, always taking care of me.

I'm drinking my coffee at the kitchen table while he makes breakfast in nothing but his boxer shorts. His back is to me as he tends to the bacon. How can a back be so sexy? His back is muscular, and my eyes travel down all of the indentations leading down to his ass. He turns to me, holding two plates, and brings them to the table.

"What are you thinking about, baby girl?"

I bite my lip before responding, "You."

"Eat your breakfast. The lawyer will be here soon."

I groan, "I'd rather suck your cock."

He intakes a sharp breath, "Eat your breakfast."

As he runs a hand through his hair.

I ask, "You're thinking about it, aren't you?"

"About what?"

"My lips around your cock, you pulling my hair, while you fuck your way into my throat."

I put a bite of pancake into my mouth, waiting for a response. After several minutes he replies, "Keep pushing, baby girl, keep it up and I'm going to fuck your dirty little mouth so hard, and I won't stop or pull back when you start to gag. I'll just let you fucking choke on my cock."

A moan escapes from my lips, "Yes, Daddy."

He gets up and sets his plate on the counter, "I'm going to take a shower. Eat your breakfast."

Does he think I don't know what he's going to do?

I wait until I hear the shower running to get out of my seat. Once I do, I walk quietly into the bathroom. As always, the door is open. I sneak in, out of his sight, I can't see his face, but I enjoy the side view. I bite my lip to suppress the moan when he takes his cock into his hand and strokes it slowly.

His back falls against the wall as he moves his hand faster, giving me a glimpse of his face. My gaze travels up and down every inch of his body. This man's body is perfect, and my eyes snap back to his dick as his breathing hastens. When his muscles tighten, I know he's close. As he explodes in his hand, my name falls from his lips like a prayer. After he washes up, he steps out of the shower and stares at me, "What are you doing in here?"

I dart my tongue out and lick my lips, "Watching my favorite show."

He grabs a towel and wraps it around his waist. As I walk closer to him, I lean forward and lick the water droplets from his chest.

"No penetration doesn't mean we can't do anything, doctor."

He pulls my hair, yanking my head back as he drags his lips up my neck, "Baby girl, you are making me fucking crazy here. I'm trying to be a good man and let you recover. But I'm human. If you don't stop this, I'm going to snap."

I kneel in front of him, gaze up at him, waiting for him to say something.

"You're hard for me so soon after coming, doctor. It doesn't seem like you're satisfied to me."

I lick the underside of his cock, and he moans, as he grabs the side of the bathroom counter.

When my tongue circles the head, he groans, and it makes my clit throb with need. I run my hands up the inside of his thighs and then slam my mouth onto his dick, taking his full length in my throat all at once.

"Jesus...Mercy...Fuck, baby girl."

He slides his hands in my hair and pulls my head on and off his cock so fast, my eyes water.

"Yes, baby, take it. Fuck, you're so good."

I grip his ass with my hands as I moan, and he comes undone, thrusting into my throat so fast, that I see stars.

"YES! I'm going to come down your pretty little throat. And you're going to swallow it all because you're such a good girl." He holds my head, pressing my face to his pelvis, as he releases into my mouth. Pulling me up by my arms, he stands me on my feet.

"I forgot how good your mouth feels," he kisses me softly.

"But now you need to get dressed, because Cyrus will be here any minute."

Turning to leave, he grabs my arm and yanks me back to him, holding me tight, "In case I haven't told you enough lately, I love you."

Gazing up into his eyes, I respond, "I love you too. And you have told me, but it never gets old."

He lets go of my arm, and I get dressed. He quickly pulls on his boxers, jeans, and a tight black t-shirt.

The doorbell rings, Liam goes to answer it, and I meet him in the living room a few minutes later.

"Cyrus, this is Mercy. Mercy, Cyrus."

I shake his hand and smile politely, "Nice to meet you."

Sitting beside Liam, he rests his hand on my leg.

"You want to adopt, Ivy?"

I nod, "Yes, very much."

"How much longer will she be in the hospital?"

I look at Liam. That's a question only he can answer.

214

"We will do another pet scan in two weeks. Until then, it's just a guess."

"Alright. We will need to schedule a home study. Are you planning on adopting her before you get married?" Cyrus asks.

"I don't want her to go to a foster home."

"What if you were the foster home? And filed for adoption as soon as you get married?"

The thought of Ivy not being in the hospital, and instead here with us, has me overcome with emotion.

I nod, "That would be perfect."

"I'll schedule the home study today. You should have a room set up for her before they come out."

Liam states, "I'll take care of it today," he glances at me, "Princesses."

She's going to love it. That girl loves princesses more than she loves anything in this world.

"I'll call you to let you know when it's scheduled."

He stands and shakes Liam's hand, and he smiles at me and leaves.

"Do you think you can manage being alone for just a little while today? I'll pick up some bedding for Ivy?"

I smile, "Yes. Or I could go with you?"

He shakes his head, "No. Not yet. You need to stay home and rest."

I sigh, "Yes, Daddy."

"Good girl, God, I love you so much."

"Hurry back, I'll miss you."

Grinning at me, he says, "I'll miss you too, dirty girl."

He gets up and leaves, and I watch him go, and my heart is full of promise for the future. I go to the kitchen and clean up the breakfast dishes. I hear the door open, and spin around thinking he must've forgotten something.

My mouth falls open as my heart races, "Nash."

"I thought he'd never leave," he says with an evil expression, "Now, you're mine."

Thirty-Nine

LIAM

I'M EXCITED as I pull into the driveway with all the princess shit. Mercy will love it, which is my favorite thing in the world, making my girl happy. I glance toward my front door, and it's wide open. What the hell have I told her about that? The door stays closed and locked. She's not supposed to open it, even if she's sure it's me. We will have words about this, that is for sure. I don't know if Nash will ever return, but I don't want to take the risk. Not when it comes to her. I need to have the code on the door changed.

I walk in, "Mercy, we talked about this," but I stop in my tracks when I realize my house has been trashed and she's not here.

The kitchen table is turned over, and there's broken glass everywhere. When I see blood on the wall, and the floor, bile gnaws in my stomach.

No. Not my Mercy. Please God, no.

Even though I know she's not here, I search everywhere for her, and it only confirms my suspicions, she's not here, she's gone.

Someone broke into my house and stole my entire fucking world. Where are you, baby? I called the police, and they said they'll be out to take a report.

Who would do this? Nash is capable of assault, but I don't think he'd kidnap her.

Finally, a police officer knocks lightly, "Police."

I walk to the door and escort him inside, and he's young. I sure as hell hope he knows what he's doing. Officer 'Robertson' his name tag says. He takes a look around and spots the blood.

"Maybe it's not hers," he says under his breath.

Somehow, I know that's not true.

He walks over to the door and inspects it, "There's no damage to the door. Either she let the perp in, he had access, or you're not being honest with me."

"What?"

Four more cops enter my house before he can answer.

They are all looking at me like I did something to my beautiful girl, as he updates them on what he knows.

"We're going to need you to come to the station," the young kid says to me.

"Please, you have to find her."

He nods, "Right."

"What station? I'll meet you there."

A slight chuckle erupts from him, "You're coming with us."

We get to the station, and I'm escorted to an interrogation room. This cannot fucking be happening.

"It'll be a few minutes before a detective comes in to talk to you, make yourself comfortable, doctor," he grins before leaving the room as if this is enjoyable for him.

I try to think. Who has her? Well, no one broke in, and she wasn't supposed to open the door for anyone. *Think Liam, think. Who has the code?* Mercy does, Xander does, and Nash. Fuck. Nash is the only one that would hurt Mercy. But kidnapping? I didn't think he'd be capable of that. I haven't been arrested, so I still have my cell phone.

First, I call Nash.

"Hi, Dad," he answers with a harsh tone.

"Where's Mercy, Nash?"

He laughs, "Somewhere you will never find her. She was yours but she's mine now. I am never letting her go. Isn't that right baby?"

I can hear her cry, and my heart breaks as panic rises in every cell in my body.

Nash laughs, "It sucks to have someone take the thing you love most in this world, doesn't it?"

"Son, please don't hurt her."

"Oh, so sad," he says, "Luckily for me, she likes it rough. But I guess you already know that."

"Give me a kiss baby," I can hear him kissing her through the phone and I've never wanted to kill my own flesh and blood more than I do right now.

"Do you want me to send you the video after I'm done fucking her?"

I gasp, "Nash if you ever truly loved her, don't do that to her. She just had surgery, she can't."

He cackles, "Oh, she can, and she will. I already knew anyway; Jessica has a bigger mouth than you know."

"Nash, please."

"The time for begging is over. You should have thought about the consequences before you stole her from me. Before you fucked her. Before you cut off my fucking money."

Tears fall down my face when he speaks to Mercy, "Say goodbye, bitch. You won't see him again, tell him it's over, you're mine now."

She sobs, and I hear him hit her.

"Goodbye Liam, I love you. I'm his now."

The line goes dead, and so do I.

I call Cyrus, "I haven't scheduled it yet."

"Cy, Nash kidnapped Mercy. I'm in an interrogation room. You have to get me out of here. I have to find her. I can't do that from jail."

"Jesus, Liam. Say nothing. I'm on my way."

A female detective comes in and sits in front of me. The sound of the metal scraping against the floor echoes in the mostly empty room.

"Where is she?"

I shake my head, "I don't fucking have her. I wish I did. I need your help; my son took her."

"Is she alive?"

"Yes."

"Tell us where she is, and I can talk to the prosecutor and try to go easy on you."

"I don't know where she is. I just told you who has her."

Cyrus walks in with a cop beside him.

"Have you charged my client?"

"Not yet," the detective answers with a scowl.

"Then he's leaving."

"Let's go, Liam," Cyrus says coolly.

I get up, and we walk out of the police station.

As we get into his car, he asks, "What the fuck is going on with Nash?"

I shake my head, "Long story short, she's been his best friend since they were kids, he recently decided he was in love with her, he's on drugs and hates me for cutting off his financial supply."

He gets into the driver's seat, "Jesus, Liam. You don't really think he'd hurt her?"

I nod, "Yeah, I do."

After telling him about him assaulting her, and the phone call, he says, "Fuck."

Yeah, that about sums it up.

He takes me to a hotel because I can't go back to my house right now, it's a crime scene. Apparently, it hasn't been processed yet.

I'm sitting in the hotel room, when Xander shows up.

I let him in, and he gives me a sad look, "I'm sorry, Liam. I'm so sorry."

"He's going to rape her. And then he's going to kill her. This is all my fault."

I sit in the chair with my elbows on my knees and my face in my hands. This is the worst day of my fucking life, hands down, no contest.

We sit there for the longest time before the banging at the door comes.

"Open up, police," they yell, "We have a warrant!"

I hand my phone to Xander. "Call Gabriel and ask him to come see me. Tell him it's urgent but don't tell him about Mercy. I don't want him getting that news over the phone. Then call Cyrus."

"Cyrus?"

"Yes, you've met. He's my lawyer."

"OPEN THE FUCKING DOOR!"

As I walk to the door, Xander says, "I'm on it."

I get shoved up against the wall within a second of opening the door, and I'm handcuffed, patted down, and read my rights.

"Ready to go to jail, asshole?"

These officers seem to have a real problem with me, and I don't understand it. I haven't done a damn thing, and they are wasting precious time that Mercy doesn't have.

* * *

I sit in the jail cell for hours, waiting for someone to tell me something. There's no sign of Xander, Gabriel, or Cyrus. It's just me alone with my thoughts when the detective stands on the other side of the bars.

"We found a body that matches her description. If it's her, you're going down for murder. This is your last chance to tell us what you did to her before things get even worse for you."

All the air escapes my lungs as I fall to the floor, dying inside. She's dead? He killed my baby girl? The only sound that escapes my throat is a sob. Mercy. No. I've lost so many people in my life, but this is the one person I can't live without.

The detective walks away, leaving me alone with my pain. If she's gone, I can't go on. I can't live without her; I don't want to. Then I hear our conversation in my head.

"If something happens, I'd like you to adopt Ivy, but if you don't want to, I understand."

I nod, "I'll adopt her if they let me."

Ivy, my God, how am I supposed to tell Ivy that Mercy is dead? She'll never forgive me if she ever finds out it's my fault. I'll never forgive myself.

Cyrus comes up to the cell, "Hey, I'm working to get you out. But if she's dead, Liam, it's a lot more serious."

I hang my head down in defeat, "If she's dead, you can leave me here to rot. I don't fucking care about anything else."

. . .

To be continued...

Afterword

I know. I know. Cliffhangers are hard. Whenever I write a book that ends with a 'what the fuck' I try very hard to get the next book to you as soon as humanly possible. Finding Mercy will be book two in the Forbidden Desires of PCH.

Currently it's set for pre-order on Amazon for November 15th. However, I'm working very hard to be able to move that date up to September or October at the latest!

You can pre-order Finding Mercy Here!

Stay up to date on all of my new releases by joining My Facebook group!

Acknowledgments

It's impossible to write a book alone. Thank you to my editor, cover designer, beta readers, and arc readers. Every single one of you means the world to me. I appreciate every single one of you.

Gabby my darling you are an absolute angel. Thank you.

To my PA's Jasmine and Chanel Ya'll put up with one of the craziest authors on the planet. Thanks for not firing me. Some days I would fire myself if I were you.

Cupcake as always you are the Dory to my Nemo.

Holly. The day before this book was finished editing you made me seriously shake my head. But you'll always be my favorite Hoe!

My readers... I love each and every one of you! Thank you for reading my dirty lil story. If you wouldn't mind a review on Amazon that would be so wonderful. Reviews make the difference between being seen and well, not being seen for authors.

About the Author

Chelle Rose is an avid reader that loves romance. You'll frequently find her raving about other authors she loves.

She loves writing and always has. Writing is her passion. Starting at the tender age of five she found herself writing song lyrics. After earning a music business degree she imagined the country music scene would be where she'd always work. However, when she decided to write her first book, Chelle knew exactly where she belonged. She's excited to share her work with you.

Chelle currently resides in Virginia enjoying the cows in her back yard. Between her family and her writing, she stays super busy and loves every minute of it. She hopes you enjoy her stories that remind us that there's hope even in life's darkest moments. After all, in the darkest night skies, the stars shine the brightest.

Also by Chelle Rose

Hard to Love Book One

Hard to Breathe Book Two

Cool Off Anthology

Made in the USA
Middletown, DE
27 July 2023